What people are saying...

"This makes it so easy to buil[...]g!
I majored in English and as [...]d
many of the words in this boc [...]t
the definitions that were prov [...] understood
their meaning. Especially wit[...] [...] the dumbed-down and questionable literature being published for young adults these days, such a series has tremendous potential to actually enhance their knowledge while upholding positive moral values."

—Teri Ann Berg Olsen, *Knowledge House*

"Burk's style is easy for the reader and geared to teenagers in the high school years. This book has 300 words that, for the most part, will be new to the reader... What an incredible way to increase the writing and speaking skills of your student!"

—Jennifer Barker, *The Old Schoolhouse Magazine*

"There are very few better ways to quickly read and actually remember 300 high-level words, such as "ruminate," "lachrymose," "salubrious" and "pulchritude." Some of the words may be recognized by many readers, but even this reader was learning new words throughout."

—Chloe O'Connor, *The Signal*

"Besides being an excellent tool to enhance vocabulary and language development, pre-teens and teens will find the story engaging. Best of all, the story steers clear of offensive language and unsavory themes."

—Anne Gebhart, *Heart of Texas*

Books in VocabCafé Series

Operation
High
School

By Judah Burk

Maven of Memory Publishing
Hurst, Texas

Operation High School

Copyright © 2010, 2012 by Maven of Memory Publishing
Hurst, Texas
www.vocabcafe.com

ISBN 978-0-9768042-9-1

The VocabCafé Book Series is intended to encourage the study and investigation of the English language. This book is not, nor does it purport itself to be, the complete and final authority on word usage and definitions. Maven of Memory Publishing is not responsible for any errors, omissions, or misunderstandings contained in this book or derived from information contained herein.

Cover and layout by impact studios

Printed in the United States of America

To my best friend Adam, I never would have had the confidence to finish this book without you. Thanks for being the Michael to my Emma.

An Introduction to VocabCafé

The purpose of the VocabCafé book series is to encourage the development of vocabulary knowledge. At Maven of Memory Publishing we believe that a good understanding of vocabulary words is crucial to lifelong success. Contained inside this novella are more than 300 words that can be helpful in improving the vocabulary of any reader, which can lead to better reading, writing, and speaking skills. It can also help improve test scores for students intending to take standardized exams.

Every vocabulary word is placed in the context of a narrative story. The storyline and sentences surrounding the words should help readers easily deduce their meanings. For easy reference and instant reinforcement, the literal definitions of every word are at the bottom of each page. At the end of each chapter there is a review of the vocabulary words featured in that section. We recommend that you go over this word review immediately after finishing the chapter in order to study the definitions while their context remains fresh.

These books were written with an intended audience of high school teenagers, although many parents find them appropriate for younger students. As a family-based company, our goal is to make a quality product that can be enjoyed by everyone. These stories contain no magic, sorcery, swear words, or illicit situations. Nonetheless, we recommend that parents read every book (not just ours) that they give their children to make sure the messages and themes coincide with their beliefs and standards.

Accompanying flash cards organized by chapter are available for purchase and highly recommended to help ensure success. Each card has the word definition and its use in the story. Reviewing these will help you in your quest for mastery of vocabulary words.

We hope this series is instrumental in helping you advance your proficiency with the English language.

Good Luck!
The VocabCafé Team

Operation
High
School

1

A MYSTERIOUS PROPOSITION

The room was completely dark except for the ring of tea candles that encircled her. The candles emitted only a small amount of light, making it hard for Emma to see anything past the tiny glow. The blindfold her captors had used on her lay by her side. Her breath grew shallow as she felt tiny bumps begin to cover her arms. Three shadows flickered across the dusty walls. She knew before she had come that it would be a long night, but now as she sat in silence, she wondered exactly how long it would take. What on earth had possessed her to agree to this lonely, *covert* gathering? No one knew where she was or who she was with, and if something went wrong, no one would be able to rescue her. It was Friday night, and her parents were out of town for the weekend. She had told them she was going to be staying at a school friend's house, a lie Emma was seriously regretting at that moment. Her parents trusted her, and she knew they wouldn't check in. For better or for worse, she was on her own.

After a few moments, Emma's eyes adjusted to the darkness, making it easier to distinguish the figures that surrounded her. She noticed a sliver of moonlight escaping from a nearby window. The people who brought her here had done their best to black out the window, but the curtain had moved, which, with the aid of the candles, provided

---

Covert   (**koh**-vert) – ADJ – secret; hidden

just enough light to give her a sense of her environment. It was a small room with a dirty, **unkempt** appearance. The floor was dusty, and the wallpaper was faded and peeling at the corners. The air was musty and in need of circulation. It looked and felt as though the room had not been touched in years. She wondered if this was an abandoned house.

Tonight's behavior was uncharacteristic for Emma. It was out of the ordinary that she told a lie, especially to her parents, and she certainly wasn't someone who went out looking for adventures. **Reticent** by nature, Emma was known for being shy and cautious. It was hard to say if this reserved attitude was due to her personality or circumstances. She had just moved to Providence, Virginia, and wasn't quite comfortable there yet. She didn't really know if she wanted to get comfortable because she didn't expect to stay there long. Her dad was in the Army, and soon enough her family would be stationed somewhere new. It wasn't as though she resented her upbringing. There were several advantages to being a military brat. By the age of sixteen, Emma had lived all over the world and experienced things other kids her age only dreamed about.

Providence was the first time she had lived in the States since she was a baby, and the American culture was surprisingly different from what she was used to. For the last several years, Emma's family had lived in a small town in Germany. It was the kind of town where people often made daily trips to the market to get the ingredients for the evening meal because their refrigerators were a fraction of the size of the ones typical in America. Although she had frequently visited the department stores in the bigger

Unkempt	(uhn-**kempt**) – ADJ – disheveled; messy
Reticent	(**reht**-uh-suhnt) – ADJ – quiet; reserved

cities of Germany, there were only a handful of shopping malls in all of Europe, and Emma never had a chance to go to one. She was surprised to learn almost every major or minor city in America had its own mall. However, the thing that struck her the most about her new home was the size of the American flags throughout the countryside. Compared to the flags of her former homelands, Old Glory was enormous and flew majestically in the sky, as if it were announcing to the world the great pride Americans have for their country. Emma, too, felt the pride of being an American because she had seen firsthand how her country's decisions impacted the rest of the world.

Emma knew she wasn't alone. Three figures dressed in black sat just beyond the candles. The entire room stood still, but the atmosphere was far from *halcyon*. The longer she sat in the quiet, the more unbearable the tension became. A knot in her stomach grew tighter as her heart beat wildly against her chest. Unsure of what to do or say, she remained unmoved and anxiously awaited her instructions.

Suddenly, a deep voice broke the silence.

"You were supposed to wear all black," boomed the mysterious voice.

"I'm, um, sorry... I don't own any black pants. I thought dark jeans would be OK," stammered Emma.

Emma hoped this answer would satisfy the voice. She meant no harm by wearing jeans, and had chosen her darkest pair just to be safe. She hadn't thought that something as minor as a wardrobe choice could get her into trouble, but now she knew better. All she could do was wait for the voice's reply. But nothing came. The room

---

Halcyon (**hal**-see-uhn) – ADJ – peaceful; calm

remained as still as the grave. Once again Emma found herself sitting silently in the darkness.

The constraints of time had no power in that tiny room. Seconds seemed like hours, and every moment dragged on endlessly. There was no knowing how long it had been since she had arrived or when she had last spoken. Had it been five minutes or forty-five? Emma had no cell phone or watch to serve as a timepiece. She didn't need to be anywhere until Sunday morning, and she started to wonder if they intended to keep her there until then. Realistically, she could remain ignorant of the purpose of this *cryptic* encounter for hours, if not days. Since the moment Emma had received a strange letter at school, the situation had grown more and more mystifying.

Tired of the silence, Emma mustered up enough courage to speak.

"Where am I?" she asked with hesitation.

"The location doesn't matter" responded a second voice. "But you're safe."

"Why have you brought me here?"

"Be patient. It is an honor that you have been asked to come here, but before we tell you everything, we have to make sure you are trustworthy."

"Trustworthy? Who am I proving myself trustworthy to? How do I know I can trust *you?*"

Her questions were met with silence. Whatever the answers were, they would have to wait. This second voice was softer than the previous one, with a sweeter tone that helped *assuage* some of Emma's fears. She started to

Cryptic	(**krip**-tik) – ADJ – mystifying or mysterious
Assuage	(uh-**sweyj**) – V – to lessen the intensity of something painful; to ease

worry less as curiosity began to take hold. There she was in the middle of the night, in a strange room with three hazy figures. Why had they chosen her? What could she possibly have done to attract such peculiar attention? She had only been at Providence High for a couple months and hadn't had the chance to make any real friends, let alone any serious enemies. If she were a victim of some *heinous* practical joke the reason for it was beyond her.

Her mind wandered back to the correspondence she had received earlier that day.

Before the letter's arrival, it had been an average Friday afternoon. She went in and out of her classes, and for the most part enjoyed her subjects. Of course, this was excluding fourth period's Intermediate German with Mrs. Huckleson. The school didn't offer many foreign language classes, but it required each student to have at least two semesters of the same language. Providence High had an unusual transfer credit policy and accepted all the classes from her former high school except her language classes. Despite knowing French, German, and some Italian, Emma was forced to complete this requirement in the classrooms of the high school. Emma chose to take German. Not only because it would be an easy A, but also because she genuinely loved learning the language. She had been excited about the prospects of a new teacher and teaching style, and was hopeful that this class would enrich her knowledge of the language. She knew at first there would be a review, but if every student was as excited about the subject as she was, she was sure the class would soon be *parsing* great works of German literature.

Heinous	(**hey**-nuhs) – ADJ – shockingly evil
Parse	(pahrs) – V– to analyze with detail, especially grammar

However, this was far from the reality of the situation. With the passing of each class period, Emma's hope of learning something new diminished. More often than not Emma found herself staring out the window as poor Mrs. Huckleson tried her best to explain the necessity of conjugating verbs. Once, in an effort to be helpful, Emma corrected Mrs. Huckleson's grammar discussion on the purpose and use of German articles. She had hoped to explain the concept more clearly for her classmates, but instead engaged in a heated argument with her teacher. Despite her good intentions Emma was left with a detention slip and a strict order to remain silent in class unless called upon. Meaning, of course, she was compelled to suffer through terrible pronunciations, misinterpretations, and a teacher who knew less about the subject than she did. Sadly there were no other options but to quietly complete both semesters. Therefore every fourth period Emma *succumbed* to her fate and grudgingly went to class.

Following her typical routine, Emma had exchanged her books in her locker and set the new ones down on her seat. It was always the same seat, the one in the third row closest to the window. After getting her stuff settled, she made a quick trip to the bathroom. Fourth period came right after lunch and she hated the thought of being bored and uncomfortable. Emma knew exactly how long it took to get to the ladies' room and back before the bell rang. Unfortunately on this Friday, she was accosted in the restroom by a blabbering blond girl and had to slip in after class had started. Mrs. Huckleson was writing the page number of the day's lesson on the blackboard. She looked up as Emma tried to sneak into class. With a disapproving

---

Succumb   (suh-**kuhm**) – V – to submit; to die

look and a shake of the head, she motioned to Emma to get to her seat. After the first day of their disagreement, Mrs. Huckleson and Emma had called an ***armistice*** to avoid further difficulties. They decided it best to stay out of each other's way and try their best to get through the next couple of semesters with as little conflict as possible. Despite this truce, it was evident by their interactions that the two had little patience for one another. As Emma slid into place, a sinking feeling filled the pit of her stomach; it would be a long hour.

The March sun kissed Emma's face as the warm sunshine poured into the classroom. Tempted by the thought of spending the entire afternoon daydreaming, Emma reluctantly returned her thoughts to the German lesson. Not wanting to waste the time she spent in the classroom, she had gotten into a habit of doing that day's homework while she waited for the period to end. It always ***vexed*** Mrs. Huckleson to see a student ignore her lesson and work on something apart from what she was teaching. However, the situation with Emma was unique, and the teacher decided as long as Emma worked on her German assignments there wasn't much she could complain about. At the very least, it kept the girl preoccupied and allowed the teacher to focus her attention on the other students.

After a while of staring out the window, Emma opened her German book. She scanned the index page to find the location of the lesson. "Simple past tense, page 52," she read. *With 52 pages down, only 200 more pages to go,* she sarcastically thought to herself. She opened the text

---

Armistice	(**ahr**-muh-stis) – N – a truce; a temporary cease of hostilities
Vex	(veks) – V – to annoy; pester; confuse

book a little bit wider and gently flipped to chapter six, unaware that that particular chapter held much more than a grammar lesson. Instead of going straight to the back of the chapter to start on the homework questions, Emma decided to skim the chapter to familiarize herself with the text. Once she reached her desired page number, she glanced down to read the overview. Much to her surprise, neatly tucked in between the pages, lay a slender white envelope. She ran her fingers over the small note; it was completely bare except for her name on the front. It was a peculiar sight but it was addressed to Emma Jones. There could be no doubt the letter was meant for her.

Curious about the contents of the mysterious note, Emma debated whether or not to open the letter in the middle of class or to wait until the bell rang and read it after class had finished. *A good student would wait until the period ended*, Emma thought. Glancing up at her teacher, Emma also remembered the scowling look Mrs. Huckleson had given her when she walked into class. *Besides, it would probably be best not to do something else today to upset Mrs. H.* She was determined to wait and read the message in her free time.

Thoughts of the letter continued to **rivet** Emma's attention. Instead of moving to the next page to get to work, Emma continued to probe the letter. She knew it would be wiser to continue on with the lesson, but she couldn't bring herself to leave the note behind. Her internal struggle continued until she caught a glimpse of the clock above Mrs. Huckleson's head. Looking at the time, she realized there was still half an hour until the bell. The agonizing thought of finishing the remaining time was too much

---

Rivet　　　　(**riv**-it) – V – to engross

for Emma's willpower, thus she gave into her inquisitive nature. Slipping the note into her lap, she proceeded to scrutinize its content.

Carefully trying to avoid any unwanted attention, Emma coughed as she tore open the envelope, hoping the sound would mask the noise of the ripping epistle. Each move was meticulous; cautiously thought out before acted. Every so often, she looked up from her work to ensure no one was looking at her. She worried someone would think from all her coughing that she was dying if she did not open it faster. Finally, the envelope opened and she slipped her hand in to retrieve the paper it held inside. Not wanting to run the risk of the papers rubbing together and making a noise, Emma slowly separated the envelope from its contents. Discreetly, she placed the letter inside her book and slipped the envelope into her book bag.

The small piece of paper looked almost identical to the envelope it had come in. Folded in a perfect square, the letter was a little bigger than the palm of her hand. Emma attentively unfolded the pad several times until it tripled its original size and more closely resembled a piece of normal paper. Adding to the *anomaly* of the mysterious letter, it was printed on customized stationary for a secret organization, not the ruled notebook paper one might expect. It was thinner than normal computer paper, and the borders were as bare as the envelope it had come in, except for a faint watermark on the bottom right hand corner. Without her reading glasses on, Emma couldn't make out the wording on the seal. The message inside was typed instead of handwritten. This meant the author had

Anomaly (uh-**nom**-uh-lee) – N – a deviation from the normal order, form, or rule

prepared the note long before the class period started. This feature did not strike Emma as particularly odd until she had finished reading what the message said.

Emma Jones,

Since the day you started at Providence High, you have struck us as someone of keen interest. We have been observing your interactions and have come to the conclusion that you would fit nicely into our exclusive brotherhood. We believe you to be the type of character which we hold in the highest regard. Therefore we extend this furtive invitation to join our secret fraternity. In order to protect the clandestine nature of this club, you must keep this invitation to yourself and share it with no one else. If it comes to light you have shared this letter or the contents of it with anyone else, your invitation will be revoked. You have the right to accept or deny this proposal.

If you choose to accept, come alone to the parking lot of the high school at 9:00 pm tonight. Leave your cell phone in your car. A vehicle will pick you up and take you to the next location. You will thus begin your initiation process. It will not be without its hardships. This is a long process, so make plans to be gone until 9:00pm on Saturday.

If you choose to deny our proposal, you must destroy this letter and speak of it to no one. We understand this may something you do not wish to do, and we will respect your decision. However, if you choose to disobey these instructions and disclose this letter, you will suffer the consequences of your actions.

Until tonight,
OIT

Furtive   (**fur**-tiv) – ADJ – secret; underhanded

Emma was stunned. She reread the letter several times to make sure she wasn't daydreaming. Once she confirmed the reality of the situation she began to look around her class to see who the author of the bizarre message might be. Whoever wrote the note had to be in this room because there hadn't been enough time for someone to deliver the note and get to another class. It had to be someone *shrewd* enough to slip the note in her book while she was in the bathroom and get back to his or her seat before Emma returned. But who, she wondered?

Emma scanned her surroundings, surveying the classroom's *milieu*. It wasn't a very large class, only about 20 students in all—and to be frank, no one stuck out as crafty enough to pull this off. She didn't know many of the students' names, but she had a pretty good grasp of their personality types. Emma recognized most of these students' faces because they all shared the same lunch period. Since childhood, she had been taught to be aware of her surroundings—to observe first and act second. Even in the most mundane situations, she found herself getting a feel for her environment—a side effect of having a father in the military. Not having anyone to talk to during lunch, Emma often spent her time observing her peers.

Providence High seemed like a typical high school, a large student body broken down into various social groups. Although there was some overlap in the different cliques, for the most part the students kept to their specific friends. The cafeteria exemplified this as specific tables were filled by members of the different societies. Every day, the same students sat at the same

---

Shrewd   (shrood) – ADJ – sly; crafty
Milieu   (mil-**yoo**) – N – environment; setting

tables. Since the students who sat together usually shared similar interests, it was easy for Emma to map out the general *coteries* of Providence High. Toward the middle of the lunch room sat the royalty of the social hierarchy, or at least those who thought they were the kings and queens of the school. Providence was on the outskirts of the capital, and many children of politicians attended school there. This group of students was universally known because of their parents' fame, and at times that popularity seemed to go straight to their heads.

Sitting close to the children of the public servants were the sports groups, who were equally famous around the school. Farther right sat the more artistically-minded students. Over the last several years, the theater department had done well at regional theater festivals. Over that time, the department had gained a substantial amount of recognition and support. Close to the theater kids sat the band members. Music seemed to follow them everywhere. Every once in awhile, the drummers started a beat on the table, and their fellow bandmates would chime in.

Directly across the cafeteria sat the math and science groups, followed closely by the computer nerds. Those cliques were more fluid, sharing many of the same members. The last group Emma had nicknamed the "ninjas." It was only one table comprised of six or seven boys. Emma wasn't sure if they actually belonged to any martial arts club, but they liked to hold mock fights, and she could imagine them in an action scene of a B-rated ninja movie. Everyone seemed to find his or her place among the variety of students at Providence High. Even

---

Coterie   (koh-tuh-ree) – N – a group of close associates; a circle of friends

students who didn't fit into a particular group found themselves sitting together and thus created a company of "loners."

With this knowledge Emma looked around at her classmates. Most of her fellow German students were of no distinct interest to her, and fell somewhere in between the loners and the semipopular groups. Out of the 20 classmates, only five caught her attention: one foreign-exchange student, one ninja kid, one cheerleader, her science class lab partner, and the junior editor of the school's newspaper. These five were the most interesting of the class, but none of them made likely candidates for the author of the letter. Still, looks could be misleading, so Emma considered the idea that one of them was more than he or she appeared to be. Emma wished she had a friend to **bandy** thoughts about her classmates, but alas she was alone.

One by one, she ruled out her remaining suspects. First, she dismissed the foreign-exchange student. A native of India, Lakshmi kept to herself and only spoke when she was spoken to. Besides, the program she was with only let her stay in America for a semester, and after finals were over, she would return to her native country. Next, Emma examined the cheerleader. Her **svelte** figure and graceful demeanor distinguished her from the other girls in the class. Emma really didn't know much about her, but as far as she could tell, she never seemed to have any interest in Emma. Although it was time for cheerleading tryouts, Emma had already proven herself to be quite the uncoordinated **lummox** during PE. Pitifully clumsy, Emma was

Bandy	(**ban**-dee) – V – to toss back and forth
Svelte	(svelt) – ADJ – slim; slender; having clean lines
Lummox	(**luhm**-uhks) – N – a large, ungainly, dull-witted person

the last person the squad would want to recruit. Next was the ninja kid, who looked like the prime suspect. He was intriguing enough to devise such a note, but he had very little motive to do so. The letter was an invitation into a club, and as far as she could tell, Ninja Kid only hung out with his karate buddies, and they were all guys. So, unless they wanted her to be the next Joan of Arc, her gender would keep her out of their group. Then there was Michael, the guy from her science class. Emma admitted to herself that there was no good reason for him to be on the list except that she actually knew him. He had always been nice to her, but their relationship consisted only of small talk and the common goal not to fail chemistry. In that way they shared a common bond, but it was barely enough to start a friendship—much less anything more significant. Last on her list was Tiffany, the soon to be editor-in-chief of *The Providence Star.* Despite the fact she was only a sophomore, Tiffany worked with *vim* and vigor for the paper and everyone knew she was being groomed to be the next editor. She would assume her new role in the fall and likely hold the office until she graduated. With the intense responsibilities of the paper, Tiffany would be in a state of *oblivion* toward the rest of the goings-on of Providence High. She wouldn't have the time or the energy to focus on anything other than her academics and the paper.

The bell rang with a loud chime, snapping Emma back to reality. Lost in her thoughts, she had missed everything that happened after she read the note. Students shuffled around as they gathered their books together. Mrs. Huckleson stood at the front, erasing the blackboard. The

Vim	(vim) – N – energetic spirit; vitality
Oblivion	(uh-**bliv**-ee-uhn) – N – total forgetfulness

room quickly cleared out as her classmates rushed to their next obligations. Emma sat conflicted and confused. She had to have missed someone when she looked around the room. By the time she stood up, the classroom was empty. Whoever had sent the note was long gone—and with that person went any hope of learning the nature of this puzzling club. She would have to wait if she wanted to find out more information about the messenger and the organization. Now she had a choice: to see where this message would take her, or leave it alone completely. Whichever path she took, she had to commit to it and accept the *repercussions* of that choice. If she decided not to go, she would have to forget about the message and not let the origin of the mysterious invitation consume her thoughts. However, if she decided to pursue this proposal, she would be daring out into the unknown. Without even a hint of who sent the letter, Emma had no idea what she was getting herself into. The message itself had been sufficiently vague, leaving her little information to make an informed decision. To make matters worse, it wasn't as if she could get anyone's advice on the matter. The choice was exclusively up to her. The question remained: *what would she do?*

Emma assembled her belongings and left the classroom. She went to her locker, put away her books, and grabbed her workout clothes. It was now 2 pm, leaving her exactly seven hours to come to her final decision. She made her way to the gym, changed for PE, and pondered her unusual dilemma.

As the night grew darker, the room became colder. It was a windy evening, and the poorly insulated building let in its share of drafts. Providence was known for its chilling nights,

---

Repercussion   (ree-per-**kuhsh**-uhn) – N – consequence

and tonight was no different. During the winter months and well into early spring, outerwear was *customary* for those who lived in this region of the country. Emma longed to be curled up in her own soft bed as she pulled her jacket closer to her body. She recalled her father's lecture on enduring harsh weather. It was one of the many survival lectures he had insisted on giving her just in case she found herself in such a situation as the one before her. Never before had she been so thankful for his advice. Emma knew it was important to keep her core warm and to think about something other than her current condition. Wrapping her arms tightly around her midsection, Emma felt her temperature rise as she focused not on the cold, but on getting through whatever the night held for her. This was just the first of many occasions that her father's military training would benefit Emma that evening.

"It's obvious that no one followed her," whispered a voice from the shadows.

"Then it is time to begin," responded another.

Sounds shuffled around her as the three figures began to walk around the room. They walked in a big circle, whispering to one another as they passed each another. The noises were meant to confuse Emma, and they worked. She couldn't tell who was speaking or where the voice was coming from.

"You have been sitting here for over an hour," spoke the deep voice. "Tell us what you have discovered."

"Excuse me?" asked Emma weakly. Her voice *quavered* with fear as she spoke.

"You have been here long enough to learn

Customary	(**kuhs**-tuh-mer-ee) – ADJ – habitual
Quaver	(**kwey**-ver) – V – to shake or tremble, as in voice or music

something of your location," replied another captor. "That is of course unless you've been sitting there this whole time feeling sorry for yourself."

They attempted to **abash** their captive by attacking her pride. Embarrassed that her demeanor gave off the impression of having a pity party, Emma was determined to prove that her hour in silence had been well spent. She paused and took her time to think about the task she was being asked to fulfill. Her captors could not expect her to know everything about her milieu. After all, she had been sitting in almost complete darkness with very little exposure to the outside surroundings. Everything she needed to answer this question had to be within her grasp. Whatever purpose to this test, she knew confidence would be a key element in her success. Emma decided to start small, with the area she was sitting in—to describe what she found there, and then move to a bigger area. Piece by piece, she used her skills of observation to paint a picture of her surroundings.

Emma looked down at the floor; she noticed the mud on the bottom of her shoes. She must have picked it up on her way into the building. It hadn't rained for a couple of days so she knew the water that wet the dirt had to have come from another source—perhaps a sprinkler system. However, if there was a sprinkler system nearby, her original assumption that she was in an isolated **derelict** building couldn't be correct. After all, people don't water the lawns of houses no one lives in. It was also obvious she wasn't in a place people visited often. Judging by the size, it could be anything from a storage shed to a small pool

---

Abash	(uh-**bash**) – V – to embarrass; disconcert
Derelict	(**der**-uh-likt) – ADJ – abandoned, forsaken

house, but there wasn't enough information to come to a conclusion as to the purpose of the building. So, she started with the facts that she did know.

"Judging by the size and condition of this place, it hasn't been used regularly for a while," said Emma. It wasn't much of an observation, but it was a place to start.

"What makes you say that?"

"The air is very stuffy in here, and it smells like mold."

"And the size?"

"The roof of the building isn't very high up, which suggests that this is the only floor."

"How many rooms are there?"

Emma *vacillated* about how to answer this question, wanting to take her time to try to get it right. She had no idea how many rooms there were. If it was a tool shed, then it was likely only one room. Yet the wallpaper on the walls suggested someone had once taken the time to decorate the place. Unless the owner had some special attachment to his or her tools, there would be no reason to dress this place up. Emma therefore ruled out the possibility of being in a place strictly used for storage. She also realized it was darker to her left than it was to her right. This of course was due to the window she had spotted earlier. If there were a window to her right, it meant the right wall faced directly to the outside. This could also mean the left side didn't. It wasn't foolproof logic, but she didn't have much more to go on. Hoping not to sound like a *dolt*, Emma made her best guess.

"There are two rooms."

"What is the purpose of these rooms?"

"This one has carpet, although not very expensive

Vacillate	(**vas**-uh-leyt)	– V – to waver
Dolt	(dohlt)	– N – stupid person

carpet, and wallpaper. It feels like a small living area. It could be either a living room or a bedroom."

"And the other room?"

"If this is a living space, then it's probably some sort of kitchen."

"There is some hesitation in your voice. Why?"

"It just doesn't make much sense for this to be a house. It's not very big, it's a mess, and either there isn't any electricity or you have decided to turn it off."

"Why do you say that?"

"It's too dark and too cold to have electricity. Not to mention there isn't a sound in this entire building. Even if you had all the lights and the heat turned off, the walls of this place are so thin, there would be at least a faint buzzing sound from the moving electrical currents. It feels more like a shell of a house than a real home."

The three shadowy figures were surprised by the accuracy of Emma's *adroit* insights. There was, in fact, no electricity in the small building, and despite its decorated interior, it was never used as a home. Emma had given them more than they had expected and although they didn't let her know it, they were pleased. Through their examination, they *ascertained* that Emma would be the perfect fourth and final member of their club.

They continued to quiz her about her location, the school, and even about Providence itself. She didn't know all the answers but tried her best. The questions continued, and Emma's head began to hurt. It was getting late and it was hard for her to keep all the information straight. Emma began to worry that the more answers she got wrong, the longer she would have

---

Adroit	(uh-**droit**) – ADJ – skillful; expert
Ascertain	(as-er-**teyn**) – V – to find out or learn with certainty

to stay out here. Little did she know, she had long since passed the test—now her captors were just trying to tire her.

"We have heard enough," spoke the deep voice.

Emma believed whoever was behind that voice was the leader. He, or at least she thought it was a he, was the one who called all the shots. He started the questions and was the one to end them.

By the time her interrogation finished, it was well after midnight. Emma's body had grown stiff from sitting in the same position for so long. Whatever was to come next, Emma wished it involved movement. Her wish was to be answered—very soon she would be getting plenty of exercise. If she had known about her next task, she would have been more careful about what she had wished for, and she would have enjoyed sitting in that tiny circle surrounded by little tea candles.

One of the figures dressed in black went around the circle and blew out the candles. Although individually they were small, the amount of light they produced together was profound. Now the room was absolutely dark, save for the sliver of moonlight. However, even this was quickly fading as the moon continued its journey.

"You have done well on your first test," spoke the softer voice. "It is now time to move on to the next task."

Emma never expected *approbation*, but somehow this bit of positive feedback gave her a small amount of reassurance. Had it been another situation, she would have been pleased with herself; however, the praise was lost on Emma as she could only focus on the second part of the voice's statement: there was to be another test. As she

---

Approbation   (ap-ruh-**bey**-shuhn) – N – praise

pondered the possibilities, she felt a presence behind her back. A hand was gently laid on her shoulder and although she couldn't see it, she knew it was motioning for her to stand up. Cold and afraid, Emma shivered as she rose. The figure knelt beside her and brushed against Emma's leg as it retrieved the black material by her feet. Before she knew it, her eyes had been covered. The blindfold was icy against her face and caused her to quiver with cold once again. Then to her surprise, the person grabbed her arms and, with a cold rope, tied her hands behind her back. It happened so suddenly Emma didn't have the time to think about struggling.

A door opened with an eerie creak and Emma was pushed out of the room and eventually led outside. Her captors stopped in front of the building to lock up. They had finished with it for the evening. Still blindfolded and with her hands bound, Emma had help walking—two people stood by her side, holding her arms and directing her steps. The third ventured out to lead the group. As they walked, Emma realized she wasn't being taken in the same direction she had come from. With every step, she felt as if she were being taken farther and farther away from civilization. Uncertain of her fate, Emma pressed on into the merciless night.

WORD REVIEW

Abash	Customary	Repercussion
Adroit	Derelict	Reticent
Anomaly	Dolt	Rivet
Approbation	Furtive	Shrewd
Armistice	Halcyon	Succumb
Ascertain	Heinous	Svelte
Assuage	Lummox	Unkempt
Bandy	Milieu	Vacillate
Coterie	Oblivion	Vex
Covert	Parse	Vim
Cryptic	Quaver	

2

AN INTRIGUING FRIENDSHIP

Farther and farther they walked. Emma's body was no longer stiff, but sore from the walking and chilly air. The wind had picked up, and the icy breeze pierced through her clothing. She felt as though an acupuncturist was sticking a thousand tiny needles all over her body. Emma had forgotten to bring gloves, and her hands felt numb. She wanted to warm them by putting them in her jacket's pockets, but the rope tied around her wrists made it impossible.

Her captors had chosen to keep the blindfold on. Although it wasn't very thick, the darkness of the night kept her from seeing through the material. She walked blindly, trusting this was a part of her initiation process and not some terrible scheme to get her alone in the woods. Emma's trust diminished as they continued to walk. Fear began to take hold. Up until that point, Emma thought the worst she could be getting herself into was a heartless practical joke meant to abash her. With every additional step she now began to think otherwise. Flashes of scenes from crime drama TV shows began to fill her head. What if she had willingly put herself in the middle of some diabolical plot concocted by a sociopath? After all, she didn't know the people she was with that night. She was beginning to feel more like a hunted *quarry* than an invited pledge.

Quarry   (kwawr-ee) – N – a victim; object of a hunt

Then they stopped. From what Emma could tell, they were about two or three miles from the little building where they started. When the journey had first begun, she tried counting her steps to keep track of where and how far they had gone. However, Emma soon realized those leading her often took her in circles. Sometimes they were small circles and she could feel them turning her around, but other times she got the feeling they were taking her in much bigger circles. In reality Emma had no idea how far they had gone. Despite her best efforts, she was just as clueless as when she first began. This lack of knowledge made Emma feel *pusillanimous* and out of control. She was at the mercy of her captors, and she didn't know if she could trust them. She was tired, cold, and scared. She felt powerless in this situation, which made her even more frightful. Emma knew that if she was in harm's way, she would have to come up with a survival plan. Her father had taught her that those who survive dangerous situations do so because they have a plan. Emma would gladly come up with a plan of action, if only she knew where to begin. She contemplated the *solemnity* of her situation and decided if the time came, she would be ready to fight.

They stood still for awhile. Emma was sure that if something awful were going to happen, this would be the time. It was very late and they could be deep in the heart of the woods. There probably wasn't anyone around for miles. With her eyes covered and her hands tied, Emma was a hostage. At this point she was practically helpless, and before she could make her move, she would have to wait

Pusillanimous	(pyoo-suh-**lan**-uh-muhs) – ADJ – lacking firmness of mind; cowardly
Solemnity	(suh-**lem**-ni-tee) – N – seriousness; gravity

for a better situation. It would do her no good to struggle now, only to put herself in a worse position. Emma quietly waited for her opportunity to get free.

Nothing happened. No one did anything but whisper to one another. As time progressed, the situation seemed more ridiculous than scary. As she stood there next to her captors, she began to realize they were just kids like her. From what she could tell, they had no intentions of harming her. She assumed the three had lost their way and were taking a moment to recover their bearings. With this thought, Emma relaxed a little. She laughed at herself for letting her imagination come up with such a wild *scenario*. Why had she thought her class-mates were really psychopaths? They now seemed like a group of kids who just wanted to have some fun and they appeared to be less organized than she originally believed. She felt silly for being so worried and decided not to get so worked up again.

However, Emma couldn't have been more wrong. She would soon learn never to assume in these types of situations. It would be a lesson she'd keep close for the next several hours. Nothing would be as it seemed—and to survive, Emma would have to stay alert.

"Sit down and keep quiet."

Thinking they didn't know what to do with her, Emma obeyed the command. With the assistance of one of the group members, she slowly sat down beside a large tree. Emma's legs had grown very tired, and she welcomed the rest. As she sat, she leaned up against the tree to support her back. Emma was now completely concerned with getting comfortable.

Scenario   (si-**nair**-ee-oh) – N – a sequence of events

Sitting complacently, Emma concentrated on trying to get warm. She rubbed her hands together, hoping to bring back some feeling to her fingers. It felt as though she had been a prisoner forever. After some time, Emma ***acclimated*** to her present condition. She forgot about everything—the blindfold, her tied hands, even the fact she had no idea where she was. She hoped this little detour would discourage whatever plans the other three had, and they could all go home and go to bed.

Lost in her thoughts, Emma was oblivious to what was going on around her. It was ***hapless*** misfortune that Emma chose this time to become complacent; otherwise she might have been better prepared for the next task. But as it was, she didn't hear her captors' conversation. She didn't notice the noise of the departing feet, and she wasn't aware that very soon she would be all alone. Had she stayed focused, she might have been able to free herself from her bonds more quickly and follow close behind those who had brought her there. It would have saved her much time and frustration.

The three others were long gone before Emma realized the whispering had stopped. She waited to see if they were ready to help her back up and continue on with their journey. She kept hoping they would pick her up and they would turn around and walk straight back to the car. She figured it had probably taken them 30 minutes or so to get where they were now, so she imagined if they started now, they would be out of the cold in about 30 minutes. She couldn't wait to start.

After a little bit Emma realized it was a lot quieter now than it had been earlier. She no longer heard whispering,

| *Acclimate* | (**ak**-luh-meyt) – V – to adapt |
| *Hapless* | (**hap**-lis) – ADJ – unlucky |

nor did she hear the sound of breathing. There wasn't any sign of her three companions. It had taken her awhile to notice, but now she was sure she was alone.

Emma was relieved at the thought of being alone, at least until she remembered her eyes were still blindfolded and her hands were tied behind her back. Panicked at the thought of being helpless in the woods, Emma struggled to get her hands free. Her movements were useless. With each attempt, the rope rubbed harshly against her wrists; every movement only served to make her bonds tighter. After a few minutes of struggling to free herself she relented; she would have to find another way to *doff* her chains. She stopped to think.

Emma thought about ignoring the fact that her hands were tied and instead getting up to try to find her way back. However, if she didn't get her hands untied then she couldn't remove her blindfold, and that wasn't an option. In her mind, walking around blind would make her an easy quarry to any number of nocturnal creatures. She would have to free herself before she could go on. It would take hard work and some creative thinking, but she was determined to do it.

Again she tried slipping her hands out of the rope. This time she moved slowly, using one hand at a time. At first she thought she was making progress but after a few minutes of valiant attempts, she realized the rope was too tight and all she was doing was giving herself a nice burn. Oh, how she wished she had brought a pocketknife with her. The rope wasn't very thick and would have been easily cut if Emma had something sharp. Emma vowed from that moment on, she would always carry a small knife in her pocket. She wondered

Doff   (dof) – V – to take off

what else she could use to tear through the rope. Leaning against the tree, she felt the texture of the bark. The bark was sharp, and she hoped it would be strong enough to slice through her bonds. Perhaps the lightweight rope, prickly bark, and just enough friction would be the right recipe to set her free. Emma began to furiously rub her hands against the bark. She used all of her strength to rub and pull. She struggled as if her life depended on it; after all, she couldn't be sure her life didn't depend on it. She *assiduously* worked and worked at the difficult task. Bark flew off the tree. She rubbed so hard her arms began to ache. Finally, Emma stopped to see if it had done any good. With great anticipation she pulled on the rope. Nothing happened. Despite her best efforts, the only damage Emma had done was to the tree, which now had a large bald spot where the bark used to be. The rope remained firm.

Emma decided to put her work in *abeyance* for the moment. She stopped moving and again started thinking. As she pondered her dilemma, she ran her hands around the rope. To her surprise, she found the knot that held the two ends together. It would take some skill, but if she could get the knot between her fingers she might be able to untie it. Carefully she twisted the rope around. The movement of the ties chafed the burn she had already received on her wrists, causing a stinging sensation to run up her arms. It felt as though she were rubbing a raw carpet burn over and over. Not letting the pain deter her, Emma didn't quit until she had the knot where she needed it. Once she had a good grasp of the tie, she carefully and assiduously began to unravel it.

Assiduous	(uh-**sij**-oo-uhs) – ADJ – carefully, attentively, tirelessly, persistently
Abeyance	(uh-**bey**-uhns) – N – suspension; temporary cessation

After a few strategic pulls, the yoke loosened and, like magic, the rope fell to the ground. It was as if someone had tied it so it could be easily untied. Emma would have saved herself a nice bit of trouble and pain if she had attempted to untie the rope first. Not wasting any more time, she used her free hands to doff her blindfold. Stumbling as she stood up, Emma brushed off the dirt and leaves she had collected while she was sitting on the ground. Looking around to make sure there were no creatures nearby, Emma set out to find her way back.

Before she left the area she stopped to look around just to be sure she hadn't left anything behind. Close to where she had been sitting was a flashlight. Thinking one of her captors must have dropped it when they absconded, Emma relished her good luck. She picked up the flashlight and turned it on. The light pierced the darkness, illuminating her surroundings. She used the tool to make a full examination of the area. Emma discovered a small piece of paper and a compass near where she had found the light. Holding the flashlight under her arm, she used both of her hands to unfold the paper quickly. Thinking she would find a letter of instructions, Emma was shocked to behold a very intricately drawn map. It was handmade but surprisingly detailed. The map showed a large green area which looked as though it was a forest. One of the markers on the map was a large tree which stood out against the rest of the **arboretum**. With a hunch, Emma turned around to gaze at the tree she had been resting on.

Arboretum   (ahr-buh-**ree**-tuhm) – N – a plot of land on which many different trees or shrubs are grown for study or display

There stood a tremendous sight. Towering above her was the colossal oak tree, its branches stretched toward the heavens, blocking out the sky. The darkness magnified its size; it was hard to tell where the actual tree ended and the rest of the forest began. Looking back at the map, there could be no doubt this tree was the one depicted in the picture. It wasn't a mistake that her captors had led her to this spot and abandoned her next to the grand tree. They weren't lost at all, but were carefully executing a masterful plan. Emma found herself in awe of how brilliant it all was. From the letter to the map, every detail had been meticulously thought out. The people who brought her there were more *wily* than she had imagined, as these intricate plans proved. She was still unsure why they would go to so much trouble, but she admired the ingeniousness of their plot.

At that moment, all the fear she had once felt was transformed into excitement. She was in the middle of an unusual adventure full of twists and surprises. With the map and compass in hand, Emma felt as though she were a character in one of her favorite childhood stories. She had always admired characters with the good fortune to stumble upon some grandiose enterprise. Emma lost sight of the cold, forgot about her pain, and couldn't remember to be tired. All she could think about was her next task. She would follow this map until it led her to her destination, wherever that might be.

She took the map and examined it closely. A small river or stream flowed to the west of the tree. She noticed another marker, a small building a little bit above the tree. She figured this building must have been the one she

---

Wily   (**wahy**-lee) – ADJ – shrewd; cunning

was held earlier. Outside of the forest, a couple of circles were drawn. Emma wasn't sure what they represented, but further above the circles was a large house. There were no instructions on the map, but she assumed the house was where she needed to go.

Emma gathered her belongings. She decided to take both the rope and the blindfold with her. The way things had been going, she figured they might prove to be useful at some point during the night. She stuffed the items into her coat pocket and took one more look at the map. Not exactly sure how she was to read it, Emma started walking in what she thought was the direction of the small building. Using the compass her captors left behind, she oriented the map to mimic her position, with the tree behind her, what sounded like the stream to her left, and the building straight ahead and a little to the right. Her reasons for heading to the building were twofold; she knew that in order to get where she needed to go, it would be best to retrace her steps, and she was very curious to see what kind of building it was. Emma walked on.

The frigid wind chapped her face. Her lips were dry and her hands were as cold as ice, but Emma didn't notice. She had an ***ardent*** desire to complete her task. The trees were extraordinarily thick and the darkness made it feel like a moonless night. Emma was thankful for the flashlight. It wasn't hard to navigate through the brush, but it was a long walk. As she continued, the woods grew even thicker and the terrain became rocky. The branches brushed against her, clawing at her clothes. A loose pebble caught her foot, causing Emma to tumble to the ground. She fell face-first against the rocks. Her forehead struck

---

Ardent   (ahr-dnt) – ADJ – passionate

the corner of a large rock, causing a considerable gash. A burning sensation ensued and a small trail of blood trickled down the side of her face. Emma had twisted her foot as she landed. Afraid she might have done more than sprain her ankle, Emma waited for a moment before she tried to pick herself up. She moved her foot carefully. Once she was certain nothing was broken, she cautiously began to stand up. She *toiled* to get up with her hurt leg making the task arduous. The pain from her head and foot made it difficult to move. She got halfway up several times, but each time she felt dizzy and sat back down. Her last attempt almost ended tragically with another fall. At that moment, Emma decided it would be best to remain seated, at least until the trees stopped spinning. Something had to be wrong— either she had gravely mistaken the distance between the tree and the small house, or she had been going the wrong direction.

Emma remembered some basic first aid her father had taught her and decided to put this little break to good use. She took out the blindfold and carefully wrapped it around her head to put pressure on her wound, which caused a sting of *cephalic* pain. She didn't know how bad it was and didn't want to run the risk of passing out.

Once again, Emma pulled out the paper map. It was then that Emma discerned her mistake. Looking at the sketch, she noticed the drawing of the woods got darker further back from the tree, the opposite direction of where she wanted to go. The deeper coloring most likely symbolized the thicker brush. Emma had been going the wrong way. But how, she wondered? Hadn't she walked

---

| *Toil* | (toil) – V – to work hard; to struggle |
| *Cephalic* | (suh-**fal**-ik) – ADJ – of or relating to the head |

straight ahead from the tree? Stopping to think, Emma remembered she hadn't checked to see which side of the tree she was sitting at. She could have been facing any direction. Perhaps that was why Emma was given a compass. She felt like such a dolt. A few minutes of setting her bearings correctly would have once again saved her time and trouble. Emma refused to let this setback *faze* her— yes, she was making several mistakes, but she was learning from them. She determined it was better to be fumbling now while she was playing a game then to make a blunder later when her life might actually depend on it.

The best thing Emma could do at that moment was to pick herself up and continue on with her quest. Before taking another step, Emma turned to face the direction she had originally been walking. She pulled out her compass and calculated her direction. She had been walking due south, so she knew to go back the way she came she needed to go north. Emma turned around, got her compass set to where she wanted to go, and started her slow and painful journey. Watching her steps and moving slowly to favor her injured ankle, Emma navigated through the rocks and trees. Soon she came upon a clearer path.

Emma came upon a familiar sight. There before her stood the magnificent tree. This second encounter was just as awe-inspiring as the first. The tree seemed ageless, as if it had always been there. For a moment Emma wondered if it had once been the tree of good and evil, and whether she was unknowingly standing in the middle of the Garden of Eden. Then Emma remembered the snake in the story and realized she was standing in the middle of the woods with who-knows-what creeping around her.

Faze   (feyz) – V – to bother; to upset

Images of snakes and spiders flooded her imagination. Emma was suddenly very thankful for the cold. Snakes were cold-blooded animals and would be hibernating this time of year. However, Emma knew snakes weren't the only creeping things in the forest at night. She wanted to quickly exit the woods and get to a place where she could see what was under her feet. She turned to the shiny compass, her trusted *bauble* to safely guide her home.

This time, Emma made the effort to plot a few points on the map and decipher which way to go. She oriented the map again. Then she decided to check on the position of this apparent stream. No longer believing the stream to be to the west, she carefully moved eastward using the flashlight to guide her progress. Her ankle was holding up fairly well, and Emma prayed it would last until she got out of the forest. It wasn't long before the beam of light flashed across what had to be the small stream on her map. Taking a minute to dip her ankle into the cool water to help reduce the swelling, Emma felt a surge of energy. Convinced she was now going in the right direction, Emma trekked on through the woods. The path was much cleaner on this side of the tree, and Emma soon began to make up time. Emma continued on her slow-footed *peregrination* through the forest. Before she knew it, she was standing at the back of a little building. Torn between exploring the hut and proceeding to her final destination, Emma decided to take a moment to look around. Pointing the flashlight directly at the building, Emma noticed it was painted a sallow yellow. Worn by weather, it looked as though it had

| *Bauble* | (**baw**-buh l) – N – a gaudy trinket; a small, inexpensive ornament |
| *Peregrination* | (per-i-gruh-**ney**-shuhn) – N – expedition; especially on foot |

once been brilliantly colored. Emma proceeded cautiously. The last time she was at this place, she had been blindfolded and bound. The evening had already been filled with surprises, and she wouldn't be shocked if someone were waiting for her to arrive. Slowly walking around the building, Emma noticed the hut had an astonishing semblance of a small home. The windows on the side of the house had shutters and little shelves under the windowsill for flowers. The front side had similar features. The colors of the house had faded, but Emma could still see the traces of the little yellow house, with its green shutters and red door. In the moonlight, this small house was a ghostly sight. It looked as it once could have belonged in a fairytale book, but the years had made the once bright exterior *wan*. A little mailbox painted purple stood on a post a few feet from the house. Upon a closer examination of the mailbox, Emma discovered faint pink writing. Her eyes scanned the script. The weather had also taken its toll on the paint, and Emma could only make out a few letters—"LVD." Those three letters brought her closer to discovering who owned the house, but without the other words, they could mean any number of things.

Disappointed, Emma returned her thoughts to the house. Clearly no one lived in it now, but could it have once been a servant's quarters? It wasn't very big, but one person might have been able to reside there long ago. The structure's purpose remained a puzzle until Emma took a closer look. Peering through the little sliver of the window that had not been covered up, Emma saw the small room she had been kept in. It looked exactly how it had felt when she had been held captive in it. A chill went down her back

---

Wan　　　(won) – ADJ – faded; pallid

as she remembered sitting in the cold, dark room. Walking to the other side, Emma looked into what she had correctly guessed was a kitchen. Shining the flashlight around the space, she took a closer look at the furniture. There were small cabinets, a refrigerator, and a table and chairs all made out of plastic. They were just toys. Emma looked back at the small living room and noticed the same thing. In fact, the décor consisted of princess furniture and small *bibelots* typical of a pre-teen's collection. Emma laughed; this once-scary building was nothing more than a little girl's dollhouse.

Emma turned her back to the house and continued on her way. Up ahead she *espied* a clearing indicating the opening of the woods. She headed directly for the outlet. First, she began to walk faster, and then without realizing it, her walk became a lopsided sprint. Excited by the possibility of being free, Emma's enthusiasm took over. In no time, Emma stood at the edge of the forest. Filled with mixed emotions, she stood there for a moment before venturing out into the clearing. Upon her arrival Emma realized she was no more familiar with what lay ahead than she was of what lay behind. By now her excitement had worn off and she was beginning to feel the effects of the long evening. Fortunately the bleeding from her cut seemed to have stopped. She was all but tempted to return to the little house to catch some sleep, but she knew quitting at that point would have made the rest of the evening pointless. Emma had to make it to the final place on the map.

She didn't need the flashlight anymore. Outside the forest, the moon shone brightly, casting a silver glow

---

Bibelot	(**bib**-loh) – N – a trinket; a small object of beauty
Espy	(ih-**spahy**) – V – to catch sight of something

across the entire yard. While in the woods, Emma had thought that once she got to the opening, she would be able to see the larger house. However, as she exited the forest, she stood at the brink of a well-manicured pasture, but with no house in sight. The field was large enough to be farmland and seemed to be *arable*, but from where she stood, there were no crops or animals in sight.

As Emma began to walk onto the property she discovered she was moving up an incline. It seemed the forest was at a bottom of a downward slope and the hill obstructed her view of the rest of the land. With all the walking she had done, and her still-delicate ankle, climbing up the hill was an unwelcome task. Still, she kept moving until she reached the apex. At the top of the mini-mountain, Emma found herself not only facing the main house, but also standing in the middle of a beautiful garden filled with water features. Before her were a couple of elegant fountains surrounded by perfectly trimmed trees. The contrast between the forest and the garden was astounding. It felt as if she were standing between two opposing worlds. Even in the darkness the beauty was breathtaking. Emma had seen enchanting gardens before, but only at the palaces of European royalty. She never imagined someone in the States being wealthy enough to acquire such a luxury. But there she stood surrounded by the soothing sound of cascading water and the sight of nature's own perfection. Emma's gaze moved from the fountains to the house, if you could call it a house. The drawing on the map had depicted the home as large, but even "large" was too small a word to describe the building. Suited nicely with the rest of the property, the exquisite mansion encompassed the

---

Arable   (ar-uh-buhl) – ADJ – fit for growing crops

horizon. Out of all of the surprises Emma had received that evening, this was by far the most startling. She must be on the property of someone of great importance to account for such opulence.

In the distance, Emma espied two figures dressed in black. Just as she had thought, those who had brought her here were waiting at the house for her. There was still some distance between the gardens and the house, but the contrast of the black clothing next to the white house made their figures distinct. Emma wondered where the third member of the coterie had gone. She also wondered how long they had been waiting for her. It was hard to tell how long she had been in the woods. Unsure of how the figures would respond to her arrival, Emma began to walk a little more slowly. Once she reached the steps of the house, she began to climb. One by one she walked up the steps.

At the top of the porch, Emma could see the smiling faces of her former captors. Expecting to be greeted with faces that **glowered**, Emma was shocked by friendly expressions. Now she really did feel like she was in an opposite world. It was evident the two were pleased with Emma. They motioned for her to take a seat and one of the two brought her a tall glass of water. Thankful for the refreshment, Emma eagerly took the glass and began to **slake** what seemed to be an unquenchable thirst. All that exercise had left her feeling dehydrated, and Emma was grateful for the unexpected hospitality. Consumed by drinking the water, Emma did not bother to look at the people who were sitting next to her. For the first time since the evening began, it was light enough for Emma

---

| *Glower* | (**glou**-er) – V – to stare angrily |
| *Slake* | (sleyk) – V – to quench; satisfy a craving |

to see their faces—yet discovering their identities was the last thing on her mind. As long as she could see their movements, Emma was happy to be sitting down and out of that dreaded snake-haunted and spider-infested forest. However, Emma did not let down her guard this time. Even if the game were only temporarily in abeyance, Emma was determined to stay alert. Emma finished her drink and set the glass down. It was time to look the other two in the eyes and see who was behind this clever plot.

Sitting on either side of her were two boys about her own age, possibly a little older. Their faces were covered in camouflage war paint, but in the moonlight the colors didn't distract from their facial features. Emma quickly recognized the boy sitting to her left. It was Ninja Kid from her German class. She was pretty sure his name was Ethan, but she was in the habit of calling him Ninja Kid, so she couldn't be sure. He must have been the one to slip the note in her book while she was out of class. Emma was quite pleased with herself because he had been her top pick for the textbook trespasser. She turned her head to the side, expecting to find another member of the ninja group to her right, but instead she recognized the face of Thomas Pickering, the high school's African American science prodigy. Emma had never met him personally but had seen his picture in the last edition of the *Providence Star*, accompanied by an article on his recent first-place finish in some national science and inventor competition. According to the article, his win secured Thomas admission to some of the most prestigious engineering universities and all but guaranteed his future recognition in the world of science. If Emma remembered correctly, Thomas was quoted as saying his career aspirations were directed toward NASA. Everyone said Thomas was a genius, and she wasn't surprised that his future goals included working for one of the most challenging and exclusive organizations in the world. They were an odd mix to be sitting together. She had never seen them talk at school and found herself surprised at their companionship. However, she wasn't entirely sure they weren't part of the same group. *Was she being held captive by the ninjas? If so, would that be a group that she would even want to join?* Emma was curious to see who the third party was; surely the identity could not be more astounding than Thomas Pickering.

Emma turned her gaze toward the gardens. There she spotted the final member of the group walking toward the steps of the house. The figure was coming from the direction of the woods. The person had a slimmer silhouette than the other two and walked with the fluid *finesse* of a dancer. It was obvious this person knew his way around the property because he never looked down to check his footing. The figure walked up the stairs but his gaze remained fixed on the house. As he drew closer to the house, Emma quickly realized the person was not a *he*, but a *she*.

This pleasing revelation **abated** her apprehension of being held captive by the ninja group once and for all. The girl's frame was thin but not petite. Her hair was slicked back in a tight bun, and it wasn't until she reached the group that Emma could distinguish its honey color. Unlike the boys' faces, hers was not covered in war paint. Emma didn't know her name, but she knew she was the daughter of someone famous. She had seen the girl around school a couple of times with the other politicians' kids, but that

---

Finesse	(fi-**ness**) – N – delicacy of movement; skill in handling a situation
Abate	(uh-**beyt**) – V – to lessen; put an end to

was all the information she had. Looking at the girl's face, Emma felt as though she had seen the girl recently. She couldn't quite put her finger on it, but it was more than the faint familiarity of seeing her in the lunch room. The feeling of déjà vu gnawed at her. They had never spoken to one another; she didn't even know her name, yet she had a sense their paths had recently crossed. The girl walked past Emma and sat in the chair directly across from her. Not wanting to annoy her by staring at her, Emma turned her gaze to the other two. She knew the source of her feeling would reveal itself soon enough—she would just have to be patient and let her mind unravel the mystery.

Once they were all seated together in the circle of chairs, Ethan stood up to speak.

"I suppose you're wondering the point of all of this," he said, in the unmistakably deep voice from earlier in the day.

Emma nodded her head in agreement.

"You have done well, and it is time we share our secret with you."

Emma listened intently. She was anxious to hear what this was all about. However, before he could continue with his explanation, the girl interrupted him.

"Before you do that, Samurai, we must first see what she has already discovered," she said.

Emma recognized this voice to be the softer one she had heard earlier in the doll house. Tired and annoyed at the thought of delaying the explanation, Emma wanted to say they must be a bunch of bored rich kids who were looking to have some fun at the new kid's expense. Knowing that her current surge of hostility was the direct result of the late night and cold atmosphere, Emma decided to appease the members, and she began to recall all that had happened over the last several hours. She talked about the letter and how Ethan had slipped it into her book while she was gone. Suddenly Emma stopped her tale and began to laugh. *Oh, what wily chicanery!* she thought. She realized that this girl was the blabbering blonde who had delayed her in the bathroom before her German class.

Emma looked directly at the girl and said, "You knew I was going to be in the bathroom before class and you deliberately held me up so Ethan would have enough time to slip the message in my textbook before I got back."

"What can I say? Your routine made it easy to deceive you," replied the girl.

"How long had you been watching me to figure that out?" Emma asked.

"About a month," replied Thomas.

"Yeah, we had already decided you were the person we had been looking for, so we waited and observed to find the perfect opportunity to send you the letter," finished Ethan.

"What I don't get is how you even noticed me."

"It was the fight with Mrs. Huckleson at the beginning of school that first brought you to our attention," said Ethan.

"Anyone willing to take on that ol' bat deserves some recognition," said Thomas.

Emma was amazed how that moment of shame could garner such attention; after all she had never meant to create a *ballyhoo*. At the time, the argument with her teacher had made her feel terrible, but looking back

Chicanery	(shi-**key**-nuh-ree) – N– trickery; deceitfulness
Ballyhoo	(**bal**-ee-hoo) – N – an uproar; a noisy attention getting demonstration

at it now, she felt a small sense of pride for her ability to stand up for what she knew was right. Mrs. Huckleson had been wrong to so quickly dismiss Emma's knowledge, and Emma had the right to let her know it. But next time, she would do it in a more private setting. Although she hadn't thought about it before, she was glad these three had taken notice of her strength, even if she hadn't appreciated it herself.

"It's getting late and we should get to bed soon," spoke the girl.

"I'm not going to bed until someone explains everything to me," Emma stated with an intensity that surprised even herself.

"I guess you do have the right to know why you were blindfolded and left in the middle of the woods," said Thomas, smiling.

The three looked at one another, trying to decide who would best explain the situation. After a moment of hesitation, Ethan stood up and took the lead. Emma was already convinced he was the leader of this unusual group, and his decision to take charge confirmed her belief. He started off by explaining that he had been her ardent *advocate* from the beginning and had strongly *advocated* for her admission to their secret society. Once they had picked her as a potential candidate, they began a series of observations to see if Ethan's initial impression of Emma was correct. Each of them had Emma in a different class, and took notes on her conduct and participation. Ethan then spoke of her superior skill at languages and her

---

Advocate   1. (**ad**-vuh-kit) – N – one who pleads a cause for
                          another
                     2. (**ad**-vuh-keyt) – V – to plead in favor for

dedication to her studies. Hearing this, Emma felt a sense of gratitude toward Ethan for his kind words. No one had ever taken that much interest in her, and she felt strangely inspired by the stranger's attentiveness. He also explained how her *aloof* attitude toward the majority of Providence High made her the ideal candidate for the secret group. Because Emma hadn't had enough time to develop strong loyalties to anyone at the school, she wouldn't have trouble keeping this a secret from anyone outside of the small group. Emma now had the "how" of the situation, but not the "why." Why would anyone go through so much trouble? It wasn't like when Romeo and Juliet had to hide their love from their feuding families, or in 1942 Germany where the lives of hidden Jews hung on the very essence of secrecy. What could be so important in the city of Providence that was worth so zealously protecting? With one word, Ethan explained everything.

"Espionage."

"Excuse me?" said Emma.

"We do what we do because it is at the very heart of espionage," he said.

"We share a common goal of wanting to work for the most elusive government agency in the world: the CIA. And it is that passion that compels us to take such dramatic lengths to keep this brotherhood a secret. We all have our reasons, but each one of us wants to be a spy. "

Ethan's comment made Emma chuckle. She didn't really believe the three people sitting next to her wanted to be actual spies. She was sure this, too, was a part of the game they were playing. She gave Ethan a "come on" look

---

Aloof (uh-**loof**) – ADJ – uninvolved; keeping one's distance

and waited for the real explanation. Emma didn't realize the solemnity of her insult. Ethan couldn't be more serious about the gang's desire to join the CIA, and they hoped Emma would share in their passion. After a long pause, Emma understood this wasn't a joke.

"You really want to be spies?" she asked in a serious tone. "Why?"

"That's none of your business," he said, clearly offended by Emma's early reaction.

"I'm sorry if I insulted you. I didn't realize you were being serious. It's not every day someone takes you out to the woods, puts you through a bunch of strange tests, and then tells you it's because he wants to be a spy."

"I guess it does seem a little odd."

"It's more than a little odd," Emma said with a smile.

The tension between the two soon dissipated. Ethan understood Emma meant no harm by her laughter, and Emma realized Ethan wasn't trying to trick her. Emma was eager to hear the full explanation of how the group began and what brought them to her, so he began the *compendium* of events that led them there that night.

"It all started freshman year," he began. "Incoming students are given a job placement test to help them see what types of career paths their personalities are suited for once they leave high school. The school believes it is a good way for students to get direction and help them make actual career goals. Many students blow it off as a silly test, but I was really curious to see the results."

"And the test told all of you that you would be great spies?"

Compendium   (kuhm-**pen**-dee-uhm) – N – a summary; an inventory

"Not exactly," explained Ethan. "I was the only one who had the CIA listed as a potential employer. Thomas scored high marks toward NASA, and Lavender was destined to be a lobbyist or some type of public relations specialist."

"So how did you three get together?"

"Well, these tests are given in the summer during freshman orientation. Every incoming student is required to attend a three-day seminar where he or she takes the test, meets with a guidance counselor, and gets introduced to future classmates. The program even includes a small group session, where the same group of students sits down with different teachers and asks questions to get to know one another better. It's sort of a trial program Providence High has been doing for the past five years to help students prepare for the transition from middle school to high school."

"So you three were all in the same small group."

"Precisely! Most students who meet in the groups don't stay friends after the program ends, but we found we all shared a common bond. One morning, the three of us arrived at school early. Since we were headed to our first small group session, we began to talk. It was there that we learned we all had an interest in espionage. Unfortunately, our conversation was cut short by the arrival of our teacher, and we decided to continue our talk after school. It was during our meeting after the session at school that we decided it would be cool to form a spy club. It started off as a joke, something fun to do for the rest of the summer, but as time went by, it became more and more serious."

"Didn't it seem weird to your friends that you three hung out together? After all, it's not like you guys are ever seen together at school."

"That's the goal," interrupted Lavender.

"The purpose of this group is secrecy. It would be harder to keep it a secret if people at school knew we were friends."

"It was easy to keep our friendship a secret during the first summer, because we hadn't really made any new school friends," said Thomas. "It was only when school began that we decided not only to keep people from knowing about the group but also to keep them from knowing about our connection to one another. This way they could never put it all together."

"So no one knows that you guys are friends?" asked Emma

"No one knows we even know each other," corrected Lavender. "Freshman year was a long time ago, and no one remembers who was in which small group."

"Why me?" Emma asked

"Because you have a critical skill none of us have; you're a gifted linguist," explained Ethan. "We all have different strengths. Thomas is a brilliant scientist, Lavender is a skilled communicator, and I'm an operations expert."

"We rotate who leads each meeting," said Lavender, "and we spend our time teaching each other different lessons from our particular strengths."

"And you need someone to teach you languages," added Emma.

"Exactly," replied Ethan.

"What if I don't want to be a spy?" Emma asked.

"That's why we spent so much time observing you to make sure you were trustworthy," explained Ethan. "Even if you don't want to be a career spy, you can still join our club, learn some important skills, and go on your way."

Emma thought long and hard about what Ethan had just said. She was intrigued by his speech. Working for the CIA didn't necessarily entice her, but joining a group dedicated to learning interesting life skills did. Although the tasks had been hard, Emma realized she had had more fun that evening than any other since she moved to the United States. If the challenges she faced that night were *harbingers* of the things to come, then she couldn't help but get excited about this club. It was more than the thought of playing spy games that appealed to her, but the idea of having a place where she belonged. She didn't know these three well, but already she felt as though she shared their bond. Despite the fact that this friendship was marked by secrecy and *stealth*, it would be something meaningful. Although she didn't know it yet, that evening Emma found something she had been missing: true friendship.

Harbinger	(**hahr**-bin-jer) – N – herald; something that foreshadows
Stealth	(stelth) – N – the act of proceeding with secrecy

WORD REVIEW

Aloof	Bibelot	Peregrination
Abate	Cephalic	Pusillanimous
Abeyance	Chicanery	Quarry
Acclimate	Compendium	Scenario
Advocate	Doff	Slake
Arable	Espy	Solemnity
Arboretum	Faze	Stealth
Ardent	Finesse	Toil
Assiduous	Glower	Wan
Ballyhoo	Hapless	Wily
Bauble	Harbinger	

3

THE POKER GAME MYSTERY

It was quite late by the time the conversation on the patio ended. Emma was very tired. The house belonged to the Wilkinses, Lavender's family, and it was agreed that the four would spend the night there. It was a large mansion with no shortage of guest rooms for the visitors. Lavender guided the way. She took Thomas and Ethan to a pair of adjoining rooms on the first floor. Their rooms were close to the back porch, and each one had a huge window facing the gardens. If the two hadn't been so tired, they might have enjoyed the view more. The four said their good-nights and Lavender led Emma upstairs to a room that was not far from her own bedroom.

All the lights in the house were dark, and Emma was surprised by how easily Lavender navigated through the darkness. From what Emma could tell, it was a very *cosmopolitan* house, full of furniture from all over the world and glass chandeliers that had to be from Europe. They walked through the large dining hall to get to the staircase. Lavender explained how they only used that room when out-of-town guests visited. Although she didn't expound, Emma understood that the Wilkinses were accustomed to hosting very important visitors. Emma knew Lavender's

---

Cosmopolitan   (koz-muh-**pol**-i-tn) – ADJ – at home in many places; internationally sophisticated

mother was a prominent politician, but she didn't have the energy to ask Lavender about it. Lavender did mention the most exciting guest who had visited was a handsome *Maharajah* from northern India the last spring. The Wilkinses hosted a ball in his honor.

As they walked up the wooden staircase, Emma's legs felt like jelly. She didn't realize how tired they were until she began to ascend the stairs. Every step took a tremendous amount of energy. She held tightly to the handrails to help herself make it up to the second floor. At the top of the staircase, Lavender guided Emma down the hallway and to her room for the night. There were four bedrooms and four bathrooms on that floor. Despite its abundant size, the second floor was occupied solely by Lavender. She was an only child, and her parent's bedroom was located downstairs near the front of the house. Tonight, however, her parents were on holiday in Europe, and the only people staying in the big house were the four friends. Across from Lavender's bedroom, Emma's room was the very last one on the hall. Lavender opened the door and turned on a lamp for Emma. She said good-night and went on to her own room.

The bedroom was incredible, decorated in green and gold. Emma felt as though she were staying in a palace. The bed was twice the size as her own back home, and she quickly discovered it was 10 times more comfortable. She had her own bathroom connecting to the bedroom, and it was just as luxurious as the bedroom itself. A huge bathtub in the middle of the room beckoned Emma to relax into its soapy comfort. Although it was already terribly late, Emma decided to take some time to soak her

---

Maharajah   (mah-huh-**rah**-juh) – N – ruling Indian prince

tired arms and legs, and clean off any dried blood, before heading off to sleep.

After her bath, Emma dressed herself in the pair of fresh pajamas Lavender had placed at the end of her bed. Clean and relaxed, Emma crawled onto the large pillow-top mattress. Although she wasn't what you'd call a *sybarite*, Emma knew she wouldn't have any trouble getting used to this luxurious type of lifestyle.

Daylight came quickly, and before Emma was ready, it was time to get up. It felt as if only minutes had passed since she had closed her eyes. Sunshine poured in through the window, lighting the entire bedroom. She opened her eyes. Lavender stood at the edge of the bed, shaking her awake.

"Emma, it's time to get dressed and ready," she said.

"What time is it?" a very groggy Emma asked.

"8 o'clock," she replied.

Emma thought Lavender was crazy. It was 8 in the morning on Saturday, they had been up all night, and they only thing Emma wanted to do was turn over and fall back asleep—a feat she was sure she could accomplish in no time. Emma's rebellious *remonstrations* would have been met with disdain if she had the guts to express them. Lavender could not care less how tired Emma felt. The day had already been planned out, and she wasn't about to let some sleepyhead get in the way.

"Get up, Emma," she coldly commanded. "Your clothes have been washed and are on the dresser for you. Breakfast will be served in 10 minutes. Don't be late."

Sybarite	(**sib**-uh-rahyt) – N – person devoted to luxury and pleasure
Remonstration	(ree-mon-**strey**-shuhn) – N – disapproval; objection

"Where are we going?"

"You will see. Your coat is on the chair next to the dresser. Dress warm; it's a chilly morning."

With that, Lavender left Emma to herself. Normally, Emma would stay in bed as long as she could get away with it, but this morning she didn't want to take a chance. She remembered why she was there in the first place, and her host's unfeeling ***behest*** was enough to get her moving. Emma threw off the covers and arose from bed. As her bare feet touched the cold floor, a shiver went through her body. Emma despised cold mornings and quickly went to her dresser to put on warmer clothes. One by one she layered her clothing. Once she was dressed, Emma reached for her coat. To her great surprise, someone had ***juxtaposed*** a large wool coat, thick-lined gloves, and a warm hat next to her poorly planned outerwear from the night before. She couldn't help but be grateful for this act of kindness. Unsure how much time she had left, Emma hurried down the stairs.

The smell of a delicious breakfast led her straight to the kitchen. Seated around the table were Ethan, Thomas, and Lavender. The three had already been served and were waiting for Emma to join them. A spread of eggs, bacon, sausage, and pancakes covered the table. The feast and the pains from Emma's stomach urged her to help herself to more than her usual plate size.

"You're late," Ethan said in a deep voice.

Nervous about his comment, Emma ***skittishly*** looked around the table, but the smiles that soon appeared on

Behest	(bih-**hest**) – N – command or order	
Juxtapose	(**juhk**-stuh-pohz) – V – to place side by side in order to compare	
Skittish	(**skit**-ish) – ADJ – nervous; cautious	

all their faces let her know he was just playing around. Everyone broke into laughter and teased Emma about being so nervous. She smiled and played along. Being generally good-natured about teasing, Emma was happy to know the group had a playful side.

The four enjoyed the hearty breakfast which had been prepared by Lavender's former nanny and current cook, Brigitte. They used the time to talk and get to know each other. During their meal, a cloud cover had rolled in and the weather looked ominous. The group had outside activities planned, but they decided it was best to wait inside and see if the storm would pass. The sky grew darker and the wind began to pick up. Large raindrops started to fall. A brilliant flash of lightning was followed by a crash of thunder. With the loud roar of the vicious weather outside, the four knew they were confined to the inside. They finished eating and Ethan, Thomas, and Lavender left the table to discuss the plans for the day, leaving Emma alone to finish her pancakes. With this divisive action, Emma was once again **relegated** to being merely a pledge of the group. Last night's conversation on the patio and this morning's breakfast had made Emma forget she was going through an initiation process. The lightheartedness of the group made Emma feel as if she really belonged. She hated the feeling of ranking beneath the other three and was ready to be a full member.

Emma was glad the storm had appeared. No part of her wanted to go back into the cold. She watched the raindrops fall, one after another. It hadn't started off as a heavy rain, but the longer she sat there watching, the harder the raindrops fell. By now the sky was a deep shade

---

Relegate   (rel-i-geyt) – V – to exile; to give a lower position

of gray. *It can't be more than 40 degrees out there,* she thought. Between the rain, wind, and March temperature, it must have felt colder than that. It was one of those mornings that begged you to sleep in, stay in your cozy pajamas, and spend the day curled up by a fire reading a good book. That was exactly what Emma wanted to do. Weary from the evening's excursion, Emma felt as though she had been at a bacchanal. Her head pounded from lack of sleep and her body was sore from all the walking, but her ankle didn't bother her anymore. She drank several glasses of water, hoping that hydrating would help her aches. Her eyes were heavy as she rested her head on the back of the chair. Once she was comfortable, her eyes began to close, and she drifted to sleep.

When Emma opened her eyes again she was surrounded by three unhappy faces. The lack of outside lighting made the room dark, but she could still clearly see the looks of annoyance. Emma quickly sat up and gave an embarrassed smile. Ethan motioned for her to stand up and follow them into the next room. Without hesitation, Emma obeyed. They walked out of the kitchen and down the hall. The entire house was dark, and apart from the occasional crack of thunder, completely quiet. They stopped in front of a closed door. Ethan lit a candle and handed it to Lavender; Lavender took it, opened the door, and disappeared. Then Ethan repeated the process with Thomas; Thomas did likewise. Then he turned to Emma, handed her a candle, and opened the door. Emma received the candle and walked into the room.

The drapes had been drawn and the room was as black as the night before. Emma felt as though she had been transplanted back to the little dollhouse in the woods. However, this was better than the dollhouse because it was warm and comfortable. Emma saw the other two candles and walked toward the light. Ethan closed the door and locked it behind him. The sound of the key locking them inside the room startled Emma. Although she knew she was not in danger, the idea of being locked in a room did not sit well with her. Certain the act was for dramatic effect, Emma decided not to think about it. Still, the feeling of uneasiness never left her.

Ethan joined the other three. One by one he took the candles and placed them on candle stands around the room. He used the last candle to light a few more. The room was still mostly dark, but the orange glow gave just enough light for the four to see one another.

"As you can see, on account of the weather, there has been a slight change of plans," said Ethan. "So, we have swapped our outside plans for inside ones."

"Since it's a rainy afternoon, we decided it would be appropriate to play a word game," added Thomas.

"A word game?" asked Emma.

"Yes, it's our own form of a detective game. We made it up one afternoon when we had nothing better to do," Lavender said, smiling.

"It's a murder mystery game," began Ethan. "One of us makes up a murder story and the others try to solve the case by uncovering the motive and the murderer."

"We take turns asking questions, and whoever solves the case first wins," explained Lavender.

"Couldn't someone keep guessing until he or she figures it out?" asked Emma.

"Not exactly," explained Thomas. "Each person can ask as many questions as he would like, but he only gets to try to solve the case once. If he guesses wrong, he's out of the game."

"You have to be absolutely sure you're right before you guess," said Ethan. "In other words, you need an airtight case... I mean like *hermetically* sealed airtight."

"And you don't want to take too long trying to figure it out," added Lavender, "because you're playing against two other players who have just as much information as you do."

"The key to the game is learning to balance working with the other players to gain information about the crime, while still keeping your suspicions to yourself," said Ethan.

"It's harder than it sounds," said Lavender, "but you'll get the hang of it."

Emma was excited about playing a game. She wasn't a very competitive person, so she didn't really care if she won or lost—she was just excited to try something sedentary. Playing seemed easy enough and didn't require being out in the weather. She was happy. However, the three were more *cunning* than Emma thought and were not about to let her off that easily, without a crafty challenge.

"To make winning more enticing," said Ethan, "we thought it would be fun to add a little bet to the game."

"What kind of bet?" asked Emma

"Well, since this is your first time playing, it would be very impressive if you could win. So here's the deal— if you win, your initiation is over, and we won't put you through any more tests. You will be equal to all of us, and we can end early and you can go back home. Perhaps even catch up on your sleep."

"And if I lose?"

"If you lose, then weather or no weather, we will continue with our original plans and go back outside."

Hermetic	(hur-**met**-ik) – ADJ – closed off; protected from outside influences
Cunning	(**kuhn**-ing) – ADJ – clever in deceiving

Emma shuddered at the thought of wandering outside in the rain. This bet was motivation enough for her to solve a hundred cases. She agreed.

Since Ethan was the mastermind behind the idea, it was agreed he should be the narrator of the story. He took some time to think about it before he started his tale. The other three got comfortable and waited to see how this would turn out. Emma was both excited and anxious. To beat her competitors, she needed *peerless* detective skills. To make it easier on Emma, the group decided it would only be fair if the story involved people they all knew. The characters of this tale would all belong to Providence High. Although Emma didn't know her fellow classmates and teachers as well as the other three, she would at least have some idea of their friends and, more importantly, their enemies.

"Last Friday, Joseph Hudson was found in his living room, dead at his poker table," Ethan began. "His body was found slumped over the table as if he were asleep. Blood and poker chips were spilled all over the table and floor; it was a *lurid* sight. According to the coroner, the time of death was sometime between one and three in the morning."

"That's an awfully late poker game," commented Lavender.

"Who were his buddies at the game?" asked Thomas.

"Seth Reese, Cory O'Reilly, and Jared Copper."

"They're all on the football team with Joseph," said Thomas.

Peerless	(**peer**-lis) – ADJ – better than all others
Lurid	(**loor**-id) – ADJ – harshly shocking

Although it wasn't smart game play for Thomas to add this information, he did so for Emma's benefit. He knew she probably didn't know much about the victim or his friends. He thought that some context would help her unravel the identity of the person *culpable* for the murder.

"Do we know what time the poker game ended?" asked Emma

"According to Seth's statement, the game ended around 11."

"Did he say why the game ended?" asked Thomas.

"Apparently, Joseph had a couple of great hands and cleaned the other three out of all their money. Seth also added that he didn't think Joseph had won fairly."

"So he was cheating his friends?" asked Lavender.

"That's what Seth believes anyway," said Ethan.

"How much was the pot?" asked Emma.

"Around eight thousand dollars."

"Seriously? What high school students have that much money to gamble with?" asked Emma.

"Joseph is notorious for hosting extraordinary poker games," explained Thomas. "He only lets in guys he knows can cough up the high stakes ante."

"But Cory isn't well off," started Lavender. "His mom's the school nurse, and didn't his father pass away a few years back?"

Lavender was also trying to help Emma out. For years, the O'Reillys went to her family's church—and, thanks to some serious seasonal allergies, Lavender had spent quite a bit of time seeing the school nurse. She had never really been friends with Cory, but their paths had crossed enough

---

Culpable   (**kuhl**-puh-buhl) – ADJ – guilty; responsible

times that she knew some information about his life. The O'Reillys were not poor, but Lavender was certain that Mrs. O'Reilly would never just give Cory a couple thousand dollars to gamble away at a poker table. He would have had to acquire the funds by some other means.

"Does Cory have a part-time job?" asked Emma.

"He does," replied Ethan. "For two or three years now, Cory has been a clerk at Movie Mania. It's really the perfect fit because movies are his *mania*, almost an obsession. I think he's seen just about every movie out there."

"How do you know that?" asked Emma.

"Because we work together," said Ethan.

"Perhaps he'd been saving his paychecks and thought a poker game would be an easy way to double his money in just one evening," said Lavender.

"It certainly would have made me mad if I lost all my savings in a poker game," said Thomas. "Especially if I lost under fraudulent terms."

"How close were Cory and Joseph?" asked Emma. "Were they good friends?"

"Hardly," replied Ethan. "Up until this last year when Cory joined the football team, Joseph was kind of a bully to Cory."

"Really?" said Emma.

"They all were," said Thomas. "Joseph, Seth, and Jared have been a tight-knit group since the beginning of high school. They're known for picking on a lot of different people, Cory included."

"So why would Cory agree to play poker with them?" asked Emma.

"Popularity," said Lavender. "Even though those

Mania   (mey-nee-uh) – N – crazed, excessive excitement three guys were mean, they are really good football players, so they're still some of the most popular guys on campus."

"So, if Cory was invited to play poker with them—" started Emma.

"His popularity status would dramatically rise," finished Thomas.

"Do you think the guys tricked Cory into playing with them so they could cheat him out of his money?" asked Lavender.

"It's possible. I wouldn't put it past those boys to do something like that," said Thomas.

"If so, they probably thought it would be an easy score—that is, until Cory found out and came back to confront Joseph," pondered Emma out loud. "You said they found the body still seated at the poker table?"

"That's right," replied Ethan.

"Did they find the money?" she asked.

"Yes, it was on the floor next to the table," stated Ethan.

"Was there any money missing?"

"Yes, according to the amounts given by Seth, Cory, and Jared, there should have been around $7,600 in the pot. Only half that much remained when the police arrived."

"That seems like a good indicator that money was the motive in this murder," said Emma.

"That's a good enough reason for me to suspect Cory," Lavender said matter-of-factly. "I'm going to guess that Cory O'Reilly murdered Joseph Hudson in revenge for cheating him out of his life savings and being a bully all those years."

"It's a good guess, Lavender, but you're wrong," said Ethan. "Cory might have been furious when he left the game, but he never came back to get even. I'm sorry, but you're out of the game."

Emma was surprised that Lavender was taken out for her guess. After all, the evidence did seem to point to Joseph being killed on account of his covetous *avarice*. Or did it, she wondered? Apart from conjectures, not much evidence had been presented in the story. Thinking back over the series of conversations, she realized it was only herself, Thomas, and Lavender who had spoken. Ethan, who knew the facts, hadn't spoken up once. The only thing they really knew about the murder was the victim, the crime scene, and what he had been doing early that evening. Even if he had been murdered by one of his poker buddies, the only person they had focused on was Cory. What about Seth? He seemed to be very talkative about the crime; he was even the person who suggested foul play in the game. Or what about Jared? No one had mentioned him since the beginning of the tale. Could he have something to do with this *convoluted* story of unsolved murder? There was more to the mystery than what they had been told. Emma needed to get the rest of the evidence before she could make her final guess.

As the search for clues continued with additional *inquisition*, Emma thought long and hard about the reasons that would inspire murder. In this story, money was the most obvious incentive, and before Lavender had wrongly guessed, Cory was the apparent suspect. With the circumstantial evidence surrounding him, anyone could have made the same mistake. Then it occurred to her—what if someone was counting on the police to make that mistake? Could it have been

---

Avarice	(av-er-is) – N –	insatiable greed for riches
Convoluted	(kon-vuh-loo-tid) – ADJ –	twisted; confusing
Inquisition	(in-kwuh-zish-uhn) – N –	the act of inquiring

that someone set up Cory as a scapegoat for the real murderer? Perhaps this was more than a tale of murder, but one of cover-ups and betrayal. If Emma's suspicions were correct, the murderer would have to be someone who knew Cory would be there that night—someone who also knew that Joseph had a habit of cheating and that Cory couldn't afford to lose. The murderer would have to be someone else at the game. This left Emma with only two suspects—Seth Reese, who was more than willing to talk to the police about the crime, and Jared Copper, who was keeping his mouth shut.

Both were equally good suspects, and without more to go on, Emma couldn't make a well-informed guess. She had two options—reveal her suspicions and run the risk of having Thomas figure it out first, or try to trick Thomas into thinking another person was culpable. The first wasn't an option—Emma abhorred the idea of going out in the cold rain. It would take some skill on her part, but Emma would have to do her best to make sure Thomas's investigation *careened* out of control. That way, even if Thomas had the same thoughts as Emma, perhaps she could convince him otherwise. If Emma could get Thomas out of the game, then she would be free to conduct a thorough investigation. Emma hated the *cavalier* attitude she had about deceiving her new friend Thomas, but it was the only way she could conceive of winning. It was a shady plan, but Emma's desperation to win compelled her to take such an action. After all, she justified to herself, this wasn't a game of teamwork.

Careen	(kuh-**reen**) – V – to swerve; to switch from side to side
Cavalier	(kav-uh-**leer**) – ADJ – marked by disdainful dismissal of serious things

"If money wasn't the motivator," Emma began, "then something equally strong must have been at the root of the murder."

Emma paused for dramatic effect before continuing her thoughts.

"The only other thing I can think of is jealousy," stated Emma. "Was Joseph dating anyone?"

"He's been dating Brittany Palmer since middle school," Ethan said.

"That's a long time to date someone. How is their relationship?" asked Emma.

"Shaky. A couple of days ago, they got into a huge fight in the middle of the cafeteria."

"Do we know the reason for the fight?" asked Emma.

"Last week he was rumored to be getting cozy with Brittany's best friend, Brooke," said Ethan. "The story could be true, but it may be just a *canard.*"

"Was there any evidence of something going on between Brooke and Joseph?" asked Emma.

"Nothing substantial. Just some gossip going around the school," said Ethan.

"A rumor isn't much to go on," said Thomas.

"True, but if Joseph didn't have a problem with cheating his friends out of thousands of dollars, do you think he'd have a problem cheating on his long-term girlfriend?"

"Good point. The willingness to deceive in a game doesn't bode well for a person's character," said Thomas.

With Thomas's words, Emma felt terrible. He was right—if you're willing to give up your morals in one area, how is that different than giving them up in

---

Canard   (kuh-**nahrd**) – N – false story; unfounded rumor

another area? She realized that winning a game wasn't a good enough reason to cheat the truth. However, she also understood there was a difference between not sharing information in a detective game and purposely stealing money from friends in a game of good faith. Emma's deception was an accepted element of the game play; Joseph's fraudulent behavior was not. It seemed hard to grasp that a similar action of deception could be right in one situation and wrong in another. However, the discrepancy was caused by the expectations of those involved. Cheating friends out of hard-earned cash for selfish gain was an *atrocity* because it exploited their trust. Misleading your opponents in a game of wit was savvy playing. Emma found herself in a moral gray area, when the right and wrong of an action lay beyond the action itself and encompassed the person's motive and the situation at hand. She knew that there are many scenarios where deception is wrong—Emma just happened to be in one where it was right. She continued playing.

"Cheating is a good enough reason to get even," added Emma.

"However, there is no evidence. No one would kill someone just because of gossip," objected Thomas.

"Unless Brittany found out it was more than a rumor," added Emma. "Perhaps she confronted Brooke about it and Brooke told her everything."

"Then wouldn't there be a double murder?" asked Thomas. "If Brittany was upset enough to get Joseph back for cheating, why would she let Brooke off?"

Thomas had made a valid argument. The affair

Atrocity   (uh-**tros**-i-tee) – N – a great wickedness

would have *estranged* their friendship and made the two girls enemies. Therefore, it would not make sense for Brittany to forgive Brooke while still wanting to seek revenge against Joseph. That is, unless Brooke had convinced Brittany it was all Joseph's fault—that, in fact, he had come to her and tricked her into betraying her best friend. If Brittany believed that Brooke was a victim like herself, she would have quickly forgiven her friend and sought revenge for both of them. It was a clever counterargument, and if Emma spun the story right, Thomas just might go for it.

"I bet Brittany and Brooke had a closer bond than Brittany and Joseph," *opined* Emma with conviction.

"Which means she would be even more upset with Brooke," said Thomas.

"True, unless Brittany didn't think it was Brooke's fault," said Emma.

"What are you suggesting?" asked Thomas.

"What if Joseph sought Brooke out and deceived her, too?" began Emma. "He could have convinced Brooke that he and Brittany had just broken up. What if she, like Brittany, was a victim?"

"That's giving Joseph an awful lot of credit in the art of chicanery," said Thomas.

"Well, if he was cunning enough to swindle his friends in poker, a game of both observation and luck, it would be easy for him to charm his way into the unsuspecting hearts of young girls," said Emma.

Emma could tell Thomas still felt an uneasy

Estrange	(ih-**streynj**) – V –	to make unfriendly or hostile
Opine	(oh-**pahyn**) – V –	to state an opinion

ambivalence toward her rendition of the tale. She thought it best not to push it, but to let Thomas come to his own conclusion. At the very least, her explanation got the group talking about possible candidates other than her two prime suspects. She didn't care which murderer Thomas picked, as long as he didn't pick the right one. Emma glanced over at Thomas, who was deep in thought. She wondered if he had uncovered her scheme and was about to solve the crime in its entirely. Perhaps he knew all along and only let Emma think she was in control of the game; Thomas was a veteran game player, after all. She kept her mouth shut and waited.

"Where was Brittany on the night of the crime between the hours of one and three?" asked Thomas.

"She was spending the night at Brooke's house," Ethan said.

"Odd for her to be spending the night at the house of the friend who supposedly cheated with her boyfriend," commented Thomas.

"Was there any evidence that placed Brittany at the crime scene?" asked Thomas.

"One of Brittany's hairs was found on the jacket worn by the victim," said Ethan.

Thomas and Emma both knew a hair found on the victim was pretty *tenuous* evidence, flimsy at best. There was no way anyone could determine when or how the hair got there. Because of the intimate nature of Brittany's relationship to the victim, one could easily conclude a number of logical situations, which did not include murder, for the appearance of her hair. Emma was afraid her brilliant scheme had failed.

Ambivalence   (am-**biv**-uh-luhns) – N – having mixed emotions
Tenuous   (**ten**-yoo-uhs) – ADJ – shaky; extremely thin

However, there was just enough circumstantial evidence to make Thomas suspect Brittany as the perpetrator of the crime. Since he didn't have any other good leads for the murderer, he decided to take a chance and guess.

"Ok, that's enough evidence for me to make my accusation," said Thomas.

"Go ahead," said Ethan.

"I believe Brittany Palmer killed Joseph Hudson on account of his infidelity," said Thomas.

"Another valiant guess," started Ethan, "However, you, too, are wrong and are out of the game. This leaves just one player left. Emma, it's your chance to solve the Poker Game Mystery."

Emma was surprised how quickly Thomas had guessed Brittany. She was sure he had picked up the flaws in the investigation. Both Lavender and Thomas had missed critical evidence needed to make a solid case. It was then she discovered her novelty to the game gave her an unfair advantage. Because this was her first time to play, Emma was more cautious in her guessing. Wanting to be absolutely sure of her pick, Emma checked and double-checked assumptions. This cautious investigative work wasn't the best way to play the game because it allowed the other players the opportunity to win first—however, jumping headlong into accusations wasn't wise either. Emma had lucked out that her opponents took their experience for granted. Next time she played, she would have to be quicker because she knew Lavender and Thomas would not make the same mistakes twice.

Now that Emma was the only player left she needed to determine the true motive for the crime. She understood the reason behind the killing would be the *crux* of the investigation. Emma had two suspects, Seth and Jared. Emma suspected Seth more than Jared, so she thought she would start her questioning there. If he wasn't the person, then she would guess Jared. One of Joseph's friends had to be behind this *execrable* deed of his murder.

"What was the relationship between Joseph and Seth Reese?" asked Emma.

"Seth and Joseph both play on the football team together," said Ethan. "They have also been best friends for years."

"What positions do they play?" she asked.

"Joseph is the head quarterback and Seth is his second-string backup," said Ethan.

"So Seth only plays when Joseph doesn't?" asked Emma.

"Correct."

"Are Seth and Joseph competitive with one another?"

"Yeah, they're always trying to one-up each other."

"Does Joseph always win?"

"No. Sometimes Joseph wins; sometimes Seth wins. They're pretty equal adversaries."

"Did Seth ever have feelings for Brittany?"

"Yes, Seth liked her first, but Joseph was suave enough to win her affection."

"Is Seth in a relationship with anyone?"

"Not really. He's gone on a few dates here and there," said Ethan. "Nothing that has lasted."

"Does he still have feelings for Brittany?" asked Emma.

"Yes. When Brittany found out about Joseph's

Crux	(kruhks) – N – the central point; the essence
Execrable	(**ek**-si-kruh-buhl) – ADJ – utterly detestable

possible affairs, she went straight to Seth and asked about it," said Ethan. "He was seen consoling Brittany."

"What did Seth tell Brittany?" asked Emma.

"He told her that Joseph would never do such a thing," replied Ethan.

"Is that true?" asked Emma.

"Not at all. Seth had his suspicions for a while, and Brittany's accusations confirmed it," answered Ethan. "After his conversation with Brittany, he was seen getting into a big fight with Joseph."

"What happened?" asked Emma.

"Things were pretty tense on the football field that day," explained Ethan, "but after a while they seemed to calm down."

"Whose idea was it to invite Cory to the poker game?" asked Emma.

"Seth's," said Ethan. The discovery of Seth's closeted feelings for Brittany confirmed Emma's suspicions. Seth had access to everything; he had the opportunity, the motive, and the ability. She hadn't asked any questions about Jared, but she felt as though she didn't have to. All signs pointed to Seth. Emma knew she could draw out her questioning until she was absolutely sure, but she was beginning to get tired, and if she was wrong, she wanted to go ahead and get the game over with. She took a deep breath and made her final accusation.

"Just to *reiterate* the facts, it was Seth who invited Cory to the poker game," she stated in summary.

"That's correct," Ethan confirmed.

"And… he had an unrequited love for Brittany."

"Perhaps."

Reiterate   (ree-it-uh-reyt) – V – to repeat

"Then it's pretty obvious. I suspect Seth Reese murdered Joseph Hudson on account of his affection for Brittany," said Emma.

"Very good, Emma!" exclaimed Ethan. "You are correct."

A wave of relief washed over her face. Not only had she guessed correctly, but in doing so, she had completed her final initiation task.

"Well, Emma, it seems that you have won the right to be our equal," said Lavender.

"Good job," added Thomas.

"You are free to do whatever you please with the rest of your afternoon," explained Ethan. "That is, until tonight at 7."

"What's happening at 7?" asked Emma.

"Your initiation ceremony," said Thomas. "You can go home now and get some rest. We'll send a car to pick you up around 6:45. "

"The dress code is formal," said Lavender.

"Don't be late," added Ethan with a smile.

With that, the three concluded the game. Emma gathered her belongings and got into a car that took her back to the high school parking lot. There she got into her own car, checked her cell phone for any messages, and drove home. By the time she reached her house, the previous evening's events were a *nebulous* memory, already fading. Had she really been held captive, tied up in the forest, and forced to find her way back? Or had it all been some crazy dream? Emma was too tired to think. She quickly changed back into her pajamas, set her alarm for six o'clock, and crawled into bed. Whatever

---

Nebulous   (neb-yuh-luhs) – ADJ – hazy; vague

had happened, she would make sense out of it after a long-awaited nap.

WORD REVIEW

Ambivalence	Culpable	Nebulous
Atrocity	Cunning	Opine
Avarice	Estrange	Peerless
Behest	Execrable	Reiterate
Convoluted	Hermetic	Relegate
Canard	Inquisition	Remonstration
Careen	Juxtapose	Skittish
Cavalier	Lurid	Sybarite
Cosmopolitan	Maharajah	Tenuous
Crux	Mania	

4

THE OATH

The sun went down early this time of year in Providence as there were a few more months till summer. Before falling asleep, Emma pulled the drapes to keep the sunshine out; however, by the time six o'clock rolled around, Emma's bedroom was completely dark. Exhausted by the previous evening's activities, she could have slept through the night, but the piercing sound of her alarm clock woke her up.

Emma had one of the most annoying alarm clocks on the market, the "Unstoppable Clockable," an alarm clock that literally runs away from the owner. Emma's mother had purchased it for her last Christmas because she was tired of hassling Emma to get out of bed in the morning. Since kindergarten, morning rituals had been a battle between Mrs. Jones and Emma. As a little girl, Emma had to be dragged out of bed to get ready for school. Generally, the only *blandishment* that could coax Emma out of bed was the enticing smell of her mother's cooking as it wafted into her bedroom. Since a hot breakfast was not always an option, Mrs. Jones had to come up with an alternative. When Emma was old enough to get ready by herself, her mother thought that an alarm clock would do the trick of waking up her sleeping beauty.

Blandishment　　(**blan**-dish-muhnt) – N – action or speech intending to entice

Unfortunately for her mother, Emma discovered the magic of the "snooze" button right away and would *squelch* the troublesome ringing like a spiteful dictator silencing protestors. Her mother had just about had it with Emma when late one evening, she watched an infomercial about the "Unstoppable Clockable," the clock guaranteed to wake even the most stubborn sleepyheads. First, the clock would make a loud, obnoxious noise. Then, before the owner could press the snooze button, it would roll off the nightstand and around the room, continuing to make the noise. By the time the owner caught the clock to turn it off, he or she would already be awake. Exhilarated by modern technology, Mrs. Jones had immediately purchased the product for her daughter and never regretted her decision. Emma, on the other hand, after a few mornings of being awakened by the jarring noise of the Clockable, was quite *penitent* for her earlier transgressions and begged her mother to remove the awful clock. But Emma's mother refused to take it back. After all, in just a few days, the Clockable had accomplished a feat Emma's mother could never do—getting Emma up the first time. As long as she lived at home and was under her mother's rule, waking up with Clockable was an *ineludible* fate.

At six, the Clockable awoke from its slumber and quickly sounded the alarm. The blinking lights from the faceplate illuminated Emma's dark quarters. Soon the Clockable was making its way all around her bedroom floor. Emma sighed at the noise. On more than one occasion, Emma had the devious plan of tossing her ridiculous

Squelch	(skwelch) – V – to put down, suppress, or silence with crushing effort
Penitent	(**pen**-i-tuhnt) – ADJ – repentant; apologetic
Ineludible	(in-i-**loo**-duh-buhl) – ADJ – inescapable

alarm clock out of her second-story bedroom window. She figured she'd tell her mother that Clockable hated that it was the most dreaded technological advancement in the world and wished to end the misery of its monotonous life by throwing itself down to the cruel earth below. She knew, of course, that her mother would never buy it, but the thought of Clockable strewn in pieces gave her a morbid sense of pleasure. Emma hated nothing more than she did her stupid alarm clock.

To the music of the unharmonious symphony playing on her floorboard, Emma tossed back the soft, warm covers of her comforter. Purchased by her father in Sweden, Emma's luxurious blanket was the envy of all her friends back in Germany. It was the perfect piece to complete her bedroom set. Emma's bed was the pride of her entire room. Filled with cozy pillows, sheets, and blankets, it was no wonder why Emma had trouble pulling herself away. Now she had no choice—she had to turn off her alarm clock.

She slowly maneuvered herself into a seated position with her feet dangling above the floor. The first steps were always the hardest. Emma's house was built in the 1920s and still retained its original hardwood floors. This amenity, among other features common with the 20s style, was the main reason Emma's mother had decided to rent this house. Emma, who enjoyed the look of the floors, did not take pleasure in the cold feel of the wood against her bare feet. Before she placed her toes onto the icy surface, Emma contemplated the pros and cons of getting up. However, her thoughts were interrupted by the penetrating sound of Clockable.

Utterly annoyed, Emma hopped out of bed to confront her admirable foe. Quickly she dressed her feet in a pair of fuzzy bamboo socks in order to *qualify* the feeling of cold her dainty toes received from the frigid floor. Emma caught Clockable underneath her dresser. The poor alarm clock was stuck between the wall and the corner of the dresser leg, causing it to have an electronic seizure. Emma reached for the contraption and relieved her irritating toy from its misery. It was now 6:03, and Emma needed to get moving to be ready in time for the ceremony.

While at the dresser, she grabbed a few clothing items to take with her into the bathroom for her shower. Emma hadn't decided what she was going to wear that night, so she thought it best to dress in her robe first and to pick out her dress once she was clean.

Unlike the setup at Lavender's mansion, Emma's house had only one bathroom on the second floor and it was down the hall from her bedroom. The house was dark and quiet. Emma's family was still out of town and wouldn't return until after church the next day. As she walked out of her bedroom and into the hallway, Emma turned on the lights. The hallway was painted a deep crimson and trimmed in a bright white. It was an elegant contrast. Although it wasn't a very large hallway, a variety of artwork was hanging on the walls. Mrs. Jones was not an art expert, but rather a *dilettante* who found great pleasure in subsidizing local artists' work. She couldn't help but purchase a new piece of art from every talented sidewalk artist she found. Mrs. Jones was not partial to a particular style or form, so her delight in street vendors' handiwork amounted to a unique collection. Emma's favorite of her mother's splurges was purchased on the Charles Bridge in Prague. Painted in watercolor, the piece depicted a scene

| *Qualify* | (**kwol**-uh-fahy) – V – to mitigate; make less harsh |
| *Dilettante* | (**dil**-i-tahnt) – N – a person who dabbles in the arts |

from the vantage point of the bridge overlooking the Prague Castle and Old Town at sunset. Every time Emma passed the landscape she had to pause. It was so peaceful. The mixture of red, yellow, and orange hues of sunset blended nicely against the red walls of the hallway. It was almost as if the walls were painted just that color for the picture.

Emma stopped, looked at her painting, and then scurried over to the bathroom. She turned the water to the highest heat setting possible and organized her stuff while she waited for the water to warm up. Steam filled the entire room, fogging up the mirror. Emma jumped into the shower and washed as fast as she could. This evening she didn't have time to waste.

Emma was in and out of the shower in no time. She grabbed for her towel, quickly dried off, then wrapped up in her robe until she found what she was going to wear. She made sure to put her socks back on to save her poor feet from touching the cold floor. Although she moved with a furious speed, Emma movements were marked by calm *unflappability*. She was excited and could not wait for the evening's activities.

Emma left the bathroom and headed to her room. She glanced up at the hallway clock as she went by. It was now 6:18. With very little time left, Emma knew how to make the minutes count. First she started to fix her hair. Because of the length and thickness of her dark brown hair, blow drying usually took the longest. To save some time, Emma had wrapped her hair in a towel to help soak up some of the extra water.

The Jones house still retained many of the original antique furniture pieces. The house had been kept by the

---

Unflappability   (uhn-**flap**-uh-**bil**-uh-tee) – N – self assurance; calm

same family, the Cook family, for generations. The Cooks had chosen to keep the place as close to its original condition as possible. Some things had been replaced—a couple of chairs, the bedroom mattresses, and all the bathroom fixtures—but as a whole, antique furniture dominated the house furnishings. When the Cooks decided to rent the place, the contract stated the furniture must stay and be well taken care of. The Joneses were not sure why the family decided to rent after so many years of living in that same house, but they were grateful to find such a place to live during their stay in the United States.

Emma's bedroom was no exception. Her furniture was made out of solid cherry wood. The deep reddish brown color was her favorite aspect of the pieces in her room. Emma also enjoyed the unusual furniture pieces such as a wardrobe and a vanity. Both were decorated with hand carvings and were of considerable size. Although a closet had been built into her bedroom 20 years before, Emma still used the wardrobe for her non-hanging clothes. Likewise, she joyfully used the vanity. She kept all of her beauty products in the drawers, and when she had the time, she used the mirror to fix her hair and on special occasions to put on some makeup. She plugged in her hair dryer and began to quickly straighten the ends of her hair. Once her hair was dried, Emma twirled it to make a simple French twist. It was the only updo she knew, and it was fast. When she was finished, Emma pulled out her makeup container. Emma didn't wear makeup that often, and when she did it was usually just powder and blush. Tonight, however, just for fun she decided to go glamorous with the addition of lipstick and eye shadow.

The clock struck 6:30, and a melodious song filled Emma's bedroom. The antique grandfather clock which stood at the edge of the stairwell began to sing its half-hour song. Its *orotund* noise resonated throughout the house. The clock was one of the few pieces of furniture that actually belonged to the Joneses. Emma's father had bought it in Sweden from an old clockmaker. With the chime, Emma realized she had only 15 minutes to finish getting ready, and she was still dressed in her robe. Hurrying from her vanity, Emma rushed to pick out her evening attire. She went straight to the back of her closet to where her nicest dresses were kept. Emma didn't have many dresses to choose from, but there was one she thought would be perfect. Emma pulled out a satin dress made out of a material the color of an *ocher* sunset. The satin material was a deep yellow, but in some lights reflected a hint of red. Emma's mother had found the material years ago and saved it for a special occasion. That occasion had come last year at Emma's previous school's winter formal. By the time of the formal, the Joneses knew they would be moving to the States. Emma's mother made her the dress as a sort of good-bye present. It was beautiful. Emma felt elegantly adorned in the luxurious gown. The design of the dress was plain. Other than the glow of the fabric, there were no adornments. The dress was sleeveless and slightly off the shoulders, stretching down just above Emma's mid-calves. Her mother once described it as tea-length dress, although Emma herself wasn't sure what that term meant.

Emma stood at the mirror admiring her reflection. Suddenly the clock in the hallway started to chime. Emma

Orotund	(**awr**-uh-tuhnd) – ADJ – marked by strength and fullness
Ocher	(**oh**-ker) – N – a range of colors from pale yellow to reddish yellow

knew it was now 6:45. Her ride would be there any second. She scurried across the room, gathering her belongings. Racing across the wooden floors, Emma began to slide. It was then she realized she was still wearing the bamboo socks. In a panic Emma reached into her closet to grab some high heels. Without looking she grabbed the first pair she could find. They were black. *Black goes with yellow, doesn't it?* Emma wondered. Whether it did or didn't, Emma didn't have the time to find something else. *Jauntily*, Emma threw off her socks and slipped on the shoes. She glanced at Clockable, who was once again resting on Emma's night stand. The faceplate read 6:47. Emma was late.

Emma made a mad dash to collect her stuff. She had her purse, her coat, a scarf, as well as the warmest gloves she owned. After putting on her outerwear, Emma quickly headed out the door. As soon as she walked into the hallway, she stopped and turned around. Emma rushed back into her bedroom and went straight for her jewelry box. She opened a couple of the tiny drawers and then quickly shut them. Finally she found what she was looking for. In the last drawer, she retrieved a slender pocket knife. Although she didn't know what exactly to expect this evening, the previous night's excursions had taught her to be prepared. Emma slipped the knife into her purse and quickly resumed her position in the hall way. Hurriedly she ran down the hall, stopping only for a moment to nod her head in approval to her favorite painting. Acknowledging the painting as she passed was her way of paying *homage* to it. Even when she was in a great hurry, Emma never forgot to recognize the work of art.

Jaunty	(**jawn**-tee) – ADJ –	lively
Homage	(**hom**-ij) – N –	respect given to acknowledge worth

She flew down the stairs and turned off all the lights except for one—the light fixture that hung directly over the staircase. Unsure of when she would return, Emma thought it best not to let the house look completely abandoned. Emma opened the front door and stepped out into the cold night's air. As she stepped out, a black stretch limousine pulled in front of her house. The vehicle was as large as her entire front yard and had to block her driveway just to park. Thankful her ride had also been late, Emma shut the door behind her and locked her house.

As Emma approached the vehicle, she noticed that the entire limousine was black, from the front to the back, including all the windows. A short, slightly overweight gentleman in his early forties opened the driver's side door. He wore a dark suit, tailored to his shape, and a hat to match. This man had a solemn expression on his face and returned Emma's eager smile with a cursory nod. It wasn't that his mannerisms were **aristocratic**; they were just very reserved and formal. Emma attributed his composure to the many years this man had probably served waiting on American diplomats and foreign royalty.

Marty—not his real name, but the one Emma gave him when she first saw him (after all, he looked like a Marty)—walked around the car toward Emma. With one suave, fluid motion, he opened the door for her and motioned for Emma to take her seat. In a soft but courteous voice, Emma thanked him. Once Emma was seated, the man closed the door behind her and walked back around to restore himself to his original position. Emma had the entire backseat to herself. This surprised her because she

---

Aristocratic (uh-ris-tuh-**krat**-ik) – ADJ – snobbish; acting like an aristocrat

was half expecting her new colleagues to be waiting inside. Instead, she sat alone in a car that was almost the same length as her entire bedroom.

Marty, whose real name was Gordon, apologized for being tardy. His use of the word made Emma chuckle softly to herself.

Gordon explained that the water from the storm earlier that day and the overall temperature had made the roads slick. Although drivers in the Providence area were used to such road conditions, Gordon thought it best to avoid stretches of roads with any bridges. Therefore they would have to take some side streets to get to their destination. Gordon was a pleasant but unremarkable sort of fellow. His voice was polished but not captivating. His appearance was pleasing but not attractive. He seemed like an ordinary man who lived a mundane existence. Gordon was a stark contrast to the grandeur of the vehicle. Emma nodded politely as Gordon explained their indirect route. She found herself having trouble paying attention to his words. The *superfluous* features of the luxury car along with her reasons for being in it compelled Emma's thoughts elsewhere.

The temperature of the limousine was warm and comfortable. Emma found herself quickly removing her outerwear and gently placing it to her side. She figured they would be in the car for a least a little bit longer and she wanted to get cozy. Gordon asked if she would like him to turn down the thermostat, but Emma shook her head *no* since she would rather ride without her coat. The truth was, Emma hated wearing coats, or any winter clothes for that

---

Superfluous   (soo-**pur**-floo-uhs) – ADJ – excessive; more than enough; extravagant

matter. Unfortunately for her, she had spent the majority of her life in colder climates, and as much as she disdained the extra layers, she much preferred them to the cold. With the warm air circulating inside the limousine and the soft leather of the seat, Emma was in complete *felicity*, cozy, comfortable, and content. Dressed in her finest, Emma was as happy as a girl of 16 could possibly be.

Gordon wasn't one for talking beyond the initial pleasantries and Emma was still too shy to strike up a conversation on her own. The next few minutes of their drive were completed in a peaceful silence. Neither of them minded the quiet, because it was born out of a lack of things to say and not an awkward situation. Emma, however, had an ***affinity*** for listening to music while in the car, so she asked Gordon if he would play the radio. There was another long silence, as Gordon ***phlegmatically*** browsed his music collection. Emma found this delay quite irritating and thought Gordon to be a lazy, uncommitted driver.

Finally, music began to play. The harmonious sounds of Richard Wagner's *Tristan and Isolde* filled the vehicle. Wagner, pronounced with a "V" sound instead of a "W," was one of Emma's favorite composers. Emma had written a research paper on the German-born composer in her music history class just last semester. In fact, it was his work on this very opera that first enticed Emma to write about him. She could hardly believe Gordon, this unremarkable man, could harbor such extraordinary musical taste. Perhaps she had been too hasty in her assessment of his qualities. A smile overtook Emma's face as Gordon glanced

Felicity	(fi-**lis**-i-tee) – N –	the state of being happy
Affinity	(uh-**fin**-i-tee) – N –	attraction; natural liking
Phlegmatic	(fleg-**mat**-ik) – ADJ –	impassive; apathetic; sluggish

back to see if the music was to her liking. Gordon returned her expression with a similar grin and then returned his gaze to the road. Neither of them said another word to each another for the rest of the drive. Both sat blissfully listening to the soft, *mellifluous* sounds of Wagner's operatic composition.

Emma had enjoyed her ride with Gordon very much and felt a sense of sadness as they pulled into the driveway of the Wilkins's mansion. With finesse, Gordon pulled the mammoth car around the circular driveway and stopped to drop Emma off at the front door. Once he got the car into position, he put it into park and unbuckled his seatbelt. Emma had no problem opening her own door, but she thought doing so might offend Gordon. Not wanting him to feel like she didn't appreciate his efforts, she unbuckled her seatbelt and readorned herself with her coat, scarf, and gloves. Once she had redressed, she sat still until he came around and opened her door.

As the door opened, Emma felt a chill come in with the evening wind. Tonight's temperature seemed colder than the night before, and Emma was thankful to be on the other side of the initiation process. Gordon gave Emma his hand and gently helped her out of the large vehicle. Once Emma had removed herself from the car, Gordon shut the door behind her.

"Thank you for picking me up and driving me here," said Emma graciously.

"You're welcome," replied Gordon.

"And thank you for sharing your CD. I really enjoyed listening to Wagner with you," replied Emma.

"The pleasure was entirely mine," he replied.

Mellifluous   (muh-**lif**-loo-uhs) – ADJ – sweetly flowing

Emma turned toward the magnificent mansion's doors as Gordon returned to the front seat of the limousine. Emma could hear the rumble of the engine as he started to drive away. Carefully, she walked over the cobblestone pathway. She remembered what Gordon had said about the slick roads and knew that ice on the ground, coupled with a pair of high heels, was a dangerous combination. There were no railings along the pathway to the door, so Emma had to watch every step. Once she made it to the front of the house, she could see the glimmer of the hallway lights through the leaded glass design of the front doors. The glass was made in such a way that Emma could only make out shadows and hazy figures of what lay behind. She took a deep breath and rang the door bell.

The robust doorbell chime could be heard through the glass doors. Soon Emma could make out the sound of footsteps as a shadow moved toward the front of the house. A tall blond woman in her late fifties greeted Emma. Lavender later explained that her name was Susan, and she was the Wilkins's temporary maid. Mrs. Wilkins' normal maid, Mary, was also on vacation, so her parents had hired Susan to keep up the house until Mary returned sometime next week. Emma was astounded to discover that even American maids received paid vacations. Susan told Emma she could make her way to the dining room for the evening's *refection*.

The house looked significantly different with the lights on. Now Emma could distinguish the features that had made the place seem so noble. She found herself standing in the doorway, staring at the exquisite chandelier above her head. It was larger than her entire body and

---

Refection   (ri-**fek**-shuhn) – N – refreshment by food and drink

hung in the center of the room. From what Emma could tell, the fixture was made of three layers, each with its own row of candle-shaped bulbs. Pieces of decorated cut glass hung from each level, connecting every piece of the chandelier together. The chandelier radiated light like an *ethereal* body floating above them.

As Emma stood staring at the chandelier, Lavender appeared. She had entered the hallway from the direction of the dining room. Lavender was dressed in a lilac-colored ball gown that aptly fit her name. Her honey-colored hair was swept up in a half updo, with some of her golden locks cascading down the side of her head. Across her neck she wore a string of pearls. Lavender made her way toward Emma and greeted her with a solemn expression.

"Susan," Lavender called out, "why haven't you taken Emma's coat?"

Emma tried to say something, but Lavender didn't give her the chance.

"Gordon said you two would be running late because of the roads, but we expected you here sooner."

Lavender motioned for the maid to come back and to hang Emma's outerwear somewhere other than Emma's body.

"Don't forget to take her purse, too," Lavender added.

Emma quickly removed her coat in order to save time. Emma also took off her gloves and placed them in her purse so she would know exactly where to find them. As she put her gloves away, Emma noticed the small pocket knife. She realized that if there were any more tasks that evening, chances were that she wouldn't get to see her purse again until it was all over. Emma didn't want to run

---

Ethereal   (ih-**theer**-ee-uhl) – ADJ – heavenly

the risk of being caught without her knife again. She would just have to bring it with her. Not wanting to arouse Lavender's suspicions, Emma devised a plan. Carefully, when Lavender wasn't looking, Emma exchanged her gloves for her knife. The effortlessness of making the switch proved her great skill in *legerdemain*. She held the knife tightly in the palm of her left hand and draped her coat and scarf over that arm to conceal the clutched fist. Emma held her purse in her right hand. Susan returned from one of the other rooms and Emma handed her the purse first. Then she used her right hand to give Susan the scarf and the coat. During the transaction Emma gently slid her left hand close to her body and turned to face Lavender.

Once Susan took Emma's belongings, she again left. As Susan departed, Lavender motioned for Emma to follow her into the dining room. They walked past the staircase and toward the heavy wooden doors that led to the Wilkins's formal dining room. The adrenaline from sneaking the knife, along with the anticipation of the evening's events, *titillated* Emma's imagination about what awaited her in the next room. Lavender opened the massive doors and led Emma inside.

This room also looked different in the light. The night before, Emma had only noticed the enormous table in the center of the room. Now with the lights on in the dining hall, Emma had the opportunity to see the elaborate decorations. It was done in a French décor, and above her on the ceiling was a magnificent *trompe l'oeil*. This painting technique was a favorite of the Baroque period, and was

---

Legerdemain	(lej-er-duh-**meyn**) – N –	sleight of hand; trickery
Titillate	(**tit**-l-yet) – V –	to excite
Trompe l'oeil	(**trawmp** ley, **loi**) – N –	a detailed style of painting that gives an illusion of being a photograph

used to make a room or wall appear to be larger. Trompe l'oeil was a French term that literally meant "trick of the eye." It always amazed Emma how realistic the imagery was in order to create the optical illusion of grandeur. Such paintings, as with the one on this ceiling, were able to depict objects three-dimensionally on a two-dimensional plane. The painting in the Wilkins's formal dining room was a mural of a daytime sky. Emma was impressed. The fresco was very realistic; with colors of cool blues and whites, the clouds looked as though you could reach out and touch them. Emma didn't consider herself very **materialistic**, but impressed by such a grandiose mansion, she could understand the desire to gain wealth.

Ethan and Thomas were already seated, and they rose when the girls entered the room. Although now an **antiquated** custom, Emma found the boys' gesture chivalrous. They remained standing until the girls found their positions and sat. Ethan was stationed at the head of the table. Emma thought that place appropriate for him considering his leadership role of the group. Thomas was sitting to his right. Both boys were dressed in their finest. Ethan wore a dark blue suit and a light blue tie, and the two tones of blue complemented each other nicely. His hair, which was usually wavy and messy, was slicked to the side. Emma thought he resembled James Bond. Thomas wore a beige three-piece suit. The light color of the suit was a nice contrast to his chocolate brown skin. Underneath, he wore a white buttoned dress shirt and a striped blue tie. They both greeted Emma with a welcoming smile. Lavender

Materialistic	(muh-teer-ee-uh-**lis**-tik) – ADJ – excessively concerned with wealth and possessions
Antiquated	(**an**-ti-kweyt-ed) – ADJ – old; outdated

took the seat next to Thomas, and Emma was given the seat to the left of Ethan. Once seated at the table, Emma gently slid the pocket knife under her lap to free her hand.

Once they were all seated, Susan came in to serve the dinner. Susan picked up each of the plates and dished out a portion of food on the four friends' plates. One by one, she served all of the dishes and took the remaining serving platters back into the kitchen. As the food was being served, Emma could hear the gentle rumbling of her stomach turn into a full-fledged *tumult*. The smell of the delicious meal got her stomach to start growling. Abashed by the noises coming from her midsection, she quickly wrapped her hands around her waist in hopes of stopping the embarrassing sound. Just when she thought her stomach had settled down and she let go of her midsection, it let out one more fearsome roar. Emma gave a half-smile to her companions. The three looked at each other and burst into a fit of laughter. Soon Emma joined in.

"Hungry, Emma?" Thomas choked out between laughs.

"I guess so," was her reply.

"Well, Susan has just finished serving us," added Lavender, "so after we bless the meal we can start to eat."

Lavender turned to Ethan and he nodded in agreement. The four bowed their heads as Ethan spoke a quick blessing over the meal. Then they dug in. The menu was simple but delicious. The cook, Brigitte, had grilled some delectable steaks for the group. There were sides of garlic mashed potatoes, steamed asparagus, and honey wheat rolls. Since it was a special occasion, Brigitte brought out sparkling grape juice for everyone to drink. Emma had never tasted sparkling grape juice, but enjoyed it very much.

Tumult   (**too**-muhlt) – N – an uproar or outburst

She found the bubbles from the carbonation tickled her noise every time she raised her glass to take a sip. Everything tasted wonderful. The meal was mostly eaten in silence due to the fullness of flavor. Every once in a while someone would stop chewing to make some observation. The others would nod in agreement or speak a short reply. Then they would all go back to eating.

Everyone finished their dinner around the same time. That evening Emma had a *voracious* appetite but did not get a second portion of anything under the strict orders of Lavender.

"You must make sure you save enough room for dessert," warned Lavender.

"Brigitte makes the best sweets," added Thomas.

"You see, Emma, Thomas has a bit of sweet tooth, so he would know," laughed Ethan.

"Do you guys come here often?" asked Emma.

"Not really," replied Ethan. "But Lavender always comes to our meetings with one of Brigitte's delicious snacks."

"We only come over when both of Lavender's parents are out of town," explained Thomas.

"So not even your parents know you guys are friends?" asked Emma, astounded.

"You see, it's not that our parents would mind our being friends," explained Lavender. "It's just that Thomas's dad and my dad go to the same club."

"And that's a bad thing?" asked Emma.

"It wouldn't be if just the two of them belonged to the club, but so do a lot of our other classmates' fathers," continued Lavender.

"Parents like to gossip about their kids and their

Voracious   (vaw-**rey**-shuhs) – ADJ – very hungry

kids' friends," explained Thomas. "It would look kind of fishy if we were always hanging out here together."

"And both of our families have been members of this club for generations," added Lavender. "Because they have a lot of *clout* in that community, people tend to listen to their gossip."

"So if you can't come here, where do you guys meet?" asked Emma.

"When it's warm we meet in Lavender's dollhouse," answered Ethan.

"And when it's cold?" asked Emma.

"It depends on whose family is out of town," smiled Thomas. "We like to make sure information about our group is as scanty as possible."

"What about Brigitte and Susan?" asked Emma.

"Well, Brigitte knows everything about the group," explained Lavender. "It is just impossible to do everything we do without having an adult involved."

"So when we need something we can't get, Brigitte gets it for us," finished Ethan.

"And Susan?" continued Emma.

"Susan only comes over on rare occasions, and doesn't really know much about what is going on in this house," explained Lavender. "My mother barely even knows her name. It would be a completely different story if Mary were here, but like I said earlier, she's on vacation."

"Which is why we chose this weekend to have the initiation and induction," added Ethan.

"What do you mean?" asked Emma

"Mary is like my mother's personal spy," responded Lavender. "She gets paid to know everything that is going on in this house and tell my mother. So we had to wait until she was out of the house, too."

"Oh," was the only thing Emma could muster up to say in response.

Just as the after dinner conversation finished, Susan brought in a new tray of *culinary* treats. Brigitte had whipped up crème brûlée, topped with an assortment of sweet berries. Emma was delighted. Crème brûlée was her favorite dessert, but she rarely had the chance to partake of such pleasure. She was very thankful that she had listened to Lavender and didn't slake her appetite with another spoonful of mashed potatoes. Every bite of the rich dessert was like eating a piece of heaven. The other three agreed with Emma—this was Brigitte's finest dessert.

Once the group finished their last bites, Susan came in and cleared the plates. Emma felt the urge to help pick up the dishes and follow Susan into the kitchen to assist her in washing them, as she would do in her own home. However, the other three stood, led by Lavender, and walked toward the opposite end of the room. Thomas was directly behind Lavender, followed by Ethan. Emma knew it was her turn to follow the group but sat for a moment pondering the dilemma of her pocket knife. She knew one of the three would likely notice it if she continued to carry it into the other room. It was then Emma had a brilliant idea.

As she rose, knife in hand and napkin in the other, she made a motion of accidently dropping the napkin from her lap. Knowing that she couldn't just leave the napkin on the floor, Emma bent down to pick

---

Culinary   (**kyoo**-luh-ner-ee) – ADJ – relating to cooking or the kitchen

it up. As she reached to retrieve her napkin, she quickly slipped the knife into her shoe. She then rose, placed the napkin on the table, and joined the group. Emma's sly *subterfuge* worked, and apart from having a minor limp in her left foot, no one noticed a thing.

Lavender led the small gang to the office they had been in earlier that day. The lights were still turned off and candles were once again used to alleviate the darkness. Two tall candlesticks stood on top of the large wooden desk in the corner of the room. Also on top of the desk was piece of paper. Ethan now took the lead and directed the group closer to the desk. Ethan, Lavender, and Thomas walked around to the other side and faced Emma directly. Emma looked first at the three figures and then at the paper. The dim lighting made the wording harder to distinguish, but after reading a few lines she could tell it was some type of contract. In just a few moments Emma would read the contract out loud and put her signature on the paper. This *affidavit* would serve as Emma's legal bond to the secrecy of the club.

Emma looked closely at the paper. In the lower right hand corner she noticed the same seal which had been on the note she had received the previous afternoon. It was bigger on this piece of paper and the letters could be made out plainly. The wording consisted of three script letters: O.I.T.

"What does O.I.T. mean?" asked Emma.

"We'll tell you once you sign the contract," Ethan replied.

Subterfuge	(**suhb**-ter-fyooj) – N – a ruse
Affidavit	(af-i-**dey**-vit) – N – a sworn written statement made before an official

Even with Emma on the brink of *affiliating* herself with the club, the group still retained some of its secrecy. Emma respected this and went on to read the contract. It was short but elegantly written. The contract stated that Emma would become a full partner in the club, entitled to all the same rights and benefits as the other members, and with these benefits, all of the responsibilities. These responsibilities included maintaining the organization's secrecy, contributing key skills, and pledging one's loyalty first and foremost to the organization and its members. There was even a clause which addressed member conduct. It was a very thorough document. Lavender had drafted it using one of her father's confidentiality contracts as a template. The resource of having a high-powered attorney for a father came in handy for the group in moments such as these. The contract also stated that the agreement was binding with no way to *repudiate* it after signing. Once her signature was on the piece of paper, she was bound by law to uphold the agreement. Emma agreed with the statement and felt no need to argue with any aspect of it. Before making the contract official, Emma was required to read out loud a clause at the bottom. This verbal acknowledgment of what the document said reflected more of a pledge of loyalty than a legal rule. The group wanted to make sure Emma understood the importance of the contract, and thus felt the need for her to proclaim it verbally. The group composed an oath which they thought might be like the one they would have to take once they joined the real CIA. Ethan pulled out a Bible and had Emma rest her left hand

---

Affiliate (uh-**fil**-ee-yet) – V – to associate oneself; be intimately united in action or interest

Repudiate (ri-**pyoo**-dee-eyt) – V – to disown; reject

on it. With her right hand raised, and her left hand on the book, Emma read the following words:

> *I, Emma Jones, do hereby acknowledge and accept the terms of this agreement set before me by the members of O.I.T. I recognize these terms to be* **incontrovertible***, and by signing this document agree to uphold these terms to the best of my ability. I recognize that it is the mission of this organization to use its talents and skills for the good of our country and mankind. I therefore pledge my loyalty, talents, and time. I will look out for the safety of my fellow comrades, and put the welfare of the group over that of my own. I make this pledge before God and my fellow countrymen.*

Ethan handed her a pen, and she signed her name at the bottom. Then Ethan, Lavender, and Thomas signed as witnesses. Once it was done, Ethan looked up at Emma.

"Officers In Training," explained Ethan with a smile.

The explanation puzzled Emma. Ethan noticed Emma's perplexed look and inquired to its origin.

"Is there something wrong?" asked Ethan.

"No, not really," replied Emma.

"Then what is it?" he responded.

"It's just I don't understand the name of the club," answered Emma. "Why is it officers in training? I thought spies were called secret agents."

Ethan smiled at Emma's naivety, and clarified that she had been misinformed. Despite the Hollywood jargon, real-life CIA spies were called officers and not agents.

"You see Emma," continued Ethan. "Agents are the paid operatives that work for the CIA officers. Calling an officer an agent is a common mistake that those who

---

Incontrovertible   (in-kon-truh-**vur**-tuh-buhl) – ADJ – indisputable

aren't in the field make. Since you are new at this we will forgive... this once."

Ethan's smile now stretched across his face. Emma now smiled, too. Never before had she met such interesting people. Now she was one of them. Emma had proven herself to be skillful and capable, and the group's growing respect for her created a foundation for a solid *rapport.*

Lavender pulled an extra bottle of sparkling grape juice from the wine chiller cabinet and poured it into four glasses. The four toasted to the group and spent the rest of the evening talking about how the group operated.

Emma was given a set of stationery, which was made from the exact same paper as her original note, along with the strict instructions to contact the group only through these letters. There were only four people in the world who had that letterhead, and no one else knew of the paper's existence. She was also instructed to always type her letters. This way, if any of the notes were found, it would be impossible to run a handwriting analysis. Spies could never be too careful. Emma was also told not to keep any evidence of the letters once she finished reading them. The best way to destroy evidence was through burning, and it was a group policy to dispose of all documentation. As for the things that the group had to keep, including each member's signed contract, they were kept in a safety deposit box in the First National Bank of Providence, under the name of Marie Wilkins. Emma then found out Lavender's first name was actually Marie. She was named after her grandmother, but since her grandmother was still alive, her parents called her by her middle name. None of

---

Rapport   (ra-**pawr**) – N – relationship of mutual under-
                  standing and trust

Lavender's school friends knew her real first name. Emma felt a sense of pride for being one of the few people privileged to this information.

Soon the clock struck 9, and the four started to say their good-byes. Church was early the next morning, and everyone needed to catch up on their sleep. Emma retrieved her coat and purse from Susan and walked out the door. There she was met by her ride. The door of the limousine opened, and a tall, skinny man walked out. Emma was surprised at how *doleful* she felt when she realized the driver wasn't Gordon, the one she expected. This man's name was William. Lavender had called a driver's service for the evening, and Gordon had ended his shift before it was time to pick up Emma. Thus, the service had sent William to pick her up. William reminded Emma of a weasel. He was a gangly man with thin, stringy hair. Although William had attempted to style his hair, he wore it in a *frowzy* manner. He had a long face and a pointy nose. Yes, he definitely looked like a weasel. Despite the fact Emma found William rather unattractive, he was just as professional as Gordon. He opened the door for Emma and waited to close it until she had taken her seat. This time the driver did not ask Emma about music—instead, he already had a live recording of the musical *Cats* playing. Emma cringed at William's lack of musical taste. She longed for the tasteful music selections of her former driver. The trip seemed much faster on the way back, and Emma was thankful to get home. She was very tired and couldn't wait to get a good night's rest.

Doleful	(**dohl**-fuhl) – ADJ – sorrowful; filled with grief
Frowzy	(**frou**-zee) – ADJ – having a slovenly or unkempt appearance

The limousine pulled up to her house and Emma said good-night to William. The wind was still cold, so Emma hurried to unlock her front door. Nothing had changed in the hours during her absence. The light above the staircase was still on and the house was just as quiet as when she had left it. Emma quickly locked herself in. She kicked her high heels off, and as the shoes soared her pocket knife *plummeted* from its hiding spot inside one shoe to the floor. The knife skirted across the hardwood floors and landed at her feet. Emma laughed at the sight. With all that had happened after dinner she had completely forgotten about her little trinket. Emma bent down to retrieve the knife and carried it up the stairs with her. Just because she had not needed it tonight did not mean it would not come in handy in the future. She carried both her knife and the box of stationery up to her bedroom. The fact that she was alone in the house did not bother her. Her neighborhood was safe, and she had set the alarm. She turned off the light and glided up the staircase to bed and the sweet release of sleep.

Plummet   (**pluhm**-it) – V – to fall hard

WORD REVIEW

Affidavit	Homage	Rapport
Affiliate	Incontrovertible	Refection
Affinity	Ineludible	Repudiate
Antiquated	Jaunty	Squelch
Aristocratic	Legerdemain	Subterfuge
Blandisment	Materialistic	Superfluous
Clout	Mellifluous	Titillate
Culinary	Ocher	Trompe l'oeil
Dilettante	Orotund	Tumult
Doleful	Penitent	Unflappability
Ethereal	Phlegmatic	Voracious
Felicity	Plummet	
Frowzy	Qualify	

5

KIDNAPPED

A loud thud awoke Emma from her slumber. Groggy from the sudden jolt, Emma looked at the clock on her nightstand. Clockable blinked 12:00. Convinced it couldn't be correct, Emma turned to check her cell phone. According to her phone, it was well past 3 in the morning. The time on the phone confirmed her suspicions that the power in the house must have gone off at some point during the night; Clockable needed to be reset. It was impossible for Emma to know how long the power had been off or when it was turned back on. However, she was thankful she didn't sleep through her alarm clock. Emma was supposed to meet her parents at church the next morning, and she would have a lot of explaining to do if she had overslept. Deciding not to reset the clock until the morning, Emma chose to set the alarm on her cell phone. She convinced herself she would get up the first time when her phone alarm rang. Once the alarm was set, she put the phone back on her nightstand and rolled over to go back to sleep.

Then Emma heard another thud. This noise was louder than the previous sound that had awoken her. Wide awake, Emma remained motionless. Could there be someone in her house? It was impossible, Emma thought. After all, she had set the security alarm; it would have gone off long before someone had a chance to get in. Emma exhaled the breath she had been holding in. Once again she had let her imagination get the best of her. She closed her eyes.

Crash! The *raucous* sound emanated from the downstairs hallway like a nuclear bomb. Emma knew she couldn't have imagined that noise. It was unlike the other two and sounded like someone had broken through one of the windows—or, at the very least, knocked over one of the antique lamps in the living room. There could be no mistake; Emma was no longer alone. Why hadn't the security alarm gone off? Her mind was racing. Then she remembered the blinking lights of Clockable. Someone had tripped the circuit breaker and cut off the power. The noises grew louder. At first Emma could only hear the shuffle of feet downstairs. Then footsteps began to ascend the stairwell. Terrified, Emma remained still. Emma's fright had caused a temporary paralysis—as much as she wanted to run, she couldn't move. Then Emma had an idea. She reached for her phone, but the fear removed all *dexterity* from her movements. In one fell swoop, she accidently knocked the phone off the nightstand and underneath her bed. Emma was making a raucous noise of her own.

She was sure whoever was in the house had heard her. There could be no hiding now; she had to find her phone and call for help. Quickly, Emma made a *sally* to escape. She attempted to quietly lower herself onto the floor but failed miserably. While trying to get off the bed, Emma got tangled up in her covers. These new bonds tripped her up and her body went crashing to the floor. Emma landed with a huge THUD. Her fall, although more loud than it was painful, was met with the quickening of the intruder's footsteps.

Raucous	(raw-kuhs) – ADJ – harshly loud	
Dexterity	(dek-ster-i-tee) – N – skill; agility	
Sally	(sal-ee) – N – any sudden start into activity; outburst or flight of passion	

Emma's right arm had broken her fall, and the *aftermath* of her clumsiness was pain. Once the shock of the fall wore off, Emma could feel the throbbing sensation of what she was afraid was a dislocated shoulder. Not letting her injury deter her, Emma reached with her left arm under the bed. Rapidly she retrieved her phone. She flipped it open, dialed the emergency number, and lifted the phone to her ear. It started to ring. Emma's heart pounded with every second. Emma heard the voice on the other side of the connection. Then right before she could say a word her phone went silent. Emma looked to see if she had lost the signal, but her phone was black. The battery had died. Emma let out a disheartened sigh. Her phone had been off the charger for the last two days and Emma hadn't taken the time to plug it in before she went to bed. She couldn't believe her terrible luck. The noises grew louder. She could hear the footsteps coming across the hallway. They were heavy and purposeful. Now was not the time for Emma to hesitate. With her one arm still sore, she used the other to crawl underneath her bed. Once completely hidden, Emma stayed as still as she could. She slowed her breathing. Emma tried to do everything she could not to give away her position. Caught in a trap, she was helpless. Emma knew her father kept a shotgun in his bedroom, but her parents' room was downstairs. Besides, it wouldn't do her any good anyway— Emma never took the time to listen to her father explain how to use it. *What good is it to have a military-trained father if he isn't home to protect me when I need him?* she thought to herself. Not that Emma could really blame her father for her current situation.

Aftermath   (af-ter-math) – N – consequence

Emma heard the creaking of the footsteps as they entered her room. The thought of a stranger entering her sacred bedchamber made Emma shudder. Then the footsteps halted. This pause caused Emma to wonder. Was the stranger looking for something in particular, or was this gesture an attempt to *coax* Emma into revealing her location? Whatever the purpose of the hesitation, Emma refused to budge. Her bed had a bedskirt that almost touched the floor. Looking through the small sliver of space between the material and the floor, Emma could make out the size of the stranger's shoes. Whoever it was wore large black shoes. They had the appearance of dress shoes, but were much cheaper looking than the pairs Emma's father owned. They were too large to belong to a woman, at least any woman Emma had ever met. As the intruder stood surveying Emma's bedroom, she began to hope the man was just a burglar looking for some easy loot. He continued to stand for what seemed like hours. Then Emma heard the sound of another pair of footsteps coming up the stairs. Until this moment Emma hadn't entertained the idea of there being more than one stranger in her house. The footsteps were lighter than the previous ones, but still sounded heavier than those of anyone she knew.

Soon the second pair of shoes joined the first. This man was also wearing the same type of shoes. They were odd choices for a pair of burglars. The men spoke in a low whisper, and by the time the vibrations of their words reached the floor, they sounded more like a soft rumble than actual words. Emma strained to make out the conver-

---

Coax   (kohks) – V – to manipulate to obtain a desired
                   outcome

sation between the two men, but her *abortive* efforts yielded only unintelligible mumbles. Then to her great delight, the men turned to leave. They took a few steps toward the doorway. Just when Emma was about to take a sigh of deep relief, she felt two pairs of hands reach underneath the bed and grab her legs. It all happened so suddenly. In a flash Emma was yanked out from underneath her bed. Kicking and screaming, she fought the intruders *vehemently*.

Unfortunately, with the combination of her injured arm and the strength of two full-grown men, Emma was no match for the attackers. Before she knew it she was gagged, blindfolded, and tied up. It was the second time Emma had found herself in this situation, and she was starting to resent it. The men carried Emma down the stairs and threw her into the back of a car. She heard the rumble of the engine and felt the car speed away from her driveway. She hoped that she wasn't the only one awakened by the noise, and that one of her neighbors had witnessed the strange events and called the police. Surely, she thought, if someone caught the description of the car, license plate number, or maybe even the two men, someone would be able to find her. It was a slim hope, but Emma wasn't ready to be discouraged yet. Then Emma's thoughts turned to her parents. She hated what discovering her missing would do to them. The worst part of the situation was the fact that church didn't start until 10 am. No one would realize she was gone for another seven hours. By that time she could be anywhere. The kidnappers could take her to a different state or even country in that amount of time. Before the police ever learned about this case, the trail would long

| Abortive | (uh-**bawr**-tiv) – ADJ – unsuccessful; fruitless |
| *Vehemently* | (**vee**-uh-muhntly) – ADV – with passion |

be cold. Even if they took her back home alive, she could be left in a *moribund* condition and no one would find her for hours, enough time to slip away to an early death. *What if it was too late for anyone to save her?* The thought of being all alone dealing with this danger started to make Emma feel *timorous*. The only thing that gave Emma even the least amount of hope was the thought this was some sort of practical joke on the part of the other members of O.I.T. Perhaps, she desperately wished, this was a spy's form of hazing.

After a while, the pain in Emma's shoulder began to subside. This was cause for some relief. Emma was thankful she would most likely end up with only a bruised shoulder from her earlier tumble. Blindfolded, Emma had no idea what type of vehicle she was riding in. As the ride progressed, the terrain became bumpier. Emma, who had not been belted in, found herself bouncing all around the car. Once or twice she even hit her head on the roof.

The length of the car ride worried Emma. Providence was not a big town and by now they were probably very far from her home. The outside noises had changed too. No longer could Emma hear anything that reminded her of the city. They were probably far out into the country by now. It was at that moment Emma wished she would have slept with her high heels on. Her little pocket knife would have come in handy at that moment.

Soon the car began to slow and then came to a stop. Emma could hear the sound of a railroad crossing. They must have stopped in front of railroad tracks. This noise

Moribund	(**mawr**-uh-buhnd) – ADJ – on the verge of death; in a state of dying
Timorous	(**tim**-er-uhs) – ADJ – full of fear

got Emma thinking. Where was the last place she had seen a railroad crossing? Certainly not anywhere in the whole county. She remembered her father mentioning some strange law forbidding railroad tracks in Beaumont County. Emma had found this to be quite peculiar—especially because of the frequency that people used railroads for transportation while she was living in Germany. It was very odd that Americans would have any major city without a railroad track. Soon the sound of the passing train faded and the car began to move. It didn't go very far though before Emma felt a sharp turn to the left and then an abrupt stop by the driver. The car engine was shut off, and the two men once again began to talk. This time their speech was loud enough for Emma to hear. The voices, although disguised by a whisper, were faintly familiar. Emma could not quite put her finger on it, but she knew she had heard them before.

"What if she doesn't have the information?" began the first voice.

"Then we will ask the others," responded the second one.

"What if they don't know, either?" continued the first voice.

"Then we'll dispose of them," responded the second one gruffly.

"I don't want to hurt them," *demurred* the first voice earnestly.

"What, then, do you propose we do?"

"Can't we just take them back to where we got them?" the first asked.

"What do you mean? 'Can we take them back?'"

Demur   (dih-**mur**) – V – to make an objection, esp. on the grounds of morals

snapped the second. "It's not like we purchased them from a department store and can return them."

The second voice *satirized* the first, and its implied criticism forced the first voice to be quiet. This harsh speech made Emma feel uneasy. She now understood that even if she collaborated with the felons, they wouldn't let her go home. Whoever it was that spoke must have been a wicked man with no feelings for Emma or her family. Emma was filled with a mix of anger and fright. If she were going to get out of there alive, she'd have to fight for her survival.

The car door opened, and the driver and the passenger stepped out of the car. Emma was ready to get out of the car. The long drive made her backside sore. Once they shut the front door, Emma expected to be helped out. She waited and waited. Nothing happened. She wondered if they had forgotten about her. While the men were out of the car she struggled to get free. She tugged on the ropes and began to loosen her bonds.

Then, just when she was about to untangle the rope, someone opened the door. Frustrated, Emma tried not to let her captors see what she had been up to. The men pulled her out of the car and guided her into a building. They pushed her onto a chair and then tied Emma to it. They had left the blindfold and gag on until they were finished. This made it harder for Emma to struggle. Once she was completely secure, the men removed her blindfold but left her mouth covered. Emma assumed it was so she couldn't scream. Once out of the darkness, Emma could make out the faces of her captors. Standing in front of her were a short, slightly overweight man and a skinny, tall man who looked like a weasel. It was Gordon and William! Stunned

---

Satirize　　　(sat-uh-rahyz-ed) – V – to criticize with mockery

at the identities of her captors, Emma continued to survey the room. There along with her were her three new friends; they were also tied up and gagged. Their *staid* expressions proved to Emma that this was a serious kidnapping, not a prank of their own devising.

Realizing this encounter was not a malicious practical joke, Emma was at a loss for the purpose of the kidnapping. Why had the limousine drivers broken into her home and taken her from her bedroom? It made sense that they would know she was home all alone, but just because they had the opportunity, that didn't give them the motive.

Emma looked to her new friends for some answers. Without speaking, she tried to get their attention. No one seemed to notice her. Emma wanted to scream, but she couldn't. She felt completely helpless. This was her worst nightmare. As she sat there trying to get their attention, Emma was dealt another surprise. The door to the building opened, and a slender silhouette entered. The shadow cast darkness around the figure, but Emma was almost certain it was a woman. As the figure drew closer to Emma, she was shocked to see Susan standing in the doorway. The morning just got stranger and stranger! Emma longed for someone to explain something, but everyone moved about the building, completely ignoring her. Emma had never had an out-of-body experience, but she was sure this is what it must feel like.

Emma watched the interactions of her three captors. From what she could tell, Susan was in charge. No longer was she the meek maid who snapped to attention at Lavender's call. Instead she behaved as a general, barking

---

Staid   (steyd) – ADJ – fixed; sober; steady

orders to her two lowly soldiers. If Susan said, "Come here," they would come. If Susan said, "Go there," they would go. Emma was sure that even if Susan said, "Run around in circles and quack like a duck," they would have eagerly obeyed. Susan was apparently a ferocious creature who could transform two adult men into **sycophants,** eager to obey her every command. Emma didn't want to discover for herself why these men were so afraid of her.

It was then that Susan pointed to Lavender, Ethan, and Thomas and ordered her two goons to take them into the other room for questioning. Emma didn't know why they had chosen to leave her behind. Perhaps it was because she was new to the group and they didn't want to waste their time with her. Or perhaps, she thought with a shudder, it was because she was to be left alone with Susan. Then Susan turned and **sneered** at Emma with contempt. It was the kind of smile Satan himself must have had when he tricked Eve to eat the apple. It was a wicked smile that made Emma's flesh crawl. Just when Emma thought all was lost, Susan turned and followed Gordon and William into the other room.

As the door slammed shut, Emma raced to untie her arms. She knew this might be her only opportunity to get free. She worked with such a fury that her hands could hardly keep up with her mind. All of her hard work paid off. Before she knew it, Emma was free. She removed her gag and threw it on the floor. Then she raced to the door. Emma knew she needed to call for help. *The car!* she thought. *Maybe one of the men left a cell phone in the vehicle.*

Sycophant	(**sik**-uh-fuhnt) – N – one who sucks up to other; self seeking flatterer
Sneer	(sneer) – V – to smile scornfully

Emma opened the door and ran outside to the black limousine. She threw open the driver's door and searched frantically. Then she saw it—a cell phone on the dashboard. Grabbing it, Emma dialed the emergency number and waited for someone to pick up. But instead of a person, she heard a loud noise from the receiver. It sounded like a large truck coming her way—*Honk! Honk! Honk!*

Emma turned to find the source of the sound. As she did, a bright light blinded her. Blinking through the overwhelming rays, Emma opened her eyes. She saw the sunshine peering through her bedroom window. The loud noise continued—only it wasn't a truck but her stupid alarm clock. It was 8, and time for her to get up and get ready for church. Clockable's unremitting, **badgering** alarm had saved her from her nightmare.

Beads of sweat rolled down Emma's face. Although she never left her bed, her body had reacted to the excitement of her nightmare if she had been really living the experience. All the adrenaline from the past couple of days, mixed with the unusual characters she had met, was a recipe for a very intense experience. This morning, Emma didn't need Clockable to pull her out of bed. The wetness from her own perspiration was enough of an incentive to get her moving. Emma threw off the covers and sat up.

The sun was bright on that March morning. It was so dark in her room the night before, Emma had forgotten to close her drapes. Sunshine now filled her bedroom. The lightness of the room was a much-welcome contrast to the darkness of her dream. Emma, who usually begrudged the sun's morning rays, found them rather soothing today. She made a mental note to listen to her dad the next time

---

Badger   (baj-er) – V – to harass

he taught her to load and shoot the shotgun. Emma even thought it wise to start sleeping with her pocket knife under her pillow, just in case.

Emma stripped her sheets and pillowcases from her bed. Now was a good time to wash her sheets. After all, she couldn't remember the last time she had done it. The thought of sleeping on month-old sheets made Emma's stomach turn. She made another mental note to herself: *Wash your sheets more often.* Her mother would have been sure to scold her if she had found out. Emma threw the dirty linens in a pile. While she was in a washing mood, she figured she might as well wash her towels from the bathroom.

The grandfather clock and its robust song chimed half past eight by the time Emma exited the bathroom. Along with her used towels Emma gathered her linens and threw them into the laundry. If she started them now, she would have just enough time to toss them into the dryer before she left for church. On her way back from the laundry room, Emma picked up her trail of dirty clothes that didn't quite make it all the way to the laundry room. Her mother was a stickler for a clean house, and Emma knew she wouldn't be pleased to see the mountain of clutter she had left along the hallway. This included the pair of black high heels left on the floor from the previous evening's excursions. Emma promptly tossed the mixture of personal effects into her laundry hamper, which had ingredients as diverse as a bowl of ***bouillabaisse*** stew. The basket was now filled with books, toys, and even a baseball bat. She would put away her things once she returned from church—at least, she told herself she would.

Bouillabaisse   (bool-yuh-**beys**) – N – a soup containing several kind s of fish and shellfish; any similar soup

It was time for Emma to get dressed for the morning's activities. Her church was an old-fashioned Baptist church that frowned upon any young woman who did not wear a dress, stockings, and heels to the service. The thought of wearing a dress was always a slight annoyance to Emma. She would much rather have the luxury of wearing pants on these chilly spring mornings. Her mother told her she should count her blessings. After all, the Joneses attended what the rest of the county called a "reformed" church, meaning the women no longer were required to wear hats. The image of a bunch of old Baptist women wearing hats in the 21st century always made Emma chuckle. One Sunday, just as a joke, Emma tried to wear one of those church hats. It itched terribly, and Emma tried to take it off several times. Her mother wouldn't hear of it, though— Mrs. Jones had **underwritten** Emma's little experiment, and she wasn't about to let her daughter waste her hard-earned money. She was forced to wear it. Emma learned her lesson that day—no more hats for her. She also wouldn't ask her mother to subsidize any more of her whims, or else she'd actually have to follow through with them.

Emma pulled out a purple wool dress she and her mother had bought in a small boutique in Austria. It was one of her favorites, and it was by far one of her warmest dresses. She paired it with a pair of black wool stockings and the black heels she had worn the night before. By the time Emma finished dressing, it was a quarter to 9. She would have to hurry if she wanted to eat breakfast and make it to church on time. Emma flirted with the idea of skipping the morning worship service so she could have enough time to make herself some chocolate chip pancakes. That was

---

Underwrite   (uhn-der-**rahyt**) – V – to sponsor; to subsidize

of course until she thought about the glower she would receive from Aunt Martha for being late. Aunt Martha—who wasn't really Emma's aunt at all, just an *officious* old busybody who liked to pry into everybody else's business—had taken a special interest in the Jones family since their arrival. Emma didn't mind Aunt Martha too much, except for her annoying habit of giving hugs to Emma every time she saw her. The woman smelled liked a musty old book. And of course Aunt Martha took it upon herself to let Mrs. Jones know every time Emma fell asleep during one of the *revered* Reverend Charles Patton's sermons. Patton was famously known for two things—his great works for the *destitute* and downtrodden population of Providence and his tremendously lengthy sermons. Emma found the latter to be his most poignant attribute.

Not wanting to run the risk of receiving a lecture from Aunt Martha on the sins of being late to church, Emma chose to grab a strawberry toaster pastry for breakfast. She knew it wasn't the healthiest breakfast, but it would at least tide her over until her family's big Sunday dinner. Emma's family always made a point to have a big meal on Sunday afternoons. Sometimes they would invite friends from church, and sometimes it would just be the three of them. It was a custom they carried over from Germany. It made Emma happy to think they hadn't left all of the European traditions behind.

Emma wrapped her pastry in a napkin and poured herself a glass of milk in a disposable cup. It was her very

Officious	(uh-**fish**-uhs) – ADJ –	annoyingly eager to help or advise; meddling
Revered	(ri-**veerd**) – ADJ –	loved and respected deeply
Destitute	(**des**-ti-toot) – ADJ –	without means of subsistence; lacking food, clothing, and shelter

own breakfast "to go." Upon her arrival home last night, Emma had laid down her outerwear on the edge of the couch. The neglect of not putting those items where they belonged benefited Emma this morning as she rushed out the door. She quickly donned her apparel. With her breakfast in one hand and a Bible in the other, Emma ran out the door.

Church was only a few blocks away from the Jones's house, and Emma enjoyed walking there if the weather permitted. The sun was high in the sky and Emma could feel its warmth as she walked down the street. On this morning, the weather in Providence was a dry cold. If it had to be cold at all, Emma liked this kind of weather best. In the sunshine, it was rather warm. Today almost felt like spring.

The night's terror had lost all its effect on Emma. On her way to church, she hardly remembered the bizarre images that had felt so real. In fact, this morning she hardly remembered any of the strange, but true, happenings of her weekend. As she walked to church, the sunshine emitted a heavenly *nimbus* around her, the halo quite appropriate for her destination. Emma could hear the sound of church bells ringing in the distance, summoning the parishioners to service. Spring was on its way, and Emma was happy.

As Emma walked, the wind began to pick up. The air had been still when she started her journey, but now that she was only a block away from her destination, she could feel the change in the weather. The sunshine, too, had changed. It was gone. Emma first noticed the lack

---

Nimbus   (**nim**-buhs) – N – halo; aura around a person; a rain cloud

of sunshine when her shadow *evanesced*. With the disappearance of her shadow, Emma glanced up at the sky. A couple of large nimbus clouds rolled in and covered the sun. This was unfortunate because Emma had forgotten to bring her umbrella. Not wanting to get drenched, Emma started to walk briskly. As the sprinkles turned into full raindrops, Emma's brisk walk turned into an all-out sprint. Determined to get to her destination on time and relatively dry, Emma went as fast as she could in that pair of high heels. Then she saw it—the *arcade* of the church entry. Emma knew if she could just make it to the covering, she would be safe. Every step brought her closer and closer. Thunder cracked just as Emma reached the safety of the arcade. When she was safely underneath it, the downpour began. It was a close one, but Emma had made it just in time.

An elderly gentleman dressed in a charcoal gray suit greeted Emma at the entrance of the sanctuary. He commented about her mad dash out of the weather, and an embarrassed Emma responded to his remark with a smile. Once inside, she could hear the music of the church choir. It was a heavenly chorus singing songs of praise. The First National Baptist Church of Providence was very traditional. The building was originally built in colonial times, and the members tried to retain as much of the original fixtures as possible. Apart from a few modern updates, such as heating, the church often felt like a museum instead of a church. The name had always struck Emma as rather odd. She had never before heard of a "First National" church. Upon her arrival,

---

Evanesce (ev-uh-**nes**) – V – to disappear; fade away; vanish
Arcade (ahr-**keyd**) – N – a covered passageway, esp. one with an arched roof

it was explained to her that the colonists gave it that name in hopes of establishing similar churches throughout the 12 other colonies. Emma found the name somewhat pretentious and in violation of the colonists' desire to escape a national church, but she never told anyone that—she didn't want to challenge this particular folklore.

As Emma walked, she noticed that she hadn't completely missed getting wet in the sudden downpour. A small trail of water followed her steps. Emma looked down at the hem of her dress. Drop after drop, a little bit of water fell. Church was a few minutes from starting, but Emma knew she didn't want to sit for the next couple of hours in a wet dress.

Walking down the hallway, Emma made a slight detour to the women's restroom. Once inside, she took off her high heels and wet stockings. She hung the stockings over one of the bathroom stalls and grabbed some paper towels to dry off her shoes. Emma finished cleaning her shoes and proceeded to take care of her wet dress. The church bathroom was equipped with a hand dryer. Emma hated using them to dry her hands, but she knew it would be just the thing to dry her dress. She turned on the machine and warm air blasted out. Emma stood in front of it, twisting her dress around to dry the hem. It was in this contorted position that Aunt Martha found Emma when she walked into the bathroom. Aunt Martha was dressed in her Sunday finest. She wore a bright peach church suit and a hat to match. The hat, which was a *meretricious* sight, had the addition of a bunch of fake flowers attached to one side. Emma had the unfortunate luck that Aunt Martha spotted her first.

Meretricious   (mer-i-**trish**-uhs) – ADJ – gaudy or falsely attractive

"Good heavens, child!" exclaimed Aunt Martha. "What on earth are you doing?"

"Good morning, Aunt Martha," was all Emma said, her mind still fixed on completing her task.

"Why, your dress is all twisted up, and your stockings are gone, too," she said.

Emma nodded.

"Where are your shoes?" gasped Aunt Martha.

Not looking back, Emma pointed with her toes toward the bathroom stall.

"You look positively sinful," said Aunt Martha.

By this time, Emma had finished drying her hem. She turned toward Aunt Martha and gave her a big smile. Then Emma grabbed her stockings.

"What would your mother say?"

Emma had no intention of acting like a *churl*, but it took everything she had not to sass Aunt Martha. She knew Aunt Martha was trying to help her. Even so, Emma had little patience for her remarks that morning. She really wanted to respond with something like, "I don't know, but I'm sure you'll find out once you tell her." This snotty thought made Emma smile—although she was pretty sure it was a sin to smile at such a comment. Emma decided she was probably in enough trouble with God for running around half-dressed in a church and being late to worship, that it wasn't worth adding insulting Aunt Martha to the list. Emma devised a much nicer response than her original *caustic* one.

"I know this looks bad, Aunt Martha, but I got caught in the rain and I didn't want to sit on the antique

| *Churl* | (churl) – N – a rude person |
| *Caustic* | (**kaw**-stik) – ADJ – marked by incisive sarcasm |

pews and run the risk of leaving water damage," Emma said with a gentle smile.

Great, Emma thought. *Now I've gone and added lying to the list.* However, the answer appeased Aunt Martha, who smiled at the sweet-hearted girl. Aunt Martha turned to the mirror, checked her reflection, fixed her hideous hat, and turned back to Emma.

"Hurry, dear. Worship has already started," she said, "and don't worry about finding a seat. I'll save you a place next to me."

With those words, she was gone. Emma couldn't believe her luck. If she felt any sense of *ennui* today, she would have to keep her yawns to herself. She prayed that the next couple of hours would pass quickly. Emma redressed and went inside the sanctuary.

The choir continued its melodious hymn. The entire congregation stood and sang along. The music selection was Emma's favorite aspect of the First National Baptist Church of Providence. The old-fashioned praise songs had a depth not found in the newer worship songs. Emma felt that these songs reflected actual struggles and deliverances of life, and not a sort of happy fluff. Of course, it was just her opinion, but she felt as though the hymns they sang every Sunday had actual meaning.

Emma spotted Aunt Martha and the seat she had saved for her. In a way, it was sweet. Emma had gotten over her annoyance with Aunt Martha and was strangely thankful that someone cared that much about her spiritual well-being. Emma might not always agree with the actions Aunt Martha took, but she envied her compassionate spirit. In a way, Emma wished she cared as much about strangers

---

Ennui   (ahn-**wee**) – N – boredom

as Aunt Martha did. Emma sat down.

Emma's prayers were answered, and her usual *torpor* was exchanged for genuine interest in Reverend Patton's sermon. She found herself rather engaged with his speech. The fire in Reverend Patton's belly burned with a passion as he *rhapsodized* about love. His sermon was on the necessity of caring for your brothers and sisters in their times of need. It was evident that the man believed in what he was saying. Waves of "Amens" and "Hallelujahs" echoed throughout the service. By the end of the sermon, Aunt Martha was brought to tears. Emma found his speech very compelling, and she decided to give a portion of her allowance every month to someone she knew was in need.

The service was wrapped up with a special offering for orphans in India. Reverend Patton himself had recently returned from a week-long mission trip there. It was this energizing expedition that inspired the morning's *bracing* message. Emma found herself hoping Reverend Patton would make a habit of visiting exotic places; it certainly did wonders for his sermons. Real-world experience turned his usual *grandiloquent* moralizing into something down-to-earth and heartfelt.

Once church was over, Emma was reunited with her parents. Alice Jones, a slender woman in her early forties, was a kind and affectionate woman. Her hair, which she was now in the habit of getting colored at the salon to cover some unsightly grays, was a light blond. Her features were soft, and despite her age, her eyes retained much of

Torpor	(**tawr**-per) – N – dullness; apathy	
Rhapsodize	(**rap**-suh-dahyz) – V – to speak or act enthusiastically	
Bracing	(**brey**-sing) – ADJ – invigorating; stimulating	
Grandiloquent	(gran-**dil**-uh-kwuhnt) – ADJ – pompous; colorful speech; bombastic in style	

their youthful blue color. Emma often imagined what her mother had looked like when she was her age. David Jones was the same age as his wife. He, too, had aged well, but his dark features were a nice contrast to his wife's features. David Jones was tall and muscular. His years in the army had given him a serious expression on his face, but with one flash of a smile, all of his harsher features would melt away. Emma's own coloring resembled her father's more than her mother's.

The three strolled together out of the sanctuary and made their way to the front of the building. Upon opening the doors, they were met with a pleasant surprise. The rain, which had caught Emma earlier that morning, had transformed into snow. There across the streets of Providence lay a small blanket of white. It was a delightful discovery. Emma ran out ahead of her parents and tried to catch some of the falling flakes. Her parents joined her at their car and dragged her away from this game. It was getting late, and dinner needed to be cooked. They left together to enjoy the weather, a good meal, and a lazy afternoon.

WORD REVIEW

Abortive	Dexterity	Sally
Aftermath	Ennui	Satirize
Arcade	Evanesce	Sneer
Badger	Grandiloquent	Staid
Bouillabaisse	Meretricious	Sycophant
Bracing	Moribund	Timorous
Caustic	Nimbus	Torpor
Churl	Officious	Underwrite
Coax	Rhapsodize	Vehemently
Demur	Raucous	
Destitute	Revered	

6

SCHOOL DAYS

Morning came awfully early for Emma the next day. Met by her usual morning friend, Clockable, sounding its alarm, Emma rolled over to try to catch it before it leaped off the nightstand, but she just missed it. Instead of slapping the snooze button, Emma hit her hand on the table. Clockable was already doing his dance on her wooden floors. The sudden sharp pain from her hand made her want to yell at the table, the morning, and most of all, her alarm clock. "Argh, this stupid alarm"—Emma's bitter *soliloquy* was interrupted by the sweet sound of her mother's voice.

"Emma, if you hurry and get dressed for school, you can have pancakes for breakfast."

Emma's mother, who in Germany had been a kindergarten teacher, was taking some time off from working. Since the Joneses weren't sure how long Mr. Jones would be stationed in Providence, her mother thought now would be the perfect time to complete some personal projects she had never had the chance to finish before. A double major in Early Childhood Education and English Literature, Alice Jones had always dreamed of writing a collection of children's stories. She had started her stories once or twice before, but something—like moving across the ocean and having to learn German—always got in her

---

Soliloquy   (suh-**lil**-uh-kwee) – N – the act of talking to one's self

way. Now that they were in the States and they didn't need her income to survive, Mrs. Jones was determined to finish. This afforded her the additional time to do special things around the house, such as make Emma breakfast on the mornings when she wasn't running late for school. Those were rare occasions, but when the opportunity was there, Mrs. Jones always took it.

The smell of homemade chocolate chip pancakes and warm maple syrup was enough to get Emma out of bed. Although she acted with a purpose, her movements were **ungainly** and uncoordinated. Emma headed out of the bedroom but tumbled twice over piles of books and clothes scattered on her floor. *Just what I need to get the week off to a good start!*

"Emma, hurry," her mother called out again.

"I'll be down in a minute!" she replied.

"Remember, you have to take the bus to school today," her mother called out.

Normally, Emma would drive herself, which afforded her extra time in the mornings to catch a few more minutes of sleep. On this day, however, Emma's parents needed to drop her car off to get its oil changed, and the best time was to do it before lunch. So today she had to ride the bus. Emma rushed to her closet, grabbed some clean clothes, and jumped into the shower. Within minutes, she was dressed and heading downstairs to partake in a delicious morning meal.

A glass of cold milk stood next to Emma's stack of pancakes. The refreshing beverage was the perfect

---

Ungainly   (uhn-**geyn**-lee) – ADJ – clumsy

counterpart to the sweet flapjacks and syrup. Emma was convinced that as long as she had a glass of milk, she could eat pancakes for every meal.

The kitchen smelled of cinnamon and spices. Emma felt as though she had entered a French bakery instead of her very own kitchen. Her mother stood at the kitchen sink cleaning the dishes. Emma's mother was a stickler for cleanliness and was extra careful to clean anything that had been *tainted* by raw poultry. Her mother knew the horrors of salmonella poisoning and refused to take any risks when she used chicken or eggs in her cooking. Emma didn't mind the attentiveness to cleaning after using eggs; what bothered her was her mother's insistence that she couldn't eat raw dough. She didn't mind so much not eating raw pancake batter, but barring raw cookie dough was too much for her. Emma, like any other 16-year-old girl, enjoyed licking the cookie bowl. It wasn't an option in the Jones house—if it wasn't cooked, Emma couldn't eat it.

The fact that Emma wasn't allowed to eat raw cookie dough was far from her mind this morning. Upon entering the kitchen, Emma was completely engrossed by the pile of pancakes with her name on it. They literally had her name on them. Emma's mother, in one of her many maternal touches, had used the can of whipped cream to write out her name. There on the top of the pancakes were the four letters, "E-M-M-A."

Emma glided to her mother, gave her a hug, and thanked her for making breakfast. Although not usually a *toady*, she began showering compliments on her mother in

Counterpart	(**koun**-ter-pahrt) – N –	one of two things that fit together
Taint	(teynt) – V –	to contaminate
Toady	(**toh**-dee) – N –	fawning flatterer; a sycophant

an effort to cover up the fact that it had taken her so long to get downstairs.

"You're the best mother in the whole wide world," Emma began.

"Is that so?"

"Yes, it's true. I'm so lucky to have a mom who's willing to make me breakfast," she continued.

"Well, you'd better eat it fast before it gets cold."

Emma could tell that her flattering remarks were amusing her mother, so she decided to continue on. After all, she thought, it never hurts to get a parent in a good mood. *Perhaps she could **cajole** her mother into making pancakes every morning if she were nice enough!*

"I bet I'm the only kid lucky enough to have a mother as nice as you."

"I'm glad you think so."

"And look, you wrote my name on the pancakes!"

"Yes, and the letters are starting to melt."

Emma took a large bite of the pancakes, and with a mouth full of food, continued on with her over-the-top flattery.

"Oh, Mom," she exclaimed, "these are delicious!"

With that comment Mrs. Jones burst into laughter. Emma smiled and continued to eat. She started to make another comment, but Mrs. Jones thought it best to *quell* her daughter's remarks before they became outright outlandish.

"Thank you, love," she said. "But now it's time for you to hurry up."

Emma smiled and continued eating her meal. David Jones walked into the kitchen to join his family. Before

---

Cajole	(kuh-**johl**) – V – to persuade by flattery
Quell	(kwel) – V – to put an end to

sitting down at the breakfast table, Mr. Jones approached his wife and kissed her on the cheek.

"It smells wonderful, dear," he said.

"I made you a stack with blueberries," Mrs. Jones replied.

Mr. Jones thanked his wife and joined Emma. He poured himself a cup of coffee and began to read his paper. Mr. Jones often sat at the table aloof during breakfast. He found the mornings to be the perfect time to catch up on international news, and he liked to drink his coffee in silence. Emma was just finishing her pancakes when her mother looked at the clock.

"Sweetie, you need to get going if you're going to catch the bus," said Mrs. Jones.

"I'm almost done," Emma said.

Emma got up from the table and moved to the trashcan to dispose of her leftover breakfast scraps. She squeezed her nose at the stink of the *offal* remainders from yesterday's Sunday dinner preparation; day-old chicken parts had a very recognizable—and unpleasant—odor. She put her dirty dishes in the sink and headed toward the door.

"Just a minute!" a voice boomed from the kitchen.

Emma turned around to face her father.

"You can't just get up and leave without saying good morning to your old man," he continued with a smile.

Emma smiled, too, and walked straight over to her father. She put her arms around his neck and gave him a kiss on the head.

"Good morning, Father," she said.

"Now that's better," Mr. Jones replied. "Good morning to you, too."

Offal   (**aw**-fuhl) – N – rubbish

It was a *sententious* greeting, but no less affectionate. Mr. Jones, who was a man of few words, still liked his daughter to acknowledge him. He waved her on, and Emma continued to gather her things for school. She retrieved her book bag and headed out the door.

"Goodbye, Mom and Dad, see you after school," she called out as she ran out the door.

Emma had a few minutes to catch the bus. The sun was up that Monday morning, and already the warm rays began to melt the snow. Emma walked along the sidewalk, splashing the puddles as she went. She was excited. Today was her first opportunity to go back to school after her adventuresome weekend. She wondered if there would be any more messages during the day or if something exciting would happen. Emma had never been a part of a club before and didn't know what to expect. Would they say hi to her today? Then she realized that was a silly question. Of course they wouldn't say hi to her—they weren't even supposed to know her.

Thoughts swirled around Emma's head as she waited for the bus to arrive. School today wasn't like any other school day; no, today it was an adventure. Today she was a spy. Emma wondered what it would be like to be a real spy, to keep secrets from all of her friends and family members, to always suspect that she was being watched or somebody was out to get her. Emma realized that to be a good spy, she would first have to think like a good spy. She wasn't exactly sure what that meant, but she was going to do it. She already had the mannerisms of a good spy. She was aloof and mysterious. No one at school knew much about her. Emma could be anyone she wanted to be.

Sententious   (sen-ten-shuhs) – ADJ – terse; pithy

The school bus arrived and Emma walked through the doors to take her seat. The bus driver, Cooper, greeted Emma with a head nod. Cooper, a man in his late thirties, never smiled; he never showed much emotion of any kind. Instead, he always wore a *jaded* look on his face, as if life had dealt him a harsh blow early on and he never got over it. Even when the students caused commotion on the bus, as they sometimes did, Cooper never looked up from the road; he just continued driving.

Emma sat next to a window near the back by herself. She was thankful to find a spot free from students *blathering* endlessly about their weekend excursions. Emma decided to use this morning's ride to catch up on homework she had forgotten. In a couple of hours, she had a quiz in her history class, so she planned to use the time to review the chapters. She pulled out her textbook and began to read. Emma's peace and quiet didn't last long though. Soon a fellow student joined her on the bench. Emma didn't look up.

"Good morning, Emma. I don't remember seeing you riding the bus before."

Surprised to hear her name, Emma looked up from her book. There, sitting next to her, was Michael from chemistry class. This surprised her even more—she had no idea he even knew her name. Michael, a tall boy with dark brown hair and a Midwestern accent, had never actually addressed her by her name. When he spoke to her in chemistry, his comments were always direct and concerned the lab assignment.

Jaded	(**jey**-did) – ADJ – dulled or worn out
Blather	(**blath**-er) – V – to talk foolishly at length about something

"Good morning, Michael," she replied. "My car is in the shop this morning."

After a few moments of silence, Emma returned her gaze to her book.

"Would you like some gummies?"

Curious, Emma looked back to see Michael furtively offering her a ***contraband*** snack. Food wasn't allowed on any of the school buses, but seeing how Cooper didn't seem to mind anything that went on, Emma gladly accepted the snack.

"Thank you," replied Emma. "Gummies are one of my favorites."

"I figured you would like them," he responded, "since you're from Germany and all."

Michael's comment made Emma blush. She wasn't exactly sure why, but she was flattered by the fact that he remembered where she was from. Not many people had paid much attention to her since she had moved to Providence. It was nice to know she wasn't completely invisible. The rest of the bus ride was traveled in silence. Michael pulled out a book of his own, and Emma returned to her history review. As she read, Emma savored the fruity flavors of the candies.

The school day progressed as any other school day. Emma found herself checking her books and locker for mysterious notes, but nothing came. She was excited to experience what life was like as a member of an exclusive fraternity. Perhaps they did missions while at school while no one was looking. Since Friday night, Providence had gotten a lot more intriguing.

Contraband   (**kon**-truh-band) – ADJ – forbidden; prohibited from import

Lavender was the first member from O.I.T. that Emma spotted. Although she hadn't known it until that morning, they shared first period AP English. Lavender sat directly across the room from her in the second row. Before class began, Emma could see that Lavender was as *voluble* as ever, carelessly chatting with a group of friends. Rather than sitting alone in her seat, Emma longed to join in on the conversation. She even got up out of her chair once, but remembered she wasn't supposed to know Lavender. Without a reasonable explanation, Emma couldn't just walk up and act like Lavender's friend. She watched as the group laughed back and forth, recounting their weekend excursions. Some girls had a mishap at the shopping mall, while others got lost on the country roads. Lavender smiled and recounted the fact that her parents were away for the weekend and shared the troubles she had with the temporary maid. She went into some detail about the maid's behavior at the dinner party, while carefully omitting the reason for the event or the guests. Emma was impressed how everything Lavender said was the truth, but still misleading. It was evident Lavender was well-versed in the art of telling partial truths. Lavender was sociable and knew just about everyone in the class. She smiled and said hello to all her friends; that is, of course, to everyone but Emma. Lavender never even looked in Emma's direction. It was like they had never met, with not a *scintilla* of Emma and Lavender's friendship.

Emma, although disappointed, was not hurt by Lavender's lack of interest. She recognized the difficulty of keeping a friendship secret with an entire classroom

---

Voluble   (**vol**-yuh-buhl) – ADJ – talkative; glib
Scintilla   (sin-**til**-uh) – N – trace; hint

of people present. If Lavender had done anything out of the normal, somebody would have noticed. Lavender was keeping up appearances, and so should Emma.

Emma didn't have much longer to dwell on the matter. The AP English *pedagogue*, Mrs. Brown, returned from a copying errand and began to pass out the morning's reading assignment. Emma's teacher, who preferred the method of active reading in class rather than passive reading at home, always started each class with a reading assignment. Students stood and read out loud in front of the entire class. Then the class spent the remainder of the period discussing what they had read. Emma hated her teacher's system. For one, the in-class reading didn't save her from having homework from the class. Instead of doing the reading at home, Emma would have to answer in-depth questions concerning the text and keep a journal on her thoughts about the class reading and discussion. Second, Emma dreaded the thought of being called upon to read. Each student would have to do it at least once and she was never ready for it to be her turn. Every morning Emma prayed that the teacher would pass her up and choose another student; until that moment her prayers had been answered. Right in the middle of Emma's silent plea for invisibility, her teacher handed her the assignment. It was an excerpt of American Indian folktales. Emma looked up at her teacher anxiously. Reading in class felt like a punishment, one that belonged to another, more errant student. After all, she was a good kid, who never caused Mrs. Brown any trouble. Emma always turned in her homework and would occasionally speak up during the class discussions. She didn't deserve this act of torture. But Mrs. Brown remained resolute.

Pedagogue   (**ped**-uh-gog) – N – teacher

"Emma, would you mind reading for us today?" asked Mrs. Brown.

Although Mrs. Brown's statement was phrased like a question, Emma knew she did not have the option of saying *no*. She desperately wanted to avoid her fate, but any sort of hesitation on her part would only make the situation worse. She gave a half-smile to Mrs. Brown, took the script, and stood up. Emma's heart began to pound. Standing up was just another part of the humiliation. Emma read four short stories for the class. Although no one else noticed what Emma considered *grievous* reading mistakes, Emma counted how many times she stumbled over or mispronounced a word. Emma was convinced there were at least a dozen obvious errors, and perhaps another 10 or so indiscernible mistakes. By the time Emma finished reading and sat back down, she was completely embarrassed. She hardly focused on anything the teacher said for the rest of the period. Emma just wanted to get to her next class. The only good thing Emma could imagine that came out of her having to read that morning was that her turn was now over. She could rest easy until the end of the semester. Unless, of course, the teacher had a special desire to torture Emma, and make her the designated reader for the rest of the semester. It was unlikely, but Emma shuddered at the thought. As soon as the bell rang, Emma was out the door.

On her way to her locker, Emma passed Ethan in the hallway. She didn't expect to see him until her dreaded fourth-period German class. It was a happy surprise. After Lavender's avoidance and her own flustered reading experience, Emma was glad for a friendly face. After all

---

Grievous   (gree-vuhs) – ADJ – flagrant; deplorable

it was Ethan who had initiated and ***championed*** Emma's invitation into the club. Ethan's efforts toward Emma's membership made Emma feel closer to him than the other two. That he had been her advocate was unexpected, but greatly appreciated. She hoped for at least a smile from him as they passed. As she walked closer to Ethan, he did smile—but much to Emma's disappointment, it wasn't at her. His smile was directed toward one of his ninja buddies coming up behind her. Ethan yelled out and quickened his step to meet up with his friend. Just as he passed Emma in the hall, a strange thing happened. Out of the corner of her eye, she thought she saw Ethan wink at her. It all happened so quickly she couldn't be sure. She turned around to get a better look, but Ethan was already walking in the opposite direction with his buddy. Emma stood in the middle of the hallway, confused.

The classroom was empty when Emma entered it. It was now time for history, and Emma decided to get to the room early to finish going over her notes for the quiz. On the bus ride earlier, Emma had spent more time eating than reading. She looked down at her watch and realized she had about seven minutes before class to cram in as much reading as possible. She sat down and opened up her book. Sitting in the quiet, Emma heard the footsteps of an approaching classmate. Distracted, she looked up from her book. There stood Thomas. He was dressed in a pair of khaki pants and a light blue sweater. She was surprised to see him there. Up until the evening on the Wilkins's patio, Emma couldn't remember ever seeing him around the campus. Knowing that he probably had an important note for her, Emma

---

Champion   (**cham**-pee-uhn) – V – to fight for; support

became *agog* at the sight of Thomas. She couldn't come up with a reason for him to be there except to bring her a message. This idea was even more probable with the absence of anyone other than themselves. Emma smiled at Thomas. His face remained expressionless and he continued to walk toward her. Emma sat up in her chair and waited for Thomas to say something or at least hand her a note. Other students would be arriving soon, so Emma expected a very brief correspondence. When he was about two seats away, Thomas turned from Emma and sat down. He, too, pulled out his history book and began to study. Thomas's action floored Emma. She had no idea he was in her class. She was also disappointed that, like her, he had come early just to study. Emma was too stunned to speak.

When Emma opened her mouth to address Thomas she was interrupted by the sound of the warning bell. Students began to rush in and take their places before the teacher came in. Mr. Wade was a stickler for starting on time. It was his strict policy that every student should be sitting in his or her seat quietly before he walked in to teach. Some of the new students who didn't know Mr. Wade as well as the others would try to test him on this policy. However, after a few class periods of being sent to detention or worse, being locked out of the classroom for the principal to find, those same students would be the first in their seats before class started. Before Emma knew it, the entire class was waiting patiently for their pedagogue to arrive.

"Pencils out and books away," a deep voice summoned as Mr. Wade walked into the classroom.

Mr. Wade was the type of man who could call an army of bustling bees to attention. With a sudden rush of

---

Agog   (uh-**gog**) – ADJ – highly excited

rustling paper, students shuffled to get their desks cleared and writing instruments out. When Mr. Wade said to do something, students jumped to comply. Emma followed Mr. Wade's orders and with great reluctance removed her history book from her desk. She knew she wasn't even close to being ready for the morning quiz and *rued* the time-wasting activities she had done instead of studying.

Mr. Wade distributed the white papers of terror one by one. Not only were his quizzes notoriously difficult, students were given one of three different versions of the quiz to remove any temptation of looking over their neighbors' shoulders. Currently, Emma was working on a B average in her history class, and she knew another poor grade on a reading quiz would make it nearly impossible for her to bring up her grade to an A.

Despite the pressure of needing to do well on the quiz, Emma found herself thinking more about Thomas's cold reaction than the quiz that was sitting on her desk. Lavender's and Ethan's responses she had expected. After all, there had been other people around. However, there had been no one but herself and Thomas in the classroom. And he hadn't even acknowledged her existence. Nothing. No "hello," no "good luck on the test," not even a smile. She was stunned and a little hurt.

Hadn't she just two days ago sworn eternal loyalty to their *confraternity*? *What exactly did that mean? Why had Thomas been so indifferent?* She knew they took pride in keeping their society a secret, but this seemed a little ridiculous. Did they seriously mean never to talk to each other

---

Rue   (roo) – V – to feel sorrow, repentance, or regret
Confraternity   (kon-fruh-**tur**-ni-tee) – N – fraternal union; a society
                   devoted to a similar purpose

in public? Emma was new at this whole thing, and from her point of view, Thomas's attempt at being secretive and *unobtrusive* was offensive.

The time allotted for the quiz was over. Emma had to guess on the last couple of questions to answer them— that is, if you can call randomly selecting a letter without reading the question guessing. Usually Mr. Wade took up the papers to grade himself, but today he gave the students the option of grading the papers themselves or having their neighbors grade them. Everyone unanimously chose to grade their own. Mr. Wade instructed them all to get out a red pen and he gave them the answers. Emma looked through her bag and found a pink sharpie. It would have to do.

One by one, Mr. Wade read off the correct answers. One by one, Emma marked her paper pink. Emma's heart sank as she continually wrote the correct answer next to her own answer. She didn't get them all wrong. In fact, she had guessed correctly on the last couple. It was ironic and sad. In the end, she wrote a 60% on the top of her paper. Emma had passed, but just barely, and that B of hers was beginning to look more like a future C than an A. *Lugubrious* about her lowered GPA, Emma sat through the rest of the period dismally waiting for class to be over. The day had started off so hopeful, with chocolate chip pancakes, beautiful sunshine, and the possibility of something exhilarating happening. Now it was turning out to be just a regular school day. Emma stopped and corrected herself—it was turning out to be worse than a regular school day.

| *Unobtrusive* | (uhn-uhb-**troo**-siv) – ADJ – inconspicuous; unassuming |
| *Lugubrious* | (loo-**goo**-bree-uhs) – ADJ – dismal; mournful; melancholy |

Emma came into her next period feeling dejected. Not only had she made a D on her quiz, but for the first time she had actual friends, and yet she still didn't have anyone to talk to. Emma had originally even been looking forward to her German class because Ethan was in it. Now after the way both Thomas and Lavender had acted, Emma didn't have much hope of conversing with him either. Up until this point Emma hadn't realized how lonely she actually was. She wondered if she really could make it through her senior year going to this school without having someone to talk to. Emma didn't mind the fact that she was shy, but she despised acting like a hermit. Although she was disappointed by both Lavender and Thomas, she wasn't mad at them. They had explained their interactions at school, although not as plainly as she now realized. Emma had known, but secretly thought otherwise, that the O.I.T. members were not friends outside of the meetings. This was the reality of the situation, and she had joined nonetheless.

Michael was already sitting at the table preparing for the day's assignment. Dread washed over her as she entered the classroom. Emma, thanks to her weekend excursions, had forgotten to read the assigned chapter. Part of her wanted to turn around and walk right back out of the classroom. She felt her head to see if she had a fever. Perhaps she could go to the nurse's office and claim that she was sick. Emma wasn't really sick, but she knew she would be if caught not being prepared for another class. Chemistry was already one of her worst subjects; the last thing she wanted at that moment was to get yelled at by Mr. Humell, her chemistry teacher. She stood in the doorway contemplating how much trouble she'd get in with her parents if she just left. She could always claim a mental breakdown. Surely there had been cases before where the stress of having no friends and failing a quiz *and* a chemistry assignment had caused a student to have a breakdown. Even if there weren't, Emma had no problem being the first. Finally, she decided the hour of enjoyment wasn't worth the week-long grounding she was sure to receive from her parents for ditching school. ***Discombobulated*** by her upsetting thoughts of imminent failure, Emma took her seat next to Michael.

"How has your day been?" Michael asked with an unusually chipper attitude.

Emma's first reaction to this question was quite ***vitriolic*** and surprisingly rude. She was upset; if she hadn't caught herself in time, she would have expressed her feelings bluntly to Michael. For fear of what might come out of her mouth, Emma chose to keep it closed and offer a half-smile in response. To make matters worse, Michael's cheery composure only served to discombobulate Emma even more. For the past couple months, he had hardly spoke a word to her—and now, on her worst school day, he decided to make an effort to be nice. *Couldn't he see that she did not want to talk to anyone?* she wondered. Poor Michael had no idea the emotional turmoil Emma was going through at that moment. Had he known, he would probably have kept to himself that day. Instead, he continued to press Emma to talk.

"How did your history quiz go this morning?" he asked.

The mention of the quiz made Emma feel sick to her stomach. She wondered why he had to bring it up. Of course, on any other day, Emma would have been flattered by Michael's friendly gestures and concern. Today just

---

Discombobulate	(dis-kuhm-**bob**-yuh-leyt) – V – to upset the composure of; frustrate	
Vitriolic	(vi-tree-**ol**-ik) – ADJ – caustic; harsh	

wasn't that day. Michael saw by the look on her face at the mention of the quiz that last period hadn't gone so well. He was a smart boy and knew that it would be best to drop the subject altogether.

"I'm sorry," he managed to say softly.

Michael's condolences *mollified* Emma's negative mood. She realized he was just trying to be friendly, and she had been rude in return. She was sorry for her previous reaction and smiled at him, her eyes full of *compunction*.

"I'm sorry for acting irritated," she replied. "It's been kind of a rough morning."

"I'm guessing the quiz didn't go well," he responded with a smile.

"Not even close to going well," she replied. "And to make matters worse, I was so worried about the history quiz that I forgot to read today's chemistry chapter."

"Oh, no! Me too," replied Michael.

Emma's heart sank. If they had both forgotten, then they were really in trouble. Emma could feel her temperature start to rise. Her face began to feel flush, and her heart began to race. She looked to Michael to see if he had a plan. Michael just looked at Emma with an enormous smile on his face. Confused by his reaction, Emma stared at him like he was crazy.

"I'm kidding, Emma," he said with a laugh. "I read it last night and even took some notes on it. We'll be fine. I've even got us started on the project."

Emma was not amused. At least not at first, but Michael continued to smile and laugh. As he did, Emma

| *Mollify* | (**mol**-uh-fahy) – V – to soften; to pacify |
| *Compunction* | (kuhm-**puhngk**-shuhn) – N – uneasiness caused by guilt; remorse |

couldn't help but find herself smiling and laughing, too. Soon her smile was as big as his. Within minutes, Emma had forgotten about her cold interactions with the members of O.I.T. and even her D on the history quiz. Michael's positive attitude had ***alleviated*** all the feelings of disappointment that her morning had evoked. His laugh was infectious, and Emma couldn't help but notice how his green eyes sparkled when he smiled.

It was on that day that Emma realized how astute Michael was thanks to his keen observations. He was very smart and could explain chemistry to her in a way she could easily grasp. She was also surprised to see how quickly he caught on to ***abstruse*** concepts and theoretical ideas. Concepts that seemed to make her mind swirl came as easy to him as learning that mixing red and blue will make the color purple. Emma found herself thinking she was lucky to have him as a lab partner. She wondered why she hadn't noticed it before that day. It was one of the best chemistry classes she had had yet. The project was actually fun, and Michael was turning out to be a very nice lab partner. It had taken them a couple months to warm up to each other, but on that morning, they began to become actual friends.

Emma knew it was time for class to be over when her stomach started to growl. She was thankful chemistry came before and not after lunch. She could just imagine how she would feel once they started mixing noxious gases together. *Oh, gross!* Once class was over, Michael walked with Emma into the hallway.

"Today was fun," he remarked.

"Yeah, it was," Emma agreed.

Alleviate	(uh-**lee**-vee-ayt) – V – to make easier; to endure
Abstruse	(ab-**stroos**) – ADJ – hard to understand

"Do you have lunch period next?" he asked.

"Yes, thankfully," she responded.

"Do you have anyone to sit with? Because you are more than welcome to sit with me and my friends."

Emma blushed at the invitation. Being shy, she didn't mind the thought of sitting with Michael, but the thought of sitting with his friends made her nervous. *Maybe she could get out of it?* She attempted to **assay** Michael's determination by making up an excuse. Hopefully, he would give up after one try. Finally she choked out a response.

"I would, but I really need to brush up on my homework for my next class," she replied.

"What's your next class?" he asked.

"Umm, German," she responded.

Emma's attempt was a failure. Michael just laughed. He knew just as well as she did that it was a lame excuse. After all, he was in the class with her. Emma was caught.

"I'll take that as a yes," he replied coyly.

"OK, it's a yes." Emma smiled sheepishly. "Thanks."

The two walked together until they split up to put away their books in their lockers. Michael made Emma promise she would not skip out on her invitation, but come join his table of friends after she got her lunch. Emma promised, and Michael departed. She quickly put her books away and headed to the cafeteria. Lunch time at Providence High School resembled feeding time at the local zoo. Students rushed into the cafeteria trying to eat everything in sight. Emma wanted to hit the lunch line before the wild pack. It didn't seem to matter when Emma came into the cafeteria—the line of students was always out the door. If she went to her locker first, there was a line.

Assay   (a-**sey**) – V – to test; to evaluate

If she went to her locker, then the bathroom, there was a line. If she went straight from class, there was a line. If she got out of class early and went straight to the cafeteria, there was a line. It just didn't make sense to her. Sometimes Emma wondered if students camped out in the lunch line just to get a good spot. Emma joined the mob to get the Monday Special. The students always commented that the only thing special about the meal was the meat the school put in it. However, after taste testing the rest of the options, the daily special was always the best. Upon arriving at the front of the line, Emma was pleased to see the meal was macaroni and cheese, a rare cafeteria delicacy. She started walking to her solo table at the edge of room—a reflex action born out of *wont* and not a malicious attempt to break her promise to Michael. Just when Emma was getting ready to set her tray down, she remembered the conversation in the hallway. Emma hesitated for a moment. She was already at her spot, and it would be so much easier just to sit down. But a promise was a promise, and Emma knew that if she broke hers, she would have to face Michael in the next class period. Emma readjusted her tray and began to scan the room, looking for her chemistry partner.

The hustle and bustle of the cafeteria *thwarted* Emma's ability to look around the room. So many students were getting their food, walking around, and talking with friends, it made it hard for Emma to see much of anything. Finally, after what seemed like an eternity of standing foolishly in the middle of the cafeteria, Emma noticed Michael's light blue polo. He was sitting at one of the smaller round tables with only a few other people. Emma

Wont	(wawnt) – N –	habit
Thwart	(thwawrt) – V –	to hinder

looked around to see what "area" of the cafeteria he was sitting in. His seating arrangement would let her know what type of people she'd be spending the next 30 minutes with. Michael's table was stationed somewhere between the computer geeks and the artists. Great, Emma thought. He's sitting in "no man's land." It was a random table which changed status from time to time depending on who sat there. She had no clue what the people she was about to meet would be like. Emma took a deep breath and, with an uncharacteristic *savoir faire*, walked straight up to the table without a trace of shyness.

When Emma arrived, she noticed a seat next to Michael with his backpack in it. Slightly confused, Emma asked if there was room for her at the table. Michael smiled, removed his bag and motioned for her to take his seat. *How gentlemanly of him*, she thought. Since he was the one to invite her, he had made sure he saved a place for her. She was thankful she would be sitting next to him since didn't plan on talking much to anyone else at the table. Michael introduced Emma to the rest of the party. Emma recognized a couple of students from her various classes, and a few were completely new faces. Emma politely said hello and sat down.

Michael's table was the closest Emma had ever sat to the center of the cafeteria. Emma felt as though she were now in the middle of all the action. Directly to her right was the ninja table. She could clearly see Ethan and his buddies goofing around. In many ways, Emma envied them. They were so bold, almost to the point of being

---

Savoir faire   (**sav**-wahr-**fair**) – N – polished sureness in social behavior

temerarious. Today the boys were acting out their own sword fight. It was Ethan on one end and a short redheaded kid on the other. The boys were talking in British accents and pretending to defend some maiden's honor. They didn't care a thing about what other people said about them, or how they responded to their bizarre cafeteria drama. They just had fun. Emma wished she were more like that.

Michael's group was nice. They talked about their classes and spring break plans. Emma had almost forgotten that spring break started the following weekend. They also brought up the upcoming Spring Fling dance that Providence High School always held the Friday before spring break. It was a way to kick off the celebration. Emma, who was partly paying attention to the conversation and partly to the ninjas, was drawn back to the table with a question directed at her. She turned to face Michael.

"Are you planning on going to the dance?" Michael asked.

"I hadn't given it much thought," she said.

Michael paused for a moment as if he were thinking. Emma wanted to turn back and watch the fight scene, but she figured Michael had something to say, and she didn't want to be rude. Just when he started to get something out, there was a sound of a large splash, and a huge gasp broke out across the cafeteria. An otherwise calm lunchtime crowd was on its way to becoming a *rout.* This particular high school had had its share of lunchroom mobs in the past.

There was Ethan covered in red fruit juice. Stunned, his head was down and his eyes looked over the red that was

Temerarious	(tem-uh-**rair**-ee-uhs) – ADJ –	reckless; rash
Rout	(rout) – N –	a rabble or mob; a defeat

dripping from his head to the floor. A pool of red liquid puddled at his feet. It was a gruesome sight, one likely to be seen in a high school horror movie. The short redheaded student stood shocked as well. Emma looked around and saw a pair of blondes laughing hysterically behind the boys. One of them had a large drink cup in hand. It was Lavender. Horrified, Emma scanned the room for another possible explanation. *How could Lavender **lambaste** her friend like that? It didn't make sense!* Sure, ignoring each other was one thing, but making one another an object for sport was a line no one should cross—especially not friends. An outbreak of laugher roared through the dining hall. People yelled, cheered, and mocked the boys.

Without thinking, Emma stood up from the table to go help Ethan. Someone had to stand up against this humiliation. As she started to walk from the table a hand grabbed her wrist. It was Michael.

"If you go over there now, you will be caught in the middle of it," he said with concern on his face.

"Someone has to do something."

"Let the teachers sort it out, Emma," said Michael. "If you're standing over there with the other girls, they won't believe you didn't have anything to do with this."

Emma knew Michael was right. It wasn't as if anyone knew she and Ethan were friends. To get involved at that moment would incriminate herself. It was ridiculous, but the best thing she could do was sit back down and avoid the situation. She hated herself for not being able to help a friend. Her thoughts turned back to Lavender, who was now explaining herself to a teacher. Lavender's cruelty filled Emma with a fiery anger. Not thinking, she blurted out her thoughts.

Lambaste   (lam-**bast**) – V – to attack violently

"How could Lavender do such a horrible thing?"

"Because she's a spoiled brat whose only concern is her own entertainment," Michael responded.

Michael didn't pick up on the fact Emma had spoken of one of the blondes by name. It didn't seem out of the ordinary to him that she would know who Lavender Wilkins was. After all, she was the daughter of the prominent Mrs. Wilkins, Providence's own Congressperson. Emma looked back toward Ethan. Upset, he made his exit from the cafeteria. His trail was marked by a dripping red line. Mockery continued at his expense. Cleaning ladies came in from the back of the food line to help with the mess. Lavender and the other blonde were now gone, too. Emma wondered what kind of *reprisal* they would receive for this deplorable action. Truthfully, she knew the only real revenge could come from Ethan and his ninja group. Emma figured the school would not give the girls much more than a slap on the wrist or semi-harsh words. They could always claim it was an accident, merely an unfortunate event. Then all they would need to do is apologize to Ethan, and perhaps promise to buy him a new shirt. Emma knew from personal experience, that no amount of money could erase the damage done to Ethan's ego. She had learned something about Lavender's character that day. Emma could find no good excuse for such behavior. It was evident, despite her ladylike upbringing, that Lavender was nothing more than a *flouter*. She didn't say much after that.

The bell rang and Emma cleared off her spot. Sadly, she threw away the majority of her macaroni. She

---

Reprisal	(ri-**prahy**-zuhl) – N –	the act of taking revenge
Flouter	(flout-er) – N –	one who participates in scornful activities

had lost her appetite after the incident in the cafeteria. She thanked Michael for asking her to sit with him and his friends. When he asked if he could walk her to their class, she politely declined. She explained she had her routine of changing books and freshening up before class. He understood and went ahead of her. Emma continued with the same routine she did before every fourth period. She grabbed her books and put them down. This time in the bathroom she wasn't held up by Lavender, although part of her wished she had been. There were some things she was dying to say to her.

Emma made it back to class just in time. Everyone was sitting in their seats—well, everyone but one. Ethan's chair remained empty after Mrs. Huckleson had shut the door and began lecturing. Emma knew he wouldn't be coming to class that period. She figured he probably had been excused to go home early that day. She sighed at his misfortune and opened her book.

There, on a half-sheet of O.I.T. paper, was a small note. She read the following words.

"We need to talk."

WORD REVIEW

Abstruse	Grievous	Sententious
Agog	Jaded	Soliloquy
Alleviate	Lambaste	Taint
Assay	Lugubrious	Temerarious
Blather	Mollify	Thwart
Confraternity	Offal	Toady
Cajole	Pedagogue	Ungainly
Champion	Quell	Unobtrusive
Compunction	Reprisal	Vitriolic
Contraband	Rout	Voluble
Counterpart	Rue	Wont
Discombobulate	Savoir Faire	
Flouter	Scintilla	

7

THE MEETING

E mma knew the note was from Ethan. There was nothing more than those four little words, but she needed no more of an explanation. She wondered if the stunt in the cafeteria had created a *schism* threatening the group's cohesion. Could it be that Ethan was planning on going solo? Perhaps not—there was a good chance he just needed someone to talk to. Emma felt a strange sense of pride that she would be the one he reached out to. Not for a second did Emma consider the note to be from one of the other members. Ethan must have dropped it off on his way home to change. She was sure of it.

The rest of her German class was uneventful. Emma found herself looking over to Michael every time her teacher would say something *unlettered* or simply untrue about the German language. Michael didn't always understand the reasons behind Emma's looks, but he would always smile back at her. Emma was just glad to have someone who she could express her sentiments to. Class seemed to drag on, and Emma continued with her tradition of doing the day's homework while in class. It wasn't a perfect system, but it worked. Soon German was over and Emma would be heading to her last class of the day, PE.

Schism   (**siz**-uhm) – N – a division
Unlettered   (uhn-**let**-erd) – ADJ – unsophisticated; ignorant

Once the bell rang, Emma hurried like the rest of her classmates toward the door. She passed Michael and said goodbye. Emma ran to her locker to grab her change of clothes. When she opened her locker, a small sealed envelope fell to the floor. Curious, Emma bent down to pick it up. In the envelope was the second half of the piece of O.I.T. paper.

"Come to Lowry's Self-Defense Academy at 9."

This letter confirmed Emma's suspicions. Lowry was Ethan's last name, and she remembered him talking about how his dad taught self-defense. She figured it must be a safe place for them to meet. Emma grabbed the note and put it in her backpack before anyone else could see what it said. She stuffed her bag in her locker and proceeded to the gym to change for PE. Today they were playing dodgeball and Emma didn't want to be late. She wasn't the most athletic girl, and being late would only make her stand out. The fact that she was a *bungler* already made her an easy target for the powerful assaults of the flying dodgeballs.

Poor Emma tried her best. She remained in the game for the first couple of rounds and at some points proved herself quite limber. After a while, she started to get rather good at the game and even knocked a couple people out herself, and for the first two rounds, she felt *indomitable*. Unfortunately, her athletic streak ran out in the middle of the third round, when a tall brunette volleyball player focused her eye on Emma. The girl

---

Bungler	(**buhng**-guhl-er) – N – a clumsy person	
Indomitable	(in-**dom**-i-tuh-buhl) – ADJ – invincible	

picked up the bouncing ball and hurled it at her. Emma swerved and tried her best to dodge it, but the ball was coming too fast. She was hit, right in the upper part of her left arm. She was out. Sweaty and tired, Emma was resigned to the sidelines. She hadn't been the best athlete, but she was proud of the way she had played. School was almost over and she was ready to go home, take a shower, and see what this meeting was all about.

Soon the final bell rang and Emma gathered her belongings from her locker. Most students chose to take showers in the locker rooms, but Emma was not quite comfortable with the idea of taking a shower in a room with 50 other girls. She preferred to go home and clean up in the privacy of her own place. She hoped whoever sat next to her on the bus didn't mind that she was a little sweaty.

Emma found herself on a different bus for her second trip ever on an American school bus. This bus was older than the first, was overdue for a cleaning, and had a very *noisome* odor. Emma then realized that whatever smell she might have accumulated during PE would be masked by the offensive smell of the bus itself. She made her way to the back of the bus. Exhausted by the day's events, she wanted nothing more than a quiet ride back to her house. She had enjoyed Michael's company that morning, but she hoped this time around he would take a different bus, or sit with someone else. Emma had a lot on her mind and didn't want to be disturbed.

The thing that consumed most of her thoughts was Lavender's betrayal. Emma couldn't help but wonder what possessed her to act that way. Was it peer pressure to keep

Noisome   (**noi**-suhm) – ADJ – offensive or disgusting up appearances? Even if it had been someone else's idea, why had Lavender gone along with it? Emma remembered the cup in her hand. It was even worse—Lavender was the one who had actually done it. In the death of Ethan's pride, Lavender was the one to pull the trigger.

Emma got her wish and remained seated by herself. The afternoon bus wasn't nearly as crowded as the morning one because of the many after-school activities students were involved in. Emma had a couple opportunities to join different clubs, but she decided to wait until the following semester before she committed herself to something. Emma now found that decision ironic considering her current club affiliation.

The bus arrived at her stop, and Emma was happy to get off. The smell had remained strong the whole time; Emma was ready for a breath of fresh air. The doors parted and she hopped off the steps onto the street. Walking was a welcome change from sitting on the dull, *flaxen* seats that matched the faded exterior of the school bus. One of her legs had fallen asleep during the ride, and it tingled as she walked toward her house. It was an odd sensation. As she walked, she thought about an excuse to get out of the house that night. It was a school night, so her parents would never let her out unless she had a very good reason. Of course, Emma didn't want to lie to her parents again; she did not want to get in the habit of acting *surreptitiously* toward her parents. Nothing good would come out of lying and sneaking out of the house under her parents' noses. She could just imagine the year-long grounding or worse. No, lying wasn't an option. She would just have to tell them

---

Flaxen	(**flak**-suhn) – ADJ – yellowish in color
Surreptitious	(sur-uhp-**tish**-uhs) – ADJ – sneaky; secret

the truth. Maybe just leave out a few key points. Whatever she decided, she would first have to get her homework done. Otherwise she wouldn't be able to go anywhere. So that's exactly what she decided to do.

Emma didn't actually have to do much convincing to get her parents to let her go to the self-defense studio. All she had to do was mention self-defense and a school friend and her parents were more than happy to approve. They even offered to take her there. Mrs. Jones saw this as a sign that Emma was adapting to life in Providence, and Mr. Jones was thrilled that Emma had taken an interest in self-defense. It was surprising how *insouciant* they both were about the matter without expressing any of the concerns Emma had expected. Emma had prepared a whole host of explanations if questions arose, but it was unnecessary. Neither one of them asked any more questions, nor did Emma feel the need to explain. There was one condition Emma was promised to abide by—to make sure she called both when she got there and when she was about to leave. Emma's parents, just like any other parents, worried when their daughter was out on the town. She agreed. It was settled, Emma could go.

After speaking with her parents, Emma returned to her room to finish her homework. She had forgotten to tell them about her poor quiz grade, and upon realizing it, Emma decided it best to wait for another time to explain. To make up for her lack of studying that morning, Emma went straight to studying history. She knew it would not do her any good on the next test if she didn't make up the chapter she had already missed. After finishing history, Emma started on chemistry. She did

___

Insouciant   (in-**soo**-see-uhnt) – ADJ – unconcerned.

not have much homework for the next day, but she had a lot of catching up to do. Emma spent the rest of her afternoon and early evening diligently hitting the books. She remained in her room for a good portion of the day, only taking short study breaks, and then a much longer one for dinner. Once dinner was done, she returned to her room. When the time came to leave, Emma had finished all of her past weekend's reading assignments, as well as everything that was due the following day.

The hallway clock chimed fifteen minutes until 9. The old grandfather's song let Emma know it was time to go. She put on her tennis shoes and grabbed her cell phone off the charger. After Emma's dream the other night, she made sure her phone was charged. If ever she were to fall into the *machinations* of an enemy, she would be ready.

"Bye, Mom. Bye, Dad," Emma called as she ran out the door.

The sun had already gone down by this time and the night wind had a chill. Emma walked quickly to her car to get out of both the cold and the darkness. Once she started the vehicle, Emma checked the gas tank. It was full. She knew her parents must have filled it up on their way back from the mechanic. Emma was thankful to have such thoughtful parents.

Emma took out the driving directions she had printed from the internet. Lowry's Self-Defense Academy wasn't far, and she had just enough time to get there. Buckled up and ready to go, Emma backed her car out of the driveway and turned onto the street.

The self-defense academy was close to 5 miles from Emma's house, just on the other side of downtown

Machination   (mak-uh-**ney**-shuhn) – N – harmful or crafty scheme

Providence. The easiest directions were to drive straight through old downtown. The older part of the city was once the heart of Providence. The city officials had done their best to maintain the integrity of the town square, and the buildings looked roughly the way they did when the city was originally built. As she drove past the old wooden and brick buildings, she could not help but imagine what the town would have been like in its glory days. She passed the old town hall, where all of the trials and city meetings used to be held. It was now a town museum. The museum was closed and all the lights were turned off. Most of the buildings had retained some of their usefulness and had been turned to something relevant for a modern age. A lot of them were antique shops or quaint stores for tourists. They were all closed at that hour. Mr. Lowry chose that area for his dojo because it was a safe neighborhood with inexpensive rent.

As she drew closer, she wondered about the kind of ramifications that the red fruit punch gag would have on the confraternity. She was curious if the hurtful prank would **ostracize** Lavender from the group. Or maybe it would sever Ethan's ties to the other two. She wondered where she would fit in if the group split.

Emma didn't have enough time to come up with an answer to that question because just then she pulled up to the academy. The lights were still on, and a couple of cars were parked in the lot. Emma turned off her car and walked in. As she walked through the passageway the door chimed, announcing her arrival. Ethan, who was standing close to the door, greeted her and led her out of the hallway

---

Ostracize   (**os**-truh-sahyz) – V – to exclude from society, by
            general consent

and into the next room. There, *blithely* standing together in a friendly circle were a man in his late forties, Thomas, and Lavender.

The sight of Lavender and Thomas was confusing. Didn't the "we" in the letter imply a conversation between two people? There they all were, laughing and smiling together as if nothing at all had happened. Emma turned to Ethan.

"Aren't you mad at Lavender?" she asked in a shocked voice.

"No, why?" he responded.

Emma didn't feel that it was necessary to recount the afternoon's activities, but Ethan seemed genuinely surprised that Emma would ask such a question. Emma, in as delicate words as she could find, tried to explain.

"You know, today in the cafeteria," she began. "The whole red punch thing?"

Ethan busted out laughing. Emma thought he was crazy. After all, he didn't think it was all that funny earlier. Ethan summoned Lavender over to help explain. It was evident Emma's version of the story needed to be *rectified* to match reality. Lavender joined them to set the record straight. Thomas remained behind and continued to talk with the older gentleman.

"You see, Emma, it was my idea for Lavender to dump the drink on me," Ethan began.

Now Emma knew he was crazy. Emma crossed her arms over her chest and looked at him. She wasn't sure what Lavender had told him, but she wasn't buying the idea that Ethan had orchestrated the plot—not after the way he

Blithely	(**blahyth**-lee) – ADV – carefree; unconcerned
Rectify	(**rek**-tuh-fahy) – V – to correct; to set right

looked in the cafeteria. Ethan realized Emma was being rather **recalcitrant** in the matter, so he continued trying to convince her.

"It's true, Emma," he continued. "The whole thing was my idea."

Emma looked at Lavender for some sort of confirmation. She stood there nodding her head in agreement with Ethan. Now she knew they were all crazy. *What type of people have I gotten myself mixed up with?* she wondered.

"Why?" she asked.

"Because of me," Lavender said. "Tiffany, the infamous gossip reporter of Providence High, was going to run a story on me in the gossip page of the school newspaper. If we hadn't pulled our stunt this afternoon, a story that could implicate our spy club would have been **disseminated** to the masses!"

Emma didn't say a word, so Lavender continued.

"She claimed to have **unimpeachable** evidence that I was running a secret sorority on campus," said Lavender. "What she had in actuality was a partial phone conversation between Thomas and me."

"How do you know this?" asked Emma.

"Because Tiffany came to me with the evidence and demanded an interview about the club. When I told her there was no club, she didn't believe me. So instead of running a front page news story on the matter, she was going to put it in the gossip page."

"That doesn't seem so bad," said Emma.

Recalcitrant	(ri-**kal**-si-truhnt) – ADJ – stubbornly defiant	
Disseminate	(dih-**sem**-uh-neyt) – V – to scatter or spread widely; to broadcast	
Unimpeachable	(uhn-im-**pee**-chuh-buhl) – ADJ – reliable beyond a doubt	

"It's actually worse. Most students read only the gossip page, and Tiffany doesn't need any proof to say whatever she wants to on the gossip pages. Everyone would believe her, and I would have had a lot of suspicion cast my way. Theories about our secret society would run *rampant* throughout the whole school!"

"So, we devised a plan to get the students talking about something else for a while," added Ethan. "People make fun of my group of friends all the time, so it made sense to pull a prank on us."

"And that's why only you were covered in red drink?" asked Emma, who was now beginning to understand the noble purpose behind the disconcerting *contretemps.*

"Yeah, we didn't think it would be fair to get other people involved," continued Ethan.

"What about the redheaded kid and the other blonde?" Emma protested.

"Ok, they were involved, but they didn't get dirty or in trouble," explained Ethan.

"But you used them," continued Emma.

"True, but we didn't force them to do anything either one of them wouldn't do on their own," explained Lavender.

Emma realized her weighty objections were now *paltry* in light of this new evidence. Up until that point, Emma was still a little bit angry at Lavender and she let her personal emotions cloud the explanation. The truth was, she didn't want to listen to Lavender. Instead, she felt the need to cavil her points. Emma caught herself

---

Rampant   (**ram**-puhnt) – ADJ – widespread; unchecked
Contretemps   (**kon**-truh-than) – N – an embarrassing event
Paltry   (**pawl**-tree) – ADJ – trivial

and stopped. She knew that if both Ethan and Lavender were saying it, then it must be true. Once she started thinking about the whole situation, she realized the plot was a brilliant *stratagem* to protect their secrets from others outside the group. Tomorrow's paper was the only one for a week. If the red punch fight made it into the paper and not Lavender's secret society, then it would be the only thing students talked about for the rest of the week. Since spring break followed the next week, no one would remember any of it. No one was harmed, and the secrecy of O.I.T. had indirectly been saved. Emma marveled at the strategy involved.

"That's why you two were both so callus this morning," gasped Emma.

"Yeah, we're really sorry about that—with everything going on we couldn't run the risk of any more suspicions," explained Lavender.

"And we wanted to fill you in, but there wasn't enough time," continued Ethan.

"Tiffany contacted me on Friday afternoon, and I only got to talk to the boys about it on Sunday," explained Lavender. "We thought it best for you to go home and get some sleep."

"You had enough excitement for one weekend, and we didn't want to involve you any more than we already had," added Ethan.

The club's actions began to make sense. Emma realized she had a lot to learn about her new friends and this organization of theirs. It was all interesting to say the least. Thomas and the older gentleman finished their conversation and came to join the rest of the group.

Stratagem   (**strat**-uh-juhm) – N – a plan to trick an enemy; ruse

Emma, who hadn't paid much attention to the man in the black martial arts gi, was now quite curious about his purpose. Ethan, who had an ***uncanny*** ability to read Emma's thoughts, noticed her curiosity and stepped in to introduce the unknown gentleman.

"Emma, I'd like to introduce you to Sensei Lowry," explained Ethan.

The man was in his late forties but had the command of a much older gentleman. The martial arts uniform he wore gave him a sense of dignity unlike many other men his age. While one might expect a grown man who dabbled in the martial arts to be immature, there was nothing ***jejune*** about him. The older gentleman bowed to Emma. His posture was as straight as a board. When he bowed, it was as though he had two separate parts which folded one over the other with ease. Emma was taken aback by the man's flexibility. At 16, she was not limber enough to bow like that; it was a wonder how a middle-aged man could do it. Emma wasn't sure how to greet a martial arts sensei. A handshake didn't seem appropriate. If he bowed, did that mean she would have to curtsy? Surely not. Emma instead chose to mimic the man's gesture and offered her own bow. It was small and not nearly as fluid as the gentleman's. However, she did the best she could.

"It is very nice to meet you, Sensei," greeted Emma.

"Welcome to my dojo," responded Sensei Lowry. "I hope you enjoy your time here."

"May I ask why we are at your dojo?" continued Emma.

"Ethan, you didn't tell the poor girl?" Sensei Lowry turned to his son.

Uncanny	(uhn-**kan**-ee) – ADJ – mysterious; extraordinary
Jejune	(ji-**joon**) – ADJ – juvenile; childish

"I wanted it to be a surprise," smiled Ethan.

Emma didn't like the sound of that. She had had enough surprises this week to last her a lifetime. She was ready for someone to explain. She turned to Lavender and Thomas, but they were gone. So she turned back to Ethan. He was still smiling. Then Sensei Lowry handed Emma a pile of white clothes. They were the training uniform for new students. Stunned, Emma turned to Sensei Lowry.

"Tonight you kids are getting a lesson in general self-defense," explained the sensei. "Ethan told me that it would be an important skill for all of you to learn."

"My dad was more than happy to offer to help," continued Ethan.

"What am I supposed to do with these lessons?" Emma inquired.

Ethan and his father laughed at her question. Emma did not find it amusing. She was sure whatever the two had in store for her would end up in her own stumbling and humiliating *pratfall*. Emma wasn't a fan of making a fool out of herself. But the two just continued to smile at her and motion for her to go change. Reluctantly Emma turned toward the locker rooms. As she headed across the room she saw Lavender and Thomas return in their own white gis. Emma knew she had been overruled in the matter. She left to go change.

When she returned, Sensei Lowry and Ethan were sparring on the mat. Sensei Lowry had Ethan in a chokehold and was teaching him how to break free. It was evident by the lack of *nepotism* shown to his son, Ethan, that

---

Pratfall   (**prat**-fawl) – N – humiliating mishap or failure
Nepotism   (**nep**-uh-tiz-uhm) – N – favoritism to family

Sensei Lowry played fair. He was serious about teaching his students the proper ways to defend themselves. He treated his son like everyone else he taught how to fight. Emma stood and watched what looked like an elegantly choreographed dance on the mat. Every step was important, and Sensei Lowry didn't let Ethan get away with sloppy work. He knew that how a student practiced would be how the student would react in a dangerous situation. Someday Ethan's life might depend on the training he had received from his father, and Sensei Lowry wasn't about to take any chances by teaching him incorrectly. Emma continued watching as she walked over to join the others.

As they stood on the sidelines watching, Lavender filled Emma in on a little bit of Ethan's family history. Since he was a little boy, Ethan had been raised solely by his father. Lavender didn't go into details about why he had only a dad, but as far as Emma could tell, the sensei was his only family. The sensei himself was a judo champion and had trained under some of the greatest masters in Japan. Sensei Lowry was not Japanese—in fact, Ethan's father was Scottish by blood—but after living a time in Japan, he now *espoused* many of the culture's finer qualities, including the strong family ties. He also strongly believed in the importance of training his children in the martial arts.

Emma listened as she looked around the room. Although she hadn't noticed it before, the room had a distinctive Japanese feel in its décor. Emma didn't know much about the differences between the Asian cultures, but there were a couple of qualities in the decorations that she did notice. There were the *fusuma*—or, in English, the sliding paper doors that separated the rooms—and a large

---

Espouse   (ih-**spous**) – V – to adopt or embrace

painting of two sumo wrestlers fighting that hung on the wall across from where the group was standing. At first, to Emma's untrained eyes, these furnishing appeared to be a random selection of Asian artifacts. It wasn't until her closer examination of the disparate decorations that she realized they had a *homogeneous* origin. Emma liked the look of the room very much. She returned her gaze to the ongoing fight.

It was amazing how quickly the sensei got Ethan into a hold, and how quickly Ethan got out of it. For every action Sensei Lowry threw at Ethan, Ethan was quick to return a *riposte*. It was evident Ethan was raised in a dojo; his father had taught him the right steps since childhood. The mat was his element, and he knew it. Ethan wasn't as good as his father, but it was easy to see his skills in martial arts were quickly improving. His strong, sharp movements had remarkable *prowess*. He had a finesse that his father didn't seem to have. Emma was sure one day he would surpass his father in skill. That day, however, was not today. Sensei Lowry had Ethan pinned down on the mat. As hard as he tried, he couldn't break free from his father's grip. Finally, Ethan surrendered.

The three standing on the sidelines began to clap for the fighters' performance. It was now their turn to join Ethan on the mat. Sensei Lowry called to the others and they came and stood opposite him, next to Ethan. First they were to start off with some stretches. Stretches, Sensei Lowry said, were the most important part of the exercise.

Homogeneous	(hoh-muh-**jee**-nee-uhs) – ADJ –	of the same kind
Riposte	(ri-**pohst**) – N –	a retaliatory movement
Prowess	(**prou**-is) – N –	exceptional ability, skill, or strength

"A fighter must be in top physical condition," the Sensei began. "He," he stopped for a moment and looked at the two girls, "or she," he said with a smile, "must always take care of the body and the mind. One of the best ways to take care of the body is to stretch out the muscles."

Emma remembered Sensei Lowry's remarkable flexibility. She longed to be as *lissome* as the Sensei, so she diligently followed his stretching instructions. They started with a brisk jog around the fighting room. The jog, the sensei told them was to help warm up the entire body. This way their muscles wouldn't be so cold when they tried to stretch them. Cold muscles could easily tear, and it was his goal to help his students not hurt themselves. So, they ran around in circles several times. Emma hadn't realized how incredibly out of shape she was until that moment. In Germany she didn't exercise because her family walked everywhere. Now that they were in the States and Emma could drive, she had retained her lack of exercising habit. She was grateful when the sensei finally told them to stop. Out of breath, Emma happily obliged.

Next, the sensei instructed the group through a round of stretches. The moves were adaptations from a Japanese style of yoga called Shin Shin Toitsu Do. It was a combination of breathing and movements developed to strengthen both the body and mind. Normally these exercises would take up the first fifteen minutes of the sensei's class, but that evening the group didn't have the time. So he shortened the routine to last about five minutes. He told them if they wanted to learn more, they would have to sign up for a class. As Emma felt how tense and sore her muscles were, the sensei's offer became more

---

Lissome   (**lis**-uhm) – ADJ – nimble; limber

appealing. She could barely bend down to touch her toes. Once the group finished their stretches, the sensei taught them a couple of key holds and how to get themselves out of them. He used Ethan as an example and went step by step on how to get an opponent in the positions and how to get themselves out of the positions. Each movement was deliberate and purposeful. The sensei cautioned to always think through the moves and never to act rashly. Students who act rashly are the ones who get themselves hurt. After he showed the group how to *fetter* their opponents in immobile positions and how to unfetter themselves, he paired the four kids up. Emma and Lavender were a pair, and Ethan and Thomas were a pair. It seemed only fair to put the girls together and the boys together. Their goal was simple—to take turns practicing the things they had just learned. Sensei Lowry remarked that the key to *vanquishing* one's enemy was to practice overpowering the opponent. Then he removed himself from the mat and watched.

At first, Emma and Lavender stared at each other, not sure what to do. Neither of them wanted to take the first turn. Emma looked over at the boys for some guidance. Ethan already had Thomas in a chokehold, and Thomas was struggling to break free. They were having too much fun. It was clear they weren't going to be much help. So Emma offered to be the first victim and their sparring begun.

The group ran several drills of the different types of holds and releases. Sensei Lowry stood on the side, offering advice when he felt it necessary or when someone asked. Whenever he saw one of the four doing something terribly

---

Fetter   (**fet**-er) – V – to restrain
Vanquish   (**vang**-kwish) – V – to conquer; overpower

wrong, he stepped onto the mat to correct their form. He also walked around, giving them each advice on how to avoid dangerous situations in the first place.

It was close to 10 when the group finished their practice drills. Ethan had asked his father for an hour lesson, and it was time for everyone to get home. Before they left, Sensei Lowry thought it important to teach his newest pupils how to throw a proper punch. It wasn't really related to the judo they had been learning, but the sensei thought it would be beneficial for the girls in the group to learn. After all, as they got older, there was a bigger chance they would get themselves into situations *inimical* to their safety. Although the sensei didn't have any daughters of his own, he knew how protective he would be if he did have one. It was his firm belief everyone, especially every girl, needed to know how to throw a punch. He wasn't a believer in useless violence; he just wanted to make sure they all knew the basics of fending off an attacker.

He instructed each student to stand with their feet planted firmly on the mat. A solid placement of the feet was an important first step. Then he said to bend the knees slightly, giving them a good balance. As he spoke, he mimed the actions with them to show them what they were supposed to do. Then he instructed them to hold their hands out as if they were holding a gallon of milk, with their hands angled slightly with their knuckle of their forefinger leading. Next he told them to bring both fists up in front of their faces right beneath their eyes. The goal was to protect the face, while still allowing them to see. The pupils followed and did exactly what he said to do. Next, he had each student bring one hand forward and at an

---

Inimical   (ih-**nim**-i-kuhl) – ADJ – hostile; harmful

angle, making sure to rotate the fist as it moved across the body. Once they got the mechanics down, he had them do it faster. Emma, Ethan, Lavender, and Thomas stood there for the next 10 minutes throwing punches at the air until their arms were heavy and tired. Once the Sensei was satisfied, he sent his students home.

Emma changed out of her white gi and returned the uniform to the sensei. He refused to take it. When Emma inquired to the reason why, the sensei explained he held back a certain number of uniforms for friends of Ethan. The one she was now holding had been ***allocated*** for that very purpose. It was hers to keep. He reminded her that she would need to wear it once she signed up for her own self-defense class. Emma thanked him for his generous gift and promised to talk to her parents about joining a class.

Sensei Lowry walked the students outside to their cars. The four friends parted. Emma got into her car and locked the door. Before she started her engine, she pulled out her cell phone to call her parents. She notified them of her return trip and started on her journey home. Emma had enjoyed meeting Ethan's dad and learning cool tips on staying safe. Now if she was ever caught in a fight she would know how to throw a good punch. Emma was glad to know the group didn't ***sequester*** their friendship from everybody's family. The importance of their secret meetings had been explained to Sensei Lowry and he had promised to respect his son's wishes. The sensei thought it was funny that the kids were so serious about their organization, but he remembered what it was like to be a kid and supported his son. As a father, the sensei was just happy to know his

---

Allocate   (**al**-uh-keyt) – V – to set aside; to distribute
Sequester   (si-**kwes**-ter) – V – to keep apart; to separate

son had a good group of friends and wasn't getting himself into any trouble. It did strike Emma as odd that the group had to be kept a secret from only Lavender's and Thomas's families. Then again, there wasn't one thing about the entire group that didn't strike Emma as odd at one point or another. She just hoped when the time came to tell her parents about the organization that they would be as cool as Sensei Lowry.

WORD REVIEW

Allocate
Blithely
Bungler
Contretemps
Disseminate
Espouse
Fetter
Flaxen
Homogeneous
Indomitable
Inimical

Insouciant
Jejune
Lissome
Machination
Nepotism
Noisome
Ostracize
Pratfall
Paltry
Prowess
Rampant

Recalcitrant
Rectify
Riposte
Schism
Sequester
Strategem
Surreptitious
Uncanny
Unimpeachable
Unlettered
Vanquish

8

EAVESDROPPING

The difference between Monday and Tuesday at school was like night and day. Emma now knew what to expect from the others in the group and didn't mind the coldness in their receptions. This time around she felt a strange sense of pride every time she was in the room with one of the other O.I.T. members. She was amazed how well they could play the part of strangers. The art of acting was *intrinsic* to being a spy and keeping the group's secret. Emma still didn't fully understand the purpose of keeping the group a secret, but it wasn't really her place to make that decision. She had only recently joined. Emma did recognize the fun in sending and receiving *arcane* notes and making plans that you couldn't tell anyone else about. It was the type of fun that felt like it should be bad, yet unlike many things done in secret, this group never did anything harmful. In fact, often the group sent themselves on missions to do mysterious acts of kindness for the community. The goal in the training was to learn how to be secretive. As long as they accomplished that goal, the mission itself could be anything they wanted it to be. Slowly, Emma began to pick up on how the organization was run and what she could expect out of being a member. Usually, the group would meet

Intrinsic	(in-**trin**-sik) – ADJ – essential
Arcane	(ahr-**keyn**) – ADJ – mysterious, known only by a select few

twice a week. During the first meeting they would learn some spy-like skill, and then on the second meeting, they would come up with some mission that would allow them to use that skill. However, since they had learned how to fight on Monday, that week's mission would be devoted to practicing those skills back at Lowry's dojo. No one in the group was able to come up with another mission that didn't involve them getting into some sort of trouble. Being a member for less than a week, Emma had only heard stories of their adventures. She couldn't wait for a chance to partake in the action.

There were also several club rules that Emma, along with the others, had to abide by. First, they never did any mission which would put them in actual danger. They decided to leave those missions until they were real spies. Second, someone apart from the group had to know where they were going. They didn't need to know why, or what they would be doing, just where they would be. Brigitte, Lavender's cook, was usually the designated person. She had been a part of Lavender's entire life, and Lavender knew she could trust her. Brigitte was their safety net in case something ever went wrong. Sometimes things did go awry; even with their precautions, and the group had gotten into sticky situations. Third, they never conducted any missions or meetings at school. There were simply too many people around and too many chances to get caught. They figured that part of being a real spy was learning to choose the situations carefully. Discretion, after all, is the better part of valor. If they needed to contact each other at school, they would do so through their notes. It was also important for their notes to be *pithy*, with limited clues for others to follow, should they fall into the wrong hands. Each note

---

Pithy   (pith-ee) – ADJ – brief; terse

should be brief, to the point, and give away as little information as possible. Emma soon found it required a lot of skill involved in writing such a letter. Once the note was read, it was to be torn up and thrown into several different trash cans, or stored somewhere safe and burned at a later time. If Emma chose to burn the letters, she must do so one at a time. She could never have two letters together at the same time. One would just be an oddity, but two could attract unwanted attention. Text messages were only used in case of an emergency. Although text messages are easier to send and receive, digital copies are stored on the person's cell phone record. The group didn't want to run the risk of having written documentation of the organization's activities. Therefore, if anyone was going to send a text message, he or she had to have a very good reason. Emma took the rules seriously, though not as seriously as the other members. To her, this whole thing was a game; to them, it was preparation for the future.

As the week progressed, Emma got better at not expressing her excitement whenever she found a letter waiting for her in her locker. The notes were always brief and always typed. The purpose of the letters varied. Sometimes they were to tell her about the plans for the rest of the week; sometimes they gave her information about the club; other times, they just told her something interesting. As part of their *tacit* agreement to maintain secrecy, the notes were never signed. Nevertheless Emma was always glad to get them and soon started to distinguish the different writing styles of the three other members. She hadn't noticed it at first, but Lavender, Ethan and, Thomas wrote in distinctive manners. Of course they were very

---

Tacit   (**tas**-it) – ADJ – implied; subtle

subtle differences; Emma noticed them only because of her keen eye for languages. The small changes were in the sentence syntax and in how each individual constructed sentences. There was also the difference in subject matter. Lavender gave Emma information about the school and what she needed to be aware of. Ethan shared information about the club itself or the week's agenda. Thomas talked about new ideas or things a spy should know. In a strange way, the *curt* correspondences told Emma a lot about each member's personality, so much more than was contained in the brief messages. Upon this revelation of her insightful skills, Emma began to wonder if she, too, were cut out to be a real spy.

Apart from the things going on with O.I.T., Emma found her own social circle expanding. Since the bus ride her friendship with Michael had continued to grow. He helped her understand chemistry and in turn she helped him with his German. She was thankful that one person could dramatically improve her two least favorite classes. She actually looked forward to going to third and fourth periods now. Since her friendship with Michael blossomed, Emma could no longer get away with eating in the cafeteria alone. Every day he insisted that she join him and his friends. On Tuesday in chemistry, when he again offered the invitation, Emma felt embarrassed to return to the table with him. Last time she hadn't paid much attention to others at the table. Now she had to go back and try to remember their names.

Upon asking Emma to come back to the lunch table, Michael recognized her uneasiness. He knew she was shy, so to help lessen her fears about interacting with new

Curt   (kurt) – ADJ – brief; short

people, he reiterated all of their names and told Emma a little bit about each one. That way, she could feel like she was meeting up with potential friends and not complete strangers. Michael's lunch group consisted of five people, including himself. With Emma, the group was six. He said that with a smile to let Emma know she was now a part of the group. Besides him there were two boys and two girls. Emma listened intently to Michael's descriptions.

"The short, kind of chubby boy is David," he began.

Michael knew him from band because they both played the trumpet. Michael also mentioned that David loved to play videogames. So if Emma knew anything about them, she would instantly become his friend. Emma assured Michael she had no clue how to play.

"I guess we'll just have to change that," was Michael's reply.

He continued with his description of the table.

"The skinny kid at the table is Ishmael," explained Michael, "but he insists on everyone calling him Rick because he wanted to better blend in at Providence High. He grew up in Afghanistan, but he's been here since the beginning of high school. He adds a nice bit of diversity to the table," Michael said with a laugh.

Rick loved everything American. He especially liked the *shibboleths* of classic TV commercials: "Where's the beef?", "Just do it!", and the like. Because English was his second language, some of the phrases didn't sound the way they were originally recorded. For the most part, his accent was light and unnoticeable, but there were times it was evident that he wasn't from this continent. His

---

Shibboleth   (**shib**-uh-lith) – N – catchphrase; slogan; something that distinguishes

friends liked to tease him about it, but it was all in good fun, and Rick didn't mind. Michael and Rick had met in math class. Both students planned on having future careers heavily centered on mathematics, so they took the hardest levels of math available at Providence High. Their class sizes were small, so they all got to know each other pretty well. Michael hoped to go to college to study architecture, and Rick wanted to be an economist someday. According to Michael, Rick was the only kid from the math classes he really enjoyed hanging out with outside of class. They both liked to make fun of each other for being nerds and enjoying the higher levels of math. Their jokes were in no way *captious*, but lighthearted and fun. That was just how their friendship worked.

"Now, the two girls are Jessica and Darcy," continued Michael. "Jessica is the brunette and Darcy is the redhead."

Michael didn't know the girls as well as the guys because each one of them were better friends with either David or Rick. Darcy and Rick volunteered together at the local homeless shelter. Darcy was also highly involved in the high school drama department and was known for her various performances in the school plays. Michael made the shameful admission that despite being Darcy's friend, he had yet to attend one of her plays. Emma agreed that it was a terrible shame.

Jessica and David were neighbors and friends from band. Michael explained that Jessica used to play the flute, but had recently changed over to the color guard. Both Michael and David agreed that Jessica's switch from their beloved band to the color guard made her a *quisling*.

Captious	(**kap**-shuhs) – ADJ – ill-natured; quick to find fault;
Quisling	(**kwiz**-ling) – N – traitor

However, they were both generous in their character and had forgiven her of her traitorous act. She was reminded of her betrayal only once a week. To Michael and David, this seemed like a more than fair situation. Jessica was a good sport and played along nicely. With that, Michael concluded his review of the table.

His tale had amused Emma, and she became more at ease with joining the lunchtime gang. Michael's descriptions had been fairly detailed as well as entertaining, and she felt as though the four other people were already her friends. Michael also mentioned that before Emma, there had been an odd number. In essence, he was the fifth wheel and felt somewhat out of the loop. Now Emma made the group six, which was a far nicer number than five. His flattery made Emma blush. She knew he was joking, but it was nice of him to say—especially coming from a math nerd.

Chemistry came to an end, and the two cleaned up their lab mess. Emma was surprised that Michael was able to give the entire history of his lunch table and still manage to get the assignment done. Emma put her books away and joined her new lunch buddies. Now that she knew something about each one of them she decided to get to know them for herself. It was a nice way to pass the lunch period.

The rest of the week continued and Emma learned more and more about both sets of friends. She learned about the members of O.I.T. through a series of notes and minor interactions. Every once in awhile, Lavender would flash her a smile or Ethan would wink at her as they passed in the hall. Thomas, however, retained a constant solemnity. He was the most reserved member of the group. He was very studious and solemn. At first Emma thought it was her—that maybe he didn't like something about her—but the more she studied him in and out of class, she realized it was him. Thomas was always reserved. This was in part due to how smart he was. Thomas never acted rashly, but was always deep in thought. It was sometimes hard for him to relate to his follow classmates, because what he had to say went over their heads most of the time. Often his comments or questions were even over the teachers' heads. So he learned to remain silent in order not to make others feel dumb. Despite the fact that he had every reason to think himself superior, Thomas was not arrogant. He viewed his superior intellect not as something to ***taunt*** others with, but as a gift given to him to do something important. He was sure it was a part of some greater plan to help mankind in the future. He wasn't sure when or how, but Thomas knew his gift was to be used for good.

Making others feel bad about themselves was not in accordance with his personal convictions. In many ways, Emma came to envy Thomas's character. He dressed and carried himself as a man well beyond his years. Thomas didn't concern himself with high school gossip or drama that went around. Nor did he worry about the things his fellows students busied themselves with. It did not matter to him if he got a date to the Spring Fling, or even what grade he would get on the next history test. Thomas chose instead to look at the world with a much grander perspective. He focused on things which he thought would last. His worldview made all of the trifling high school cares and concerns seem like the ***nugatory*** affairs that they were. It was evident Thomas Pickering was mature far beyond people twice his age. His perspective made Emma stop and think about how she could better view the world.

Taunt	(tawnt) – V – to mock; insult
Nugatory	(**noo**-guh-tawr-ee) – ADJ – worthless; insignificant

Emma's lunchtime friends were very different. They enjoyed laughing and discussing every matter of high school politics. Since most of them were involved in different aspects of extracurricular activities, they always had something to say about what was going on in Providence High. Each one of them had an opinion on the academic and social dynamics of the school.

On Wednesday, when the much-awaited issue of the *Providence Star* came out, Emma's lunch table was full of things to say. They discussed the red-juice horror of Monday and their thoughts and opinions on some of the well-known members of the high school high society. Jessica and Darcy particularly, had some choice words to say about Lavender and her prank. The girls were in unanimous opinion that the politicians' children were nothing more than spoiled brats who expected everyone else to do something for them. Their thoughts were full of tacit envy, and Emma wondered how many of the politicians' students they actually knew. Emma halfway listened as she flipped through the few pages of the newspaper. She scanned the headlines for anything that would incriminate her own secret society. One article featured the expansion of the high school library and how the construction was scheduled to be completed over spring break. The sports page consisted mostly of articles about how the rugby team was doing. Providence High School didn't offer much in the way of spring sports, but rugby was a local favorite. The paper was filled with a little bit of everything going on at the school, including Lavender's inauspicious debut on the gossip page, but nothing about any secret societies and their connections to the school. Emma felt a strange sense of relief.

The Providence Star even included a two-page spread dedicated to the planning of the Spring Fling dance, with photographs from the previous year.

"Apparently the student events committee expects an even better turnout at the dance this year," commented Emma.

"Really?" asked Darcy.

"Yep. The student senate has been preparing for the dance all year," Emma said sarcastically.

Emma enjoyed school dances, but she never understood the *maudlin* sentiments most girls had about them. To her, it would be a night to have some fun with friends and nothing more. After her *wry* remark, it was clear the other two girls at her table didn't share her opinion. Instead, they expressed the same slightly hurt look on their faces.

"Don't you like school dances?" asked Darcy.

"It's not that. I just don't understand the big deal people make out of them," Emma responded, hoping to get herself out of the hole she had dug.

"What do you mean 'big deal?'" inquired Jessica.

"You know...going out and buying an expensive new dress, worrying about whether my hair and makeup are perfect," continued Emma.

"So you don't like to get dressed up?" asked Jessica, clearly confused by Emma's answer.

"No, I like to get dressed up. I just don't like to fuss about it," replied Emma.

"So everyone who worries about those things is making a fuss?" interjected Darcy.

Emma could tell as hard as she tried, this conversation was not going her way. She could continue to try to explain how she didn't feel the necessity of making

---

Maudlin	(**mawd**-lin) – ADJ – silly and overly sentimental
Wry	(rahy) – ADJ – disdainfully ironic

a big deal out of getting dressed up, or she could say something to pacify her new acquaintances. If Emma felt the need to stand up for what she believed in, then she wouldn't have let the conversation go. However, some fights were just not worth winning.

"No, I think it's important to try to look your best, and it's fun to get dressed up for dances," she said. "I just like to concentrate on the having fun part and try not to worry about whether everything is perfect."

This answer seemed to appease both Jessica and Darcy, and they changed the subject from grilling Emma to other aspects of the dance. They wondered if Student Senate had found a better D.J. and what type of snacks would be served. Emma didn't care what they talked about, as long as it didn't involve an interrogation. She turned to look at Michael, but he had a peculiar expression on his face. What Emma did not know was that before her little speech about school dances, Michael was gathering enough courage to ask her to go with him. He was a hopeful *aspirant* to be her date. He had been trying to ask her since Monday, but things like the great red-juice fight had always gotten in the way. He had been determined to ask her today before the end of the lunch. Now his courage was shot. He thought he understood what Emma was saying, but he was afraid that she thought the whole thing was silly. Michael didn't want Emma to think that about him. He also didn't want to jeopardize their friendship by asking her to the dance and making it weird between them. At that moment Michael decided it best to leave things as they were.

Aspirant   (**as**-per-uhnt) – N – someone who aspires

Emma, of course, had no idea her blunt words had left Michael feeling **aggrieved**. Had she known the type of trouble her remarks might cause him, she would have kept her mouth shut. Truthfully, Emma would be happy to go with him. She enjoyed his company tremendously and thought they would have a wonderful time. If Michael had expressed his fears, Emma, too, would have been able to offer some **remedial** comments to put his mind at ease. Unfortunately for him, he remained silent. As it went, Emma was completely ignorant of the situation. She left the lunch table completely unaware of her almost-date. School continued uneventfully.

The day flew by and soon Emma was back at her house. As she sat at her desk in her pajamas, Emma felt her eyes begin to get heavy. It was late, and Emma was in her bedroom finishing up her last bit of reading for the day. She planned to go to bed early that evening, so she had already said goodnight to her parents. Music played softly in the background to help block out any unwanted distractions. In an uncharacteristic manner, Emma's English teacher had assigned at home reading as she wanted the students to spend more than 45 minutes concentrating on the text. Emma was a diligent student and had only 10 more pages to go, and Emma did not want to drag them out any longer than she had to. Lost in concentration, Emma did not hear the sound of her cell phone ringing. The deep philosophical words of William Faulkner and the gentle harmony of Vienna Symphony Orchestra masked the ring. The phone went quiet. Again, the phone began to ring; again, Emma

Aggrieved	(uh-**greevd**) – ADJ –	troubled or distressed in spirit
Remedial	(ri-**mee**-dee-uhl) – ADJ –	tending to remedy

missed the call. It rang for a third time. Emma, who was at this time on the last page of her reading assignment, concentrated on every word. The music, which found its purpose as a distraction from any outside noises, was doing its job perfectly. It was if the orchestra knew when the phone would ring and adjusted its volume to cover it up. As the ring tone grew louder, the song also reached its *crescendo*. It was a war of melodies, and the robust Vienna Symphony Orchestra won. When Emma put her book down, her phone was silent, and once again a gentle harmony played.

Emma returned her book to her backpack to ensure she would have it for class the following day. She was tempted to shut off her lamp and crawl directly into bed. Her warm, soft mattress beckoned her to curl up and fall blissfully into sleep. She pulled back the covers and tucked herself in. Halfway to sleep, Emma remembered she had left her phone on her dresser. She was already *sedentary* and had no desire to move. Tempted to leave it there until the morning, Emma remembered her promise to always keep it charged. She debated with herself for a moment about getting up and plugging it in. She was torn. Emma finally realized she would have an easier time going to sleep if she knew her phone was being charged. Reluctantly, she pulled back the covers and hurried over to her dresser. Then Emma did something she rarely did, she checked it for missed calls. She wasn't exactly sure why she did it, but something inside of her said to look.

Crescendo	(kri-**shen**-doh) – N – the climactic point; peak
Sedentary	(**sed**-n-ter-ee) – ADJ – settled; characterized by little exercise

Looking at the display, Emma was surprised to see three missed calls and a text message. The calls were from the same number, one she didn't recognize. It was nearly 11, and she wondered who would need to get in touch with her so badly that they would call three times. She toggled to her inbox to read the text.

"Emergency meeting. Come to the parking lot of the school as quickly as you can."

There was no name attached to the message, but Emma knew immediately who, or at least what group, it was from. Emma contemplated her situation for a moment. It was late, her parents would never agree to letting her go, and she was already in bed. Whatever they had to say, couldn't it wait until the next day? She had already made plans to meet at the dojo, her parents had already said yes, and it wouldn't involve her getting out of bed. It was decided; Emma would stay. She sent her reply.

"Already in bed. Parents won't let me out. See you in the morning."

Satisfied with her answer, Emma went to put her phone on the charger and crawl back in bed. Before she had a chance to get back to bed, she got a reply that **rebuffed** her earlier response.

"Emma, you have to come. We have a once in a lifetime opportunity, and we can't let you miss it. See you in 10 minutes."

Rebuff   (ri-**buhf**) – V – to snub; beat back

It seemed the message wasn't a request but a command. The urgency of the text intrigued Emma, and she was curious what could have happened between the afternoon at school and that evening that had gotten the entire group in an uproar. Whatever it was, it had ***obtruded*** the group's attention and was also ruining her good night's rest. Emma scurried around her room trying to change as quickly as she could, while still making as little noise as possible. Although she was now curious about what was going on, she still didn't know how she would be able to get out of the house. If her parents were in the living room they were between her and the front door. If they were in their bedroom they were between her and the back door. To ***augment*** the seriousness of the situation, Emma needed to get down the stairs without making any noise—a feat that was nearly impossible on the old 1920s wooden staircase. Once she made it downstairs, she couldn't be sure where her parents were, and she ran the risk of picking the wrong direction and getting caught.

Nevertheless, Emma knew it must be important so she was determined to make it out of the house unnoticed. Once dressed, Emma stopped to ponder her dilemma. If she couldn't get out the front or the back door, there was always a window. Emma moved to her window to see if it could be of any use. She opened her blinds and looked out. It was useless. Even if she managed to quietly get the screen off, once she got out the window, there was nothing but the ground to catch her fall. The thought of jumping out a two-story window seemed even more ridiculous than the idea of trying to sneak out of the house in the first

---

Obtrude	(uhb-**trood**) – V – to force oneself upon; to intrude
Augment	(awg-**ment**) – V – to make more intense

place. Then Emma remembered the bathroom window. It was big enough to squeeze through, and the tree just outside of it might be usable to help her down. It would be tricky, but it just might work.

Before leaving her bedroom, Emma turned her radio back on. She hoped the music would cover any extra noises that might arouse her parent's curiosity. Emma often fell asleep to music, so it wasn't odd to leave the stereo playing well after her bedtime. Emma grabbed her keys and cell phone and tiptoed across the hallway. Every noise made her heart flutter. She was sure at any moment her parents would turn the lights on her and ask her what she was doing. How could she explain? It wasn't as though she could simply say, "I got a text from a friend about an important meeting." But she couldn't lie to her parents. The only solution was not to get caught. Placing one bare foot lightly in front of the other, Emma made it the bathroom.

In the bathroom Emma stopped to put her shoes on. She had made sure to grab her tennis shoes for the climb down, but hadn't wanted to run the risk of having them squeak across the wooden floor. Once her shoes were on she opened the window. There stood a large magnolia tree brushing up against the house. The branches looked sturdy enough to hold Emma's body weight. At this point, Emma was standing on the toilet looking out of the window. Without giving it much thought—she knew if she stopped to think about it she'd back out—Emma hoisted herself backwards out the window. She put her legs out first to help guide her onto the branches, while keeping her arms secured on the window frame. The balancing act between the tree and the window reminded Emma of her early gymnastic days. She started and ended gymnastics at the age of seven, when a bad fall broke her right arm. It was an incident Emma did not want to repeat. Emma **grappled** the window sill, trying not to slip and lose her balance as she reached for the tree. She remained in this precarious situation for longer than she cared to. Once Emma's feet were planted on the tree, she slowly shifted her weight from the bathroom window to the tree. She painstakingly removed one arm from the window to the tree, and then moved the other. Soon she was hugging the tree. Emma looked back at the open window. She knew it would be best to try to close it, but the thought of hanging over the open ground between the tree and the window was unappealing. She had come that far; she thought it best not to press her luck. Quickly Emma shuffled down the truck. It was easier than she had imagined. Finally she made it to the ground. Suddenly, Emma heard a sound. Without thinking, she dove behind a **laurel,** part of the thick landscaping surrounding the house. A car drove swiftly down the street.

Once the car was out of sight Emma stood up, brushed off dirt and leaves, and ran to her car. She had gone through a lot of trouble to get to this meeting. Whatever they had to tell her, it had better be worth it. Inside her car, Emma pulled out her cell phone to let them know she was coming. It was now 11:08.

"Just made it out of the house. On my way."

Emma carefully backed the car down the driveway before turning on the headlights so as not to foil her valiant efforts. She drove quickly through the black streets, trying not to think about the trouble she would get in if her

---

Grapple	(**grap**-uhl) – V– to seize
Laurel	(**lawr**-uhl) – N – a small evergreen bush

parents discovered she was missing. The night sky was dark, and *opaque* clouds completely covered the moon. Emma did not mean to speed, but all the excitement of a secret meeting and sneaking out of her house gave her a lead foot. She glanced down at her speedometer and realized she was going 50 miles per hour in a residential zone. Going 20 miles over the speed limit would not only get her an expensive ticket, but also a reckless driving charge. It hadn't been that long since she took her driver's license test, so she remembered all too clearly the possible jail time for a reckless driving offense. She could just imagine the reaction from her parents when they found out she was out of the house when she called them with her one phone call. Emma put her foot on the brake. Nothing was worth that kind of punishment. The rest of the way, Emma kept a *trenchant* eye on her speedometer to be sure she didn't drift back above the speed limit in her haste to get to her destination.

Soon, her maroon sedan pulled into the parking lot of Providence High. Emma noticed a couple of cars parked in the darkest part of the lot. Emma knew they had parked in the shadows so as not to attract any unwanted police attention. On her ride there, she also remembered the curfew law they would be breaking if their meeting went past midnight. This was the highest risk mission Emma had ever been a part of. Emma parked her car in the shadows.

The passenger's side door of the navy van opened. The door bore the sign of Lowry's Self-Defense Academy. Emma immediately knew the driver. Emma joined the

---

Opaque	(oh-**peyk**) – ADJ – not translucent; not allowing light to pass through
Trenchant	(**tren**-chuhnt) – ADJ – keen; sharp

other three group members in the van. Everyone sat in silence waiting for her to get settled. As she eased into the front seat, she could feel the tension. All eyes were upon her. The clock on the dashboard read 11:21. Not wanting to endure any *revilement* from the others as punishment for her lateness, Emma offered the first words.

"I'm sorry it took me so long," said Emma.

Her apology was overshadowed by the anticipation of finding out the reason for this spontaneous meeting. Everyone turned to Lavender. Not knowing what to expect, Emma turned to Lavender, too.

"When I came home from school, I overheard my mother tell Brigitte to plan on cooking for an extra person," Lavender began. "When she left, I went in and asked Brigitte who was coming. She didn't know, so I went to talk to my mom to see if she could fill me in on the details. When I asked my mom about it, she explained it was a work thing. Being curious, I continued to ask her about it. At first she didn't want to give me the details, but my persistence won out and she gave in. "

As she talked, Lavender's words came faster and faster. Lavender was so excited that she had forgotten to take a single breath since beginning her tale. By the end of her last sentence she was completely out of oxygen. Ethan stopped her and made her take a long, deep breath before she could continue. After a long pause and a cleansing breath, Lavender continued her story:

"It turns out the visitor was Officer Jack Hawkins from the CIA," continued Lavender.

The mention of Officer Hawkins served to build tension exponentially in the van. They knew whatever else

---

Revilement   (ri-**vahyl**-muhnt) – N – scolding; harsh language

Lavender had to say could possibly change the course of their lives. After all, Lavender was talking about a real-life CIA Officer.

"Officer Hawkins is a home-based officer assigned to assess national security threats from foreign nationals," explained Lavender.

"Why would a home-based officer be meeting with a congresswoman?" asked a puzzled Thomas.

"Because my mom is a part of the National Security Committee in the House of Representatives," explained Lavender. "The officer has been tracking a new threat that he wanted my mom to bring to the attention of her committee."

"What kind of threat?" inquired Emma.

"A group of neo-fascist *renegades* who want to take down the White House."

Lavender made this statement in a rather matter-of-fact manner, which Emma found to be very unsettling. Either she was making up the entire story for a laugh, or she didn't recognize the solemnity of her last statement. Emma wasn't sure which one it was, but if it was the first, Lavender surely did not understand what a joke was. Beginning to doubt Lavender's credibility, Emma started to ask her some questions.

"And your mom just told you all of this when you asked."

Emma's skepticism was far from hidden.

"Oh, no, I barely got the name of the visitor out of my mom," she replied. "Those types of meetings are highly classified."

"Then how did you find out about it?" inquired Emma.

"Because I excused myself from dinner early and

Renegade   (**ren**-i-geyd) – N – traitor

hid in my mom's study closet," explained Lavender. "I knew the reason for Officer Hawkins's visit had to be important."

Lavender didn't feel remorseful for eavesdropping. Since she planned to be an officer herself, in her opinion, Officer Hawkins was her *compatriot*, not just in nationality but also in career choice. Her hiding place had proved to be quite useful in the past when listening in on her mother's business meetings. She had expected to hear some interesting aspects of the CIA, but never in her wildest dreams did Lavender expect to come upon a real plot of *subversion.* Most of Congresswoman Wilkins' meetings consisted of budget increases and lobbyist support. The majority of Lavender's experience with the government came from what she heard behind her mother's closed door. This was the first time Lavender had overheard something interesting. The group begged Lavender to continue with her story. She more than willingly complied. Lavender thought it best to start from the beginning.

"Officer Hawkins recently returned from his field assignment in Southern Italy," Lavender explained. "Part of his assignment while he was there was to monitor the resurgence of Italian terrorists. There have been some serious threats made by a group known as the Cani Rossi—or, in English, the Red Hounds—to undermine the Italian government. The group is known for its strong ties to Mussolini's ideology and is well-versed in Giovanni Gentile's writings as well."

Lavender's debriefing was almost a word-for-word reiteration of what she had heard earlier in her mother's

---

Compatriot	(kuhm-**pey**-tree-uht) – N – fellow countryman; a colleague
Subversion	(suhb-**vur**-zhuhn) – N – an attempt to undermine the government

study. She spoke with authority and conviction, despite the fact that she only understood some of what she was saying. Although the kids had read about fascism when they studied World War II, they only had a *superficial* knowledge of the term's meaning. All they knew was when someone said "fascism", it was synonymous with the word "bad." Lavender continued.

"Once Officer Hawkins returned to America, it was his job to monitor different Italian websites to stay current on the situation there. While searching the internet, he found some American websites that espoused unmistakably similar doctrine to that of the Red Hounds." Lavender's excitement rose as she spoke. "Because the website is targeted at Americans, the CIA loaned Officer Hawkins to a FBI joint-tasked force. The CIA only has jurisdiction overseas, and cannot act on American soil. However, given Officer Hawkins' expertise on the organization, he has been an invaluable asset to the investigation and has been allowed to follow the group's activity for the last several months. He is now convinced there is a Cani Rossi terrorist sleeper cell hidden in America."

"Does the Officer know where the sleeper cell is located?" asked Ethan.

"Right here in Providence!" exclaimed Lavender.

Lavender was almost out of breath when she finished her last statement. Her words were unbelievable. A group of secret terrorists hiding in their own city! Everyone sat quietly soaking in all that they had just heard.

"But if it's a sleeper cell, then why does Officer Hawkins think the group is a national security threat?" asked Emma.

Superficial   (soo-per-**fish**-uhl) – ADJ – on the surface; shallow

"Because he believes the group is planning an attack on American soil to help ignite the attacks in Italy," explained Lavender. "If the group can successfully carry out a terrorist attack here, then it will boost their activity abroad. According to Officer Hawkins, the political unrest that is stirring in Italy has reached its boiling point. If the Red Hounds can demonstrate their power by striking America, then they have the chance to successfully remove any doubt of the extent of their power. Other groups will be too terrified to question them. They will then be able to go on to commit all kinds of malicious deeds, from disrupting political operations to *razing* governmental buildings, leaving ruin and rubble in their path.

"It makes sense," interjected Thomas. "America is the most powerful country in the world. If the Red Hounds can do something that causes chaos and confusion here, they will have no trouble causing terror in their own country."

"Exactly," said Lavender.

"So, why bring all this information to your mom?" asked Emma.

"Because the CIA doesn't think the Red Hounds are a serious threat and have treated Officers Hawkins's intel with contempt," said Lavender.

"If the CIA doesn't think it's a threat, then why bring it to Congresswoman Wilkins?" asked Emma.

"Because according to the website, the group is planning something big, and soon," Lavender said, with a sense of urgency.

Officer Hawkins had been in the CIA long enough to know sometimes the best way to get action was to get politics involved. His dinner with Congresswoman Wilkins

---

Raze   (reyz) – V – to erase, destroy

was a clever *gambit* to bring attention to his suspicions. He hated to admit it, but the threat of a terrorist attack was sometimes not enough to get his superiors' backing. Especially since his evidence was limited, and based more on his experience with the group than cold, hard facts. If he wanted to succeed at getting someone to listen to him, he needed help from an important influence. Congresswoman Wilkins had worked with Hawkins before and knew that he was a good officer. This was precisely why he had come to her for help that night. The National Security Committee would be meeting soon, and he needed her to bring his intel to the table. She agreed to speak on his behalf. It was her plan to persuade the group to look into the possibility of an Italian plan of rebellious *sedition* within its government.

"What else does he know about the group?" asked Ethan.

"The group he has been following are Americans," said Lavender. "However, they're of Italian descent. From what Officer Hawkins could tell, they were all sent to the University of Milan to study."

"And it was there they were introduced to the ideologies of Mussolini?" inquired Thomas. "So we are dealing with home-grown terrorists who were radicalized overseas?"

"Precisely!" answered Lavender. "Officer Hawkins thinks that during their four years in Italy, they were recruited by the leaders of the Red Hounds and trained as a sleeper cell. So, they got their degrees, moved back to the United States and have been waiting for their next orders."

Gambit	(**gam**-bit) – N – a scheme to gain an advantage; clever maneuver
Sedition	(si-**dish**-uhn) – N– treason; insurrection against lawful order

"Does Officer Hawkins know where in Providence they are located?" asked Thomas.

"He has tracked down a warehouse near the docks," answered Lavender. "That's why he thinks they are planning an attack."

The leader of these scheming *rogues* had recently purchased an old building on the docks of Providence Harbor. Officer Hawkins was awaiting permission from the FBI leadership to investigate the premises, but hadn't gotten the clearance from his supervisors yet.

"Did you by any chance get the address?" asked Ethan.

"Yeah. It's 1353 East Briar Street," responded Lavender. "Why?"

"Just because Officer Hawkins can't go, doesn't mean we can't!" proclaimed Ethan.

Rogue   (rohg) – N – a dishonest person; scoundrel

WORD REVIEW

Aggrieved	Maudlin	Subversion
Arcane	Nugatory	Sedentary
Aspirant	Obtrude	Sedition
Augment	Opaque	Shibboleth
Captious	Pithy	Superficial
Compatriot	Quisling	Tacit
Crescendo	Raze	Taunt
Curt	Rebuff	Trenchant
Gambit	Remedial	Wry
Grapple	Renegade	
Intrinsic	Revilement	
Laurel	Rogue	

9

THE PLOT

"What?" exclaimed the rest of the group in unison.

"Think about it! Officer Hawkins can't go to the warehouse because of all the red tape," explained Ethan, "but there's no reason we can't go."

"How about the fact that it is a warehouse full of known terrorists?!?" exclaimed Emma.

"They're only *alleged* terrorists," corrected Ethan. "Besides the CIA doesn't think they're a big threat, so why should we?"

"Because we aren't the CIA!"

"Yet," said Ethan. "We aren't the CIA *yet.*"

"So, we go, check out the warehouse, and see what's going on," said Lavender. "Then we go home. It doesn't have to be a big deal."

"Lavender, you can't be serious," said Thomas.

"Why not? We talk about doing stuff like this all the time," said Lavender. "Now we have a chance to really be spies and you want to turn it down?"

"This could be our only chance to do something like this," added Ethan.

"When would we go?" asked Emma.

"Tonight—it would have to be tonight," responded Ethan.

Excitement had overtaken the group's ability to reason clearly. Despite the fact that this mission went against all of their rules, Lavender and Ethan were sold on the scheme. The two bounced back and forth ideas of what they needed and how they would do it. Thomas and Emma couldn't believe their ears. Slowly, Thomas began to waver. He, too, longed to be an officer and agreed with the others on this once in a lifetime opportunity. Soon even he joined in with the plot. It was agreed this would be only a surveillance mission. They wanted to gather information about the group and see for themselves if they posed any real threat to the United States. It would be simple and it would be safe. They would take notebook paper with them and compile a ***dossier*** of their findings. If they found anything of interest, they would send it to the CIA as an anonymous tip. That way, it was a win/win situation. They were convinced it was a brilliant idea. Emma, the most reserved member of the group, was not as convinced, but knew this mission was already ***ineluctable***; there was no way to talk the group out of the idea. Thus, instead of worrying, she, too, got excited. It would be a real spy mission!

To be safe, the group decided on new ground rules. First, they would keep a safe distance between themselves and anyone at the warehouse. Second, if they found out anything important they would take it to the authorities. Third, if the situation became dangerous at any time, they would ***truncate*** the mission immediately. Everyone agreed.

Ethan was already behind the wheel and was designated as the official driver. Emma became the copilot. She plugged the address Lavender had given

Dossier	(**dos**-ee-ey) – N – a file containing detailed records
Ineluctable	(in-i-**luhk**-tuh-buhl) – ADJ– unavoidable; inescapable
Truncate	(**truhng**-keyt) – V – shorten by cutting off

them into Ethan's GPS. They were about 10 minutes from their destination.

The majority of the drive was in silence. Everyone was nervous and excited at the same time. It was late and the docks were basically empty. To map out the territory and to get a feel for the environment, the kids drove slowly around the docks. Most of the buildings were completely dark except for the outside lights. The florescent bulbs and the blackness of the sky cast an eerie, yellow glow around each of the doors. The cold air mixed with the water on the bay, creating a fog that added to the creepiness of the entire situation. Ethan parked the van *askew* behind a couple of dumpsters at the edge of the warehouses, hiding it from anyone's vantage point and angled for an easy escape.

The four walked in the shadows. The warehouse in question was at the far end of the row of buildings. They were careful to avoid any lights and kept themselves hidden in the darkness. The clear *disparity* between the four high school students and the normal dock clientele meant they would stand out if noticed, so staying under cover was vital. If caught, it would be hard to explain why they were there after midnight on a school night. They couldn't be seen.

No one was in sight as the group made their way down the row of warehouses. Many of the buildings were rusted and falling apart. They reeked of decay and neglect. Windows were broken, and some had holes in the middle of the doors. It was little wonder why a group of renegades

---

Askew	(uh-**skyoo**) – ADV – out of line; in a crooked position
Disparity	(dih-**spar**-i-tee) – N – lack of similarity, difference

would pick such an environment to house their schemes. No one took notice of the all-but-abandoned docks. As the spy club made its way toward the other side of the dock, the structures made a gradual shift from completely falling apart to only minor decay. Many of the newer warehouses had roofs and almost all of their windows still intact. They weren't much to look at, but compared to the previous warehouses, were rather well-kept. The buildings were numbered by 10. Faster than expected, they were standing in front of warehouse 1330 with only two more buildings to go. Even if they hadn't seen the number, the four friends could have guessed which building they were looking for. It was the last on the row of warehouses, and the only one with its lights on. The group approached it with caution. From what they could tell, there was no one outside, but they couldn't be too careful.

The warehouse had once been painted a dark red, but now had a ***pied** and *mottled** appearance caused by weather and rust. It was a mix of reds and dark browns. The side of the building facing the other warehouses, the direction the students came from, was windowless. This was unfortunate because it meant the group needed to make their way around the building just to get a look at the inside. The front side of the building faced the parking lot. It would have been a lot easier for the group to walk around that side of the building to get to the side with the windows. However, that path was lit by an overhead light. It was also closest to the front door, making it impossible for the students to hide if someone happened to pull into the parking lot or come from the inside. If they wanted to see what was inside, they would have to go around the back.

Pied   (pahyd) – ADJ – multi-colored

The backside faced the bay. Luckily, the edge of the building did not extend out into the water; there was a small wooden platform in between the land and sea. The platform jutted over the edge of the water like a mountainous *crag* over a deep valley. The lack of light was fortunate because the darkness would maintain the group's stealth. However it was inopportune because it made it impossible to see if the wood had rotted or not. There was no way, except by putting pressure on the boards, to see if the wood was strong enough to hold their weight. From the looks of the rest of buildings, the group didn't feel too sure on the odds of that being in their favor. They decided to take the path one at a time, with the lightest person going first. That would be Lavender. She would carefully walk across it, and at the first sign of trouble, turn around and come back to the rest of the group. The water was too cold and deep to risk falling in.

Lavender lowered herself down onto her hands and knees. She decided it would be easier to test the strength of the wood that way. Crawling would more evenly disperse her weight across the wooden panels and allow her to feel if there were any holes or rough spots. It would be a long crawl. The wooden pathway stretched as long as the warehouse, about 70 feet. Another reason for the crawl was because there were windows that faced out into the bay. Lavender didn't want to run the risk of being spotted walking along the backside of the building. Once Lavender reached a few feet down the path, Emma was to follow. After Emma would be Thomas, and last would be Ethan. Lavender made small movements at first, *scrupu-*

Crag   (krag) – N – a steep rugged rock or peak

lously examining every piece of wood as she crawled across it. It wasn't a very wide pathway, only two to three feet wide at the widest part. Lavender stuck close to the building. She figured the wood would be the strongest closest to the actual structure. She also knew that if one advancing motion went *awry*, she would topple into the water. It was a plunge she didn't want to take.

The wood was damp from the recent rain and snow. Thankfully, most of the snow was gone, leaving behind only frigid water, which regrettably only added to the moisture in the boards. Lavender could feel the cold water seeping through her jeans at her knees. The texture of wet wood made her hands feel clammy. Every time she set her hands down, she couldn't help but worry about the possibility of splinters. After a successful couple of feet, Lavender felt Emma's presence on the platform. The wood gave way slightly as she joined, and it made a small bounce. Lavender's heart jumped at the movement. If the wood dipped with just herself and Emma, she shuddered to think what it would be like to have the boys on the platform, too. Lavender quickened her movements to put more distance between herself and the rest of the group.

Emma followed closely behind Lavender's footsteps. The thought of being on an old platform made her nervous. Soon Thomas joined the group and the wood dipped farther and didn't come close to rising back to its original height. The movement of the wood was an ominous sign. Lavender hadn't made it to the end yet so all three were on the platform together. The darkness made it impossible to see one another, and Ethan had no way to

---

Scrupulous	(**skroo**-pyuh-luhs) – ADJ – very thorough
Awry	(uh-**rahy**) – ADV – off course

tell how long to wait before joining them. One thing was certain—the boards didn't seem like they would be able to hold all four students at once. Lavender would have to make it off before Ethan began.

Emma couldn't see Lavender, but prayed that she was close to the end. Emma wanted nothing more than to get off the platform as quickly as possible. She moved as swiftly as she could while trying to maintain her balance and avoid putting too much pressure on the wood. As she crawled, her thoughts wandered to the icy temperature of the water below and considered what would happen if the boards snapped with the weight of the students. She shuddered in *tremulous* fear at the thought of tumbling into the freezing water. To make matters worse, once on the other side, they would have to make it back again. Not letting herself dwell on the tasks of the near future, Emma trudged on.

After a couple of minutes, the wood moved again. This time the movement was coupled with an unsettling cracking noise. Emma couldn't see the rest of the group, but she was sure the movement of the wood and the breaking sound were a direct result of the four members being on the wooden platform all at the same time. Soon, she was convinced, something would break. Emma scurried to the edge. Almost running, Emma did her best to remove her weight from the desolate pathway.

Hurrying into the darkness, Emma almost didn't notice the change of texture under her hands and knees. It took her a moment to realize that she was no longer crawling on damp wood, but on wet dirt. A small pebble first caught her attention when it rolled underneath her

---

Tremulous   (**trem**-yuh-luhs) – ADJ – fearful; trembling

hand, causing a substantial amount of discomfort. The sudden halt from moving so quickly nearly caused Emma to go headfirst into the ground. She caught herself and slowly crawled over to the side of the building where Lavender was sitting. The two waited in silence for the boys to join them. Soon both Ethan and Thomas were by their sides. Once reunited, they made their way to the windows.

They decided that Ethan would be the first one to look. The agreement, although a silent one, was understood by the entire group. As the leader, Ethan took the responsibility of making the first step. Once up, he motioned to the others to follow. Slowly, three small heads rose up next to his to look into the window.

Inside was a large room filled with tables that had tools on top of them. At first glance the room didn't look like anything special—a few workstations here and there with random equipment scattered along. Apart from the unusual location, nothing about the warehouse seemed out of the ordinary. That is, until the group spotted a row of tables in the far right corner. They were off to the side and covered by stained sheets. The covering lay over the majority of the tables, but it was pulled back ever so slightly on one to reveal a ghastly sight. There, spread out on the table, was a large *arsenal* of weapons. Although they couldn't tell if the guns were illegal, it was obvious there was something unusual about the amount of firepower hidden under the blankets. Lavender pulled out the notebook and the pen and began to write down descriptions of the room.

The group scanned the rest of the warehouse. No one came in or out of the large workroom. The windows on the side of the building provided only a small picture

Arsenal   (**ahr**-suh-nl) – N – a collection of armaments

of what was going on. The tables of tools were too far from view to make any meaningful assumption of their purpose. Apart from the tables of weapons, there was little information to be gathered from that particular vantage point.

Frustrated at the thought of not getting more out of this surveillance excursion, Ethan left the window and began to look for a way inside the building. The rotting condition of the wood made it easy for him to find exactly what he was looking for. He dug into the soil around the disintegrating baseboards and *exhumed* a broken panel. Ethan tugged on the panel, revealing a fairly large opening into the building. Before entering the building, he motioned to the group to see if anyone had entered the large work room. After getting clearance, Ethan crawled into the warehouse. Stunned by his behavior, the rest of the group wasn't sure what to do. They looked back and forth, and reluctantly followed him one by one through the hole. Once the four students crawled through the opening, they congregated at the closest corner to continue their clandestine cause.

It was no warmer inside than outside. Light *emanated* from a few overhanging bulbs which seemed to be left on to ward off intruders. The four friends hovered close to the corner, motionless for several minutes, waiting to see if they had just crawled into a trap. The room was silent, except for the occasional creaking floor common to all old buildings. The group gradually emerged from their hiding place, slowly at first, and hiding behind different tables and equipment as they eased forward. As time passed they grew bolder. They changed from a crawl to a crouch, then to a standing position.

Exhume	(ig-**zoom**) – V – to unbury; unearth
Emanate	(**em**-uh-neyt) – V– to flow out; originate

Eventually they moved around the room freely.

The first thing the group wanted to explore was the arsenal of guns on the table in the opposite corner. The sheets were large and hung to the floor, making it impossible to know for sure what was underneath them without removing them. They wanted to be sure of their suspicions before they drew any conclusions. They had learned long ago that things aren't always what they appeared to be. Ethan pulled out his cell phone and began to take pictures of the warehouse. He wanted documentation of what they saw in case they needed to bring the information to the CIA. On their way over to the covered arsenal, they passed rows of equipment and material. Barrels of what appeared to be cleaning chemicals were scattered throughout the warehouse. There were odd tools and pumps. It looked as though they had stumbled into an old plumber's warehouse. It was an unusual assortment for a warehouse on a dock, but nothing particularly dangerous. The group expected to find bomb-making equipment, but they saw nothing to support those suspicions. Lavender kept the notebook out, documenting everything they saw. So far the only thing that suggested a possible terrorist attack was the large *surplus* of guns, certainly more than needed for security for this one building.

Closer to the weapons table was a table of science supplies. It looked just like the lab table Emma used in her chemistry class. Scattered atop the table were half-filled beakers, flasks, test tubes, and safety equipment along with ring racks, tongs, and Bunsen burners. There were weights for measuring powder and measuring cups for liquids. Although some of the equipment was in crude

---

Surplus   (**sur**-pluhs) – N – amount greater than needed

condition, the setup had everything anyone would need for a home science lab. The group would have spent more time examining the science equipment, but as they stood there they heard the sound of the closing of a car door. Soon they heard the chatter of people talking outside the front of the warehouse.

The broken panel which had served as the doorway into the warehouse was well across the room. One or two of the students would have been able to make it there in time, but it was unlikely they all could get out before someone entered the warehouse. The open room made it impossible to find a place to hide if they didn't make it; they would have to find another place to go. Terror caused the group to freeze. They had only seconds to find a hiding place.

Suddenly Emma had an idea. She was standing next to Lavender and grabbed her hand pulling her toward the covered tables. Ethan and Thomas followed. The four dove underneath the coverings and hid themselves safely behind the curtains. It was the best place to be; that is, as long as those coming in didn't want the guns. Thomas was the last to make it under the covers. He hid himself just in time; a group of men entered the room right as he pulled the sheet down. Underneath the sheet, it was impossible to see what the men looked like. They stood in the doorway talking with one another. The distance between the front door and the gun tables made it hard for the group to understand what the men were saying. Although the thought of being in a room with a group of potential terrorists was frightening, it was a terrific scenario for the four friends to gather important information. Assuming they didn't get caught, the men's arrival was a fortunate event. The group sat quietly as the men moved from the doorway toward the middle of the room. Their steps were heavy, suggesting the men were not small in size. At one point each member of the group was tempted to sneak a peek of the men, but no one dared to reveal their hiding place.

Once the men were closer to the tables, their voices could be distinguished clearly. It sounded as though there were three distinct speakers, but the group might have been much bigger if there were others present who didn't speak. Anxiety grew as the men approached the tables closest to the kids. Now they would be able to overhear their plans. The men walked around the room surveying the different tables. They were quiet now and appeared to be concentrating.

Then one man with a particularly raspy voice spoke up. The kids' ears perked up to listen to what he had to say. They needed anything that might give them a clue into the purpose of the strange *farrago* of materials in the warehouse. The man spoke in a gruff tone.

"Tutto abbiamo pronto per domani la notte?" he asked.

Confused, the students turned to one another to see if any of them had understood him. With puzzled faces they all shrugged their shoulders. Not one of them had gotten a word of what the man had said. Hope was not lost, however, as a second man spoke up. The group listened with their entire concentration, hoping they might have just missed what the first guy said.

"Sì, noi il recieved l'ultima spedizione in un paio di ore fa," he replied.

The four friends were stunned. Although they knew they were seeking out a known Italian terrorist group, they had never suspected that the men would actually speak Italian. This surveillance mission was a lot harder than they originally anticipated. The men continued with their

---

Farrago   (fuh-**rah**-goh) – N – confused mixture; hodgepodge

conversation. The four friends felt hopeless. Any effort to uncover the Red Hound's secretive **perfidy** was thwarted by a language barrier. Suddenly, Thomas took the pen and the notebook from Lavender and started to write something down. Once he was finished, he turned to Emma. The paper read:

"Do you know Italian?"

Emma grabbed the paper and wrote down her reply.

*"I speak a little Italian, but my knowledge of the language is **subpar**."*

Thomas took the paper again and scribbled down, *"Do your best."* With his reply he handed the pen and notebook to Emma. The potential for valuable information **necessitated** a translation of the men's conversation, and Emma's knowledge of languages made her the perfect candidate for the task. Nervous about her inabilities, Emma hesitated in her translation. She, more than anybody else, knew how tricky translating languages could be. Depending on the person's knowledge of the vocabulary and the speaker's dialect, two words with completely opposite meanings could sound the exact same. Thoughts and ideas were very easily lost in translation. Nevertheless Emma was the group's only hope of figuring out what the men were saying. All she could do was try.

Emma listened intently and began to furiously scribble down words and phrases she heard. There was no way she would be able to directly translate the conversation from the men's speech, but if she could write them down and see the words, there was a good

---

Perfidy	(**pur**-fi-dee) – N – treason; treachery
Subpar	(suhb-**pahr**) – ADJ – below average; not qualified
Necessitate	(nuh-**ses**-i-teyt) – V – to make unavoidable

chance she could grasp the point of the conversation. Emma had a knack for seeing the **orthography**, the written characters of a foreign language, and putting the words together into a meaningful context. It wasn't as useful as being fluent in the actual tongue, but for situations like this one, it was the next best thing. All the others could do was sit back and wait.

The men's speech stopped abruptly. The sudden halt in speaking caused Emma to jerk up from her notebook. She looked at the rest of the group with wide eyes. Terror made her face white. The other three were dying to know what she had heard, but were too afraid to ask. Slowly Emma turned her notebook around and pointed to the word "pistola" next to which she had written "guns." The rest of the group didn't need any more translation to know the group of men were now walking toward the gun table. The heavy footsteps they had heard when the men first entered the warehouse now sounded like the robust thumping of marching soldiers. Each footstep mirrored the uniform pounding of Thomas, Ethan, Lavender, and Emma's hearts. Their terror amplified the noise. The sounds of the approaching footsteps were **omnidirectional,** overwhelming the kids with the sense that they were surrounded. The noise of their beating hearts also filled their eardrums. It was impossible for them to distinguish between the two thunderous noises.

The footsteps stopped directly in front of the table which housed the group. The light from the overhead

Orthography	(awr-**thog**-ruh-fee) – N – a part of language study that deals with letters and spelling
Omnidirectional	(om-nee-di-**rek**-shuh-nl) – ADJ – coming from all directions

hanging lamps revealed the shadow of the men's legs. The shadowy figure was distorted and larger than life. The presence of these threatening legs only added to the tension. The men stood for a while in silence. The four held their breath, waiting and praying that the men would soon leave so they could get out of the building. As the men stood next to the table, the group realized the severity of their plight. They had willingly put themselves in a situation that was potentially very dangerous. No one knew where they were. If they got out of there safely, they were determined never to attempt such a foolish endeavor again.

Finally, after an eternity of silence, the men turned and started walking toward the front of the building. An enormous sense of relief overwhelmed the members of the O.I.T. group and they let out a great sigh in unison. Unfortunately for them, the release of tension by all of them at once caused the metal table to move ever so slightly. No one had taken the time to notice the gun table was on wheels. Their movement caused the wheels to creek. They knew at once they were in trouble. The sound of footsteps rushing toward them only served to confirm this. Within moments, the sheets were ripped away revealing four very frightened faces hiding below the table.

The removal of the protective sheets brought a feeling of **consternation** to the young spies. The group had been caught; there was nothing for them to do but try to escape. They scurried out from the table but their movements were too slow. The men grabbed the students and yanked them from underneath the table.

Consternation   (kon-ster-**ney**-shuhn) – N – dread that results in utter confusion; dismay

As they pulled, the four struggled to get free. There were three men to the four of them. The men were strong but the four friends did everything they could to break their holds. One man had the two girls and the other two had Ethan and Thomas. Emma and Lavender were caught by their arms and were being dragged into the middle of the room. In the midst of their panic, the girls remembered the lesson from Sensei Lowry. They knew their only hope for survival was to make this attack as difficult as possible for the perpetrators. Together they dropped their weight to the floor, causing the man's arms to buckle. They kicked and dragged their feet trying to put as much pressure on the man's body as possible. Even if they couldn't outfight him with strength, they knew they could make this experience as painful as possible for the man. Thomas and Ethan were likewise enacting lessons from the night at the dojo. Ethan, the more experienced of the two, quickly freed himself from the burly Italian's grip and raced to help Thomas. It was a scramble from all sides. Hair was pulled, shins were kicked, and pain was inflicted on everyone involved. The unsuspecting terrorists didn't know what to think. They had never anticipated the presence of high school students in their warehouse, much less students who knew how to put up a fight. The trouble the students caused caught them off guard just as much as their presence.

Thomas and Ethan freed themselves just around the time Lavender and Emma were released. Once away from the men's grip, the group rushed toward an exit. One of the men was standing in the direction of their original entrance point. Although he was temporarily disposed from the fight, the group knew it wouldn't be wise to try to run past him. Even if just one of them were caught by his hand they would all be in trouble. They looked around and saw the pathway to the front door was clear. Without saying a word, they all ran toward the exit. If they could get out the door they were sure they could make it to the van. Once safely out of the docks, they would call the police.

The door was heavy, but Thomas managed to throw it open. His strength came from a mix of adrenaline and the knowledge that behind that door was freedom. He wasn't about to let anything stand in the way of getting out of there safely. The door swung open with a massive thud. The group bounded toward the open air only to be stopped by a very large, very angry-looking Italian. He was as tall as he was wide, with a thick, dark beard and ebony eyes. He stood there with his hands on his hips and a grimace on his face. The husky Italian looked at the four teens standing in front of him; a wicked smile appeared on his face. They wouldn't be getting out that way and he knew it.

Panicked, the group turned in opposite directions, just missing the burly arms of the giant who stood before them. To their horror the other three men had regained their strength and were now racing toward the four friends. They were angry. The embarrassment of being beaten by kids brought fire to their eyes and they moved forward with a newfound *vendetta* against the teens. With quick steps, the men soon encircled them. They had nowhere to go. There was one man for each of them now, and all their hope for escape was gone. Their arms were quickly bound. Emma closed her eyes tightly, hoping that when she woke up it would all be just another dream. It was no use—she was wide awake and

---

Vendetta   (ven-**det**-uh) – N – enmity marked by bitter hostility

the four friends found themselves trapped in the middle of a dangerous *intrigue*. There they stood at the mercy of the Cani Rossi.

Intrigue   (in-**treeg**) – N – evil plot; use of underhanded schemes

WORD REVIEW

Arsenal	Exhume	Pied
Askew	Farrago	Scrupulous
Awry	Ineluctable	Subpar
Consternation	Intrigue	Surplus
Crag	Necessitate	Tremulous
Disparity	Omnidirectional	Truncate
Dossier	Orthography	Vendetta
Emanate	Perfidy	

10

STATE OF EMERGENCY

The terrorists quickly grabbed the children and removed them from the warehouse. Unsure what to do with four meddlesome youngsters, the men decided to stick them in a nearby van, far enough away from each other so they wouldn't be able to untie one another. Their unexpected presence *spawned* a frenzy of agitated discussion among their captors as they determined how to deal with this new situation. Four nosy American children would have four sets of worried parents, and those worried parents would soon call the police. The men knew that once the police were involved, the FBI, and possibly the CIA, wouldn't be far behind. They couldn't take a chance on waiting for their original date—they had to act quickly. The arrival of the group of friends set the plot into motion. It would be now or never for the Italian gang. They had put in too much time, effort, and money for things to go wrong now. They decided it would be best to take the children with them and dispose of them once everything was done. The four men discussed this new plan as they pulled the children to the van. Their conversation was a mix of fast Italian and broken English. Although Emma and her friends didn't fully understand what was going on, they knew they had stumbled upon something big.

Spawn   (spawn) – V – to bring forth

Once the children were secure in the van, the Italians left the giant to keep watch over them. Any grand hopes of escape were dashed as the husky man sat in the back of the van between the girls and the guys. His vicious smile *extorted* a sense of fear from the four novice operatives. They were terrified of him, and with good reason. One strike from this monster and any one of them would not be able to see straight for a week. Now wasn't the time to try to escape. They just had to wait for a better opportunity. Emma, Thomas, Lavender, and Ethan sat quietly thinking about their next move. Their spy training allowed them to be calm and *reflective* even in the face of such danger.

The rest of the terrorists scuttled around the warehouse, angrily muttering *imprecations* in Italian. Fortunately for the youthful spy gang, they had been left without blindfolds. They watched the action intently, hoping to gain as much knowledge as possible about the plot. The men were in a state of emergency, running back and forth gathering materials, tools, and weapons. They loaded the cargo piece by piece into the van, working fast and furiously. It was obvious they were on a mission. The vans were quickly filled and closed. There were three vehicles total, including the one that carried the frightened students. Once the vans were packed, the group locked the warehouse and started the engines. The execution of the plot was messier than the Cani Rossi had hoped, but they had never planned a scenario for an intrusion of high school students. At the very least, the O.I.T. group felt good

Extort	(ik-**stawrt**) – V – to wrest or wring from a person by violence
Reflective	(ri-**flek**-tiv) – ADJ – marked by meditation or cogitation
Imprecation	(im-pri-**key**-shuhn) – N – malediction; curse

that they had unnerved the organization enough to cause them to be sloppy. Hopefully their carelessness would *undermine* some aspects of their plan. The van began to move, and the students were taken along with all the other cargo. They had unwillingly become a part of the plot.

The three turned to Emma. They knew she had the most knowledge about what was going on, but hesitated to ask because of the hairy man sitting at her right. It was possible the man spoke only Italian, but they didn't want to run the risk that he also understood English. At this point they seemed like innocent bystanders who were in the wrong place at the wrong time. It would only harm them to reveal their knowledge of the organization and its terrorist plot, however limited it might be. There was still a chance they would let the four go once they accomplished whatever terrible deed they had in store for Providence. At least that was what the kids chose to believe. Once they had a moment to themselves, they would ask Emma what she had learned.

The road was bumpy and the vans took the curves of the streets with reckless speed. They were in a rush to get to their destination. Emma prayed that the unsafe speed would catch the attention of a passing policeman, but no such officer passed their way. It was the middle of the night, and the part of town the gang was headed toward was all but abandoned. They were going to the industrial section that fell outside the normal patrol routes of the Providence PD. The Cani Rossi knew they had until 5:30 in the morning before the workers would arrive to the various factories in the area. As far as they were concerned, it was more than enough to do their job and get out before anyone knew they had been there.

Undermine   (uhn-der-**mahyn**) – V – to impair; to work against

The vans pulled into the back of a large facility, the Great Regions Water Purifying Center. It was the water purifying center, as well as reservoir, for not only Providence's water, but also for Washington D.C. and the surrounding suburbs. This building connected to a network of pipes, rivers, and water towers that ran throughout the countryside. Any type of destruction to this plant would cause a massive water shortage for at least three of the county's most important cities. Although the watering plant was one of the most significant buildings in the entire state, it was left unguarded due to its lack of national security appeal. When making up plans to protect the nation, no one ever considered the water supply. That is, until *after* the terrorist's plot that night.

Once the materials were completely unloaded and dragged into the water treatment plant, the Italian giant hauled his human cargo into the building. He had two students in each arm and carried them with the ease of a couple of shopping bags. By the time the students were unloaded with the rest of the cargo material, only Emma knew, thanks to her Italian language skills, of the ***opprobrious*** purpose of this malevolent visit to the capital's watering plant. The rest of the group stood, or hung as the case was, in ignorance. The Cani Rossi knew that water was the one economic resource the American government had overlooked. It was their intention to poison it and cause mass hysteria across the nation. This one act of terror would show how vulnerable the country's defenses were. It didn't matter to them if one or a 100,000 people were killed in the process—they were doing this to send a message. The

---

Opprobrious   (uh-**proh**-bree-uhs) – ADJ – disgraceful or shameful

lack of consideration for human life was ***reprehensible***. The evil men had neither remorse nor fear of ***perdition***.

The lights remained off. Instead of turning on the power, which might have cast suspicion, the men had set up floor lanterns all across the main building. They were small camping lanterns that were light sensitive. It was a clever solution to the darkness. The men had obviously thought through their scheme. The presence of the lanterns along with the sound of dripping water gave the building an unusual feel. The atmosphere resembled that of a cave, and the men who held the four captive appeared in the darkness as miners.

The other three men not responsible for restraining the kids worked diligently at assembling some contraption near the base of one of the biggest water pumps. They wore head lanterns to help light their workstation. The grisly man herded the four children out of the way of work. Although they were already tied, their captor put the four in pairs and tied them back-to-back on the floor. He tied Emma to Ethan and Lavender to Thomas. The mix of boys and girls was to help keep the weight unevenly distributed, making it harder for them to try and escape. Once his hostages were taken care of, the man joined the other three with their work. The machine they were building was complex and would take too much time without the aid of the human gorilla.

Among the four terrorists was a particularly interesting man. Although the students didn't know him, his name was Duilio Maroncelli, a noteworthy Italian scientist. Duilio considered himself a ***cabalist*** having studied ancient

---

Reprehensible	(rep-ri-**hen**-suh-buhl) – ADJ – deserving rebuke
Perdition	(per-**dish**-uhn) – N – eternal punishment; utter destruction
Cabalist	(**kab**-uh-list) – N – one versed in secret sciences

chemistry during his time at the University of Milan. His unique talents in chemistry garnered the attention of the Agenzia Informazioni e Sicurezza Esterna, or ASIE, the Italian equivalent of the CIA. He trained with the ASIE after graduating from the University; however, he soon defected and went into private practice once his antigovernment and pro-fascist sentiments were discovered. His ***proclivity*** for both science and anarchy made him a prime candidate for the Cani Rossi. Duilio was the mastermind behind the water plot. He, along with three other colleagues, assembled the destructive machine that he originally designed in the ASIE.

Once the kids were alone, Emma informed her friends of the plot to poison the area's water supply. Her words were quick and hushed, because the bear man came to check on them from time to time. Because they didn't have all the information, they had no way of knowing how much time they had left before the chemicals were to be dumped into the reservoir. The only thing they could tell was the men weren't going to dump the materials in directly. They had assembled some sort of machine and welded it to the pipes. Sparks lit up the room as the men finished putting the contraption together. It got bigger and bigger. It was a large machine made to hold an enormous amount of powdered chemicals.

While the men worked, the four friends inched closer and closer together. Because they were tied in pairs, they had to work together in order to move without attracting any unwanted attention. Their movements quickly halted as the approach of heavy footsteps came their way. As the men approached the completion of their

---

Proclivity   (proh-**kliv**-i-tee) – N – natural leaning; predisposition

machine, the husky man's visits became shorter and less frequent.

The machine was finished and welded tightly to the main pipes. The location of the device was essential; it was placed directly connected to the main reservoir in order to contaminate the most water. Once the powder mixed with the water, it would start a chain reaction; the water contaminated by the powder would then contaminate the rest of the reservoir water. All the Cani Rossi needed to do was make sure they had enough of the powder for a lethal dosage of their mixture and the water would do the rest. It was a wickedly ingenious plot.

The machine served a twofold purpose. First, the group needed a device large enough to hold the lethal dosage of chemicals. Second, the toxic mixture was made up of two distinct chemicals. Although harmless by themselves, together they made a deadly combination. The chemicals were both generally colorless and could mix with the water without detection. Well, almost without detection; when mixed together the two chemicals yielded a deadly, *fulsome* smell. Once completely mixed into the water, it wouldn't be a problem; however, it was a potential danger for those doing the mixing. The terrorists had overcome this potential danger by installing a timer onto the device. Once the machine was loaded and ready to go, they would set the timer for five minutes, allowing them time to escape before the fumes filled the room. Unfortunately, their four unwanted guests would be left behind to suffer.

Once the assemblage was complete, the prison guard no longer came to check on the group of four. He and the others were far too concerned with loading the

---

Fulsome   (**fool**-suhm) – ADJ – repulsive

chemicals. The O.I.T. members knew now would be the only time to concoct a subterfuge. They weren't exactly sure what to do, but right now would be their only chance to escape. Emma and Ethan scooted closer to Lavender and Thomas. Emma, who had gotten into the habit of always carrying her pocket knife after that first fateful night, whispered to the other two to help her get her shoe off. Puzzled, Lavender and Thomas complied with her request. As the shoe came off, a small black knife fell onto the floor.

The sight of the small object had a magical effect on the group. It was like a tiny *talisman*, there just to bring them good luck. That knife was a way to help them break free and possibly intervene in the devious plot. Emma used her foot to kick the small knife over to Lavender and Thomas. Ethan, who was still tied to Emma's back, sat helpless in the rescue attempt. He was forced to move with Emma and couldn't see exactly what was going on. The knife landed closest to Lavender and she wiggled her body around to get a better grip on it. Ethan and Thomas faced the gang of outlaws and kept watch as the two girls worked to pass off the knife. After several valiant, although unsuccessful attempts, Lavender finally got a handle on the small knife. Together with the help of Thomas, they cut through their bonds.

As the kids enacted their escape, the four deadly men diligently worked to empty the chemicals into their machine. The men's' movements were slow and deliberate, since they couldn't risk mixing the chemicals prematurely. Their actions engrossed their attention, leaving little room to be concerned with the movements of their soon-to-be-former captives.

Talisman   (**tal**-is-muhn) – N – a charm

The terrorist's preoccupation with the device was fortunate. The loud racket made from the spilling bags of power masked the furtive noises made by the rustling students. Once Lavender and Thomas were free they helped their other two friends untie themselves. The ropes were cut and tossed off to the side. Emma grabbed the pocket knife and put it into her pocket. She then turned to Thomas and whispered to him.

"What will happen if the chemicals get mixed in the water supply?"

"Depends on what kind of chemicals they have," he replied.

"Do you think you can identify the chemicals?" she asked.

"Not unless I get a close look at the symbols on the containers," he responded. "Even if I can identify them, I don't have the tools needed to counteract the reaction."

Thomas's outstanding science ability was only so helpful in a situation like this one. He had the ability to determine the type of reaction that would be caused by the materials, but no way to stop the reaction from occurring. Once the chemicals reached the water, it would be too late.

Ethan motioned to the others to join him behind a large group of pipes. He had a plan. Thomas was the only one who knew anything worthwhile about chemicals and chemistry, therefore it would be his responsibility to try to find out what types of chemicals the Cani Rossi were pouring into their machine. Even if Thomas couldn't stop the chemical reaction, the information would be important to give the CIA once they got out of the water plant. Any data they could give to the right authorities could be crucial. Because of the amount of danger involved, Lavender was to go with him. If the group stayed in pairs, it would be easier to help each other out if one of them got into trouble. Ethan and Emma were to find a way to escape the building and try to get help. Once the plan was set, the four broke into their two teams. Lavender and Thomas went one way, and Ethan and Emma went another.

Time, however, was on the terrorists' side. The four captives freed themselves at the same moment as the Italians finished pouring in the chemicals. The device was complete; all they needed to do was set the timer. Suddenly a loud bang shook everyone inside. The sound of gunfire caused the terrorists to scramble toward their weapons. As they reached for their own guns, Duilio ran back to the machine. They had come too far and had done too much to let the intruders stop the plan from working. Even if the four didn't make it out alive, Duilio was determined for the plan to succeed. He switched the timer on. A flash of red numbers appeared in the darkness: 5:00... 4:59... 4:58... 4:57... The countdown continued.

The loud bang had come as a complete shock to everyone inside. Little did anyone know that the arrival of the four wannabe spies at the warehouse was more than just a nuisance as the Cani Rossi had originally thought. While the men viewed the intrusion as a minor obstacle, their involvement would be the major downfall of the entire plot. The sudden emergence of activity, which resulted from the change of plans, was a red flag to the Officer Hawkins' joint-task force. Several FBI Special Agents and CIA officers had been watching the warehouse. There had been an observation team stationed for weeks, but up until that point, there had been no suspicious activity. Men came and went from the warehouse, but all the evidence the team had of terrorist activities was circumstantial. They were about to give up on the warehouse as a dead-end when the Cani Rossi decided to make their move that night. The team had intercepted a frantic cell phone call from one of the Cani Rossi men during the mad dash to the water plant. This call explained that the organization had to move quickly due to the unexpected intruders. That was all the evidence the task-force needed to make their move. The sloppiness of the execution, along with the hints that possible hostages were involved, had led the joint-task force to that very water plant. Upon arrival, the CIA-FBI team surrounded the building. The agents and officers followed closely behind the Cani Rossi vans, but held back and waited for the most opportune time to begin their attack. One wrong move and the team could turn the already hostile situation into a deadly attack. However, now was the time to move.

Guns fired in all directions, creating a raucous noise reverberating throughout the halls of the watering plant. Gunshots hit pipes, causing water to shower down and fill the halls. Thomas and Lavender had disappeared in their mission and were nowhere to be found. Emma and Ethan took cover behind another set of pipes. At one point Ethan had the idea to try to stop the machine's timer, but Emma pulled him back to the safety of the shelter. Now was not the time to get in the way. The shower of water and bullets made the entire plant a battlefield; it was safest to stay hidden and let the war before them play out. Ethan reluctantly agreed.

The squad of trained FBI Special Agents and CIA Officers stormed the halls of the watering plant. Their footsteps could be heard throughout the building. The men of the Cani Rossi knew they were outnumbered and cut off from their escape. In a last-ditch effort to save themselves, the men of the Italian terrorist group ran out into the halls with their guns blazing.

Gunfire ensued for a moment longer, then stopped completely. Echoes of the blasts continued on, but it was evident no more shots were being fired. Silence came, and with it an odd sense of *serenity*.

A CIA officer dressed in all black was the first to approach the main room. He looked around and saw the massive machine constructed on the watering pipe. The officer carefully approached the device.

Relieved that it was over, Ethan and Emma started to reveal themselves from their hiding place. Just when they were about to stand, Ethan pulled Emma down together. He pointed to a shadow in the corner. There stood Duilio with a 9mm pistol in hand. The officer's back was turned to him, giving Duilio the element of complete surprise. Duilio raised the pistol and aimed. Unsure of what to do, Emma looked at Ethan. Without giving it much thought, she screamed.

"Look out behind you!"

The officer whipped around to reveal his own handgun. In a fluid motion the officer aimed his gun and shot Duilio's shoulder. The force of the bullet threw Duilio to the floor and knocked the 9mm from his hand. The gun dropped and slid across the floor. Within moments, two Special Agents joined the officer and took Duilio into custody. Understanding the urgency of the situation, the officer raced back to the device. There were only seconds left in the countdown, but he was trained to handle situations such as this one. With great care, the man disarmed the chemical tube and shut it down with three seconds remaining. It was all over.

Serenity   (suh-**ren**-i-tee) – N – state of peacefulness

Once the coast was clear, the two friends emerged from behind the pipes. With their hands in the air, they slowly approached the armed men. It was obvious the two high school students weren't a part of the Italian terrorist organization; however, they felt no need to take any chances. After all, they had put themselves in enough danger for the night.

As they approached, one of the Special Agents had a stern look on his face. This was no place for children, and he was curious how a pair of high school students had gotten themselves involved in such a situation. As he began to scold the two, Thomas and Lavender appeared with three other adults, two men and one woman. Thomas was in the process of explaining the machine and the types of chemicals they were using. He and Lavender had succeeded in indentifying the substances and their potential reactions in the water. Once the group was reunited, a CIA officer in a dark suit began to speak with them. He was one of the men who had entered with Thomas and Lavender.

"That is enough, Special Agent Rodgers," he began. "Ethan and Emma, my name is Officer Hawkins. I just finished hearing from your friends here how you all got involved in this terrorist activity." He turned to Lavender first. "As you well know, eavesdropping on matters of national security is a Federal crime. Not to mention getting yourself seriously endangered."

The group looked down for fear of the consequences of its involvements. The officer continued.

"However, without your involvement, we would never have caught this plan in time," he began. "Therefore, the agency, the bureau, and the president himself, is willing

244 ••• Operation High School

to grant **amnesty** for any wrongdoing."

The officer broke out into a smile.

"Now, I understand you four hope to be spies one day. Well, the agency could use some go-getters like you in the future. If you promise to stay out of trouble and stop meddling in national security, I think we might be able to find a place for you after college."

Officer Hawkins reached into his inner jacket pocket and pulled out some business cards. He handed one to each of the students.

"Give me a call after graduation."

With that, the officer turned and walked away from the group. Stunned, they each held the cards tightly in their hands. Other members of the task-force motioned for the group to follow them. It was late and time for them to get home. Because of the national security secrets involved with foiling a terrorist plot, the four friends were sworn to secrecy. They were never to talk about this night—ever. The students didn't mind, because that also meant that the government wasn't going to tell their parents. As long as they could sneak back into their houses without getting caught, they wouldn't get grounded for their excursion. If their parents noticed their absence, the government wouldn't be there to help **rescind** any punishments or consequences. They were dropped off next to their van and in no time, Ethan returned his friends to their cars at the school. It was close to five in the morning by the time Emma made it home. The sun was starting to peak through the night sky, and there were only two more

Amnesty	(**am**-nuh-stee) – N – an official pardon for a group of people who have violated a law or policy
Rescind	(ri-**sind**) – V – to cancel; to annul

precious hours of sleep before Clockable would sound his alarm. Emma climbed back up her tree and crawled through the window. She tip-toed across the hallway floor and snuck back into her bedroom, where she took a very short nap before school.

The world seemed a little bit more dull that morning. The excitement from the evening's excursions had colored Emma's perception. Classes seemed less interesting and her mind often drifted off to the thrilling world of being a spy. As she daydreamed, Emma found herself drawing *effigies* of the Italian gangsters with distorted faces and unintelligent expressions. Her cartoons made her smile. She and her friends had been instrumental in taking down a group of terrorists. She may not have wanted to join the CIA before, but that taste of excitement had Emma hooked. Someday she, too, would be a spy.

She didn't know it at the start of third period, but Emma's next big adventure was just around the corner. As she sat lost in her thoughts, Michael tried to help explain the properties of water molecules and their importance to all life on earth. He seemed frustrated by her lack of attention, and finally put his pencil down and addressed Emma directly. Normally Michael didn't let his emotions get the best of him, but he was *infatuated* with Emma and this passion finally took control.

"I've tried to find a good time to ask you this and never had the nerve," Michael began, determined. "Emma Jones, will you please go to the dance with me tomorrow night?"

Surprised by both his question and the sincerity

Effigy	(**ef**-i-jee) – N – a likeness of someone, especially in expressing ridicule
Infatuated	(in-fach-oo-eyt-ed) – ADJ – possessed by a passion, often foolishly

with which he stated it, Emma returned Michael's ***suppliant*** request with a smile.

"Of course I will," she replied.

Emma's answer brought the color back to Michael's face. All frustration left at once and he began to smile, too. Michael picked up his pencil to once again explain chemistry. Emma did her best to listen, but her thoughts were now on her newest escapade: tackling her first date!

Suppliant   (**suhp**-lee-uhnt) – ADJ – humble and earnest

WORD REVIEW

Amnesty	Infatuated	Rescind
Cabalist	Opprobrious	Serenity
Effigy	Perdition	Spawn
Extort	Proclivity	Suppliant
Fulsome	Reflective	Talisman
Imprecation	Reprehensible	Undermine

GLOSSARY

Abash - (uh-**bash**) - V - to embarrass; disconcert - page 27 - chapter 1

Abate - (uh-**beyt**) - V - lessen; put an end to - page 50 - chapter 2

Abeyance - (uh-**bey**-uhns) - N - suspension; temporary cessation - page 38 - chapter 2

Abortive - (uh-**bawr**-tiv) - ADJ - unsuccessful; fruitless - page 117 - chapter 5

Abstruse - (ab-**stroos**) - ADJ - hard to understand - page 153 - chapter 6

Acclimate - (**ak**-luh-meyt) - V - to adapt - page 36 - chapter 2

Adroit - (uh-**droit**) - ADJ - skillful; expert - page 29 - chapter 1

Advocate - (**ad**-vuh-kit) - N/V - 1. one that pleads a cause for another 2. to plead in favor for - page 53 - chapter 2

Affidavit - (af-i-**dey**-vit) - N - a sworn written statement made before an official - page 105 - chapter 4

Affiliate - (uh-**fil**-ee-yet) - V - to associate oneself; be intimately united in action orinterest - page 106 - chapter 4

Affinity - (uh-**fin**-i-tee) - N - attraction; natural liking - page 95 - chapter 4

Aftermath - (**af**-ter-math) - N - consequence - page 115 - chapter 5

Aggrieved - (uh-**greevd**) - V - troubled or distressed in spirit - page 196 - chapter 8

Agog - (uh-**gog**) - ADJ - highly excited - page 147 - chapter 6

Alleviate - (uh-**lee**-vee-ayt) - V - to make easier; to endure - page 153 - chapter 6

Allocate - (**al**-uh-keyt) - V - to set aside; to distribute - page 181 - chapter 7

Aloof - (uh-**loof**) - ADJ - uninvolved; keeping one's distance - page 54 - chapter 2

Ambivalence - (am-**biv**-uh-luhns) - N - having mixed emotions - page 78 - chapter 3

Amnesty - (**am**-nuh-stee) - N - an official pardon for a group of people who have violated a law or policy - page 244 - chapter 10

Anomaly - (uh-**nom**-uh-lee) - N - a deviation from the normal order form or rule - page 19 - chapter 1

Antiquated - (**an**-ti-kweyt-ed) - ADJ - old; outdated - page 100 - chapter 4

Approbation - (ap-ruh-**bey**-shuhn) - N - praise - page 30 - chapter 1

Arable - (**ar**-uh-buhl) - ADJ - fit for growing crops - page 47 - chapter 2

Arboretum - (ahr-buh-**ree**-tuhm) - N - a plot of land on which many different trees or shrubs are grown for study or display - page 39 - chapter 2

Arcade - (ahr-**keyd**) - N - any covered passageway, esp. one with an arched roof - page 128 - chapter 5

Arcane - (ahr-**keyn**) - ADJ - mysterious; known only by a select few - page 185 - chapter 8

Ardent - (**ahr**-dnt) - ADJ - passionate - page 41 - chapter 2

Aristocratic - (uh-ris-tuh-**krat**-ik) - ADJ - snobbish; acting like an aristocrat - page 93 - chapter 4

Armistice - (**ahr**-muh-stis) - N - a truce; a temporary cease of hostilities - page 17 - chapter 1

Arsenal - (**ahr**-suh-nl) - N - a collection of armaments - page 218 - chapter 9

Ascertain - (as-er-**teyn**) - V - to find out or learn with certainty - page 29 - chapter 1

Askew - (uh-**skyoo**) - ADV - out of line; in a crooked position - page 213 - chapter 9

Aspirant - (**as**-per-uhnt) - N - someone who aspires - page 195 - chapter 8

Assay - (a-**sey**) - V - to test; to evaluate - page 154 - chapter 6

Assiduous - (uh-**sij**-oo-uhs) - ADJ - careful; attentive - page 38 - chapter 2

Assuage - (uh-**sweyj**) - V - to lessen the intensity of something painful; to ease - page 14 - chapter 1

Atrocity - (uh-**tros**-i-tee) - N - a great wickedness - page 76 - chapter 3

Augment - (awg-**ment**) - V - to make more intense - page 199 - chapter 8

Avarice - (**av**-er-is) - N - insatiable greed for riches - page 73 - chapter 3

Awry - (uh-**rahy**) - ADV - off course - page 216 - chapter 9

Badger - (**baj**-er) - V - to harass - page 123 - chapter 5

Ballyhoo - (**bal**-ee-hoo) - N - an uproar; a noisy attention getting demonstration - page 52 - chapter 2

Bandy - (**ban**-dee) - V - to toss back and forth - page 23 - chapter 1

Bauble - (**baw**-buhl) - N - a gaudy trinket; a small, inexpensive ornament - page 44 - chapter 2

Behest - (bih-**hest**) - N - command or order - page 64 - chapter 3

Bibelot - (**bib**-loh) - N - a trinket; a small object of beauty - page 46 - chapter 2

Blandisment - (**blan**-dish-muhnt) - N - action or speech intending to entice - page 85 - chapter 4

Blather - (**blath**-er) - V - to talk foolishly at length - page 141 - chapter 6

Blithely - (**blahyth**-lee) - ADV - carefree; unconcerned - page 170 - chapter 7

Bouillabaisse - (bool-yuh-**beys**) - N - mixture of things - page 124 - chapter 5

Bracing - (**brey**-sing) - ADJ - invigorating; stimulating - page 132 - chapter 5

Bungler - (**buhng**-guhl-er) - N - a clumsy person - page 164 - chapter 7

Cabalist - (**kab**-uh-list) - N - one versed in secret sciences - page 235 - chapter 10

Cajole - (kuh-**johl**) - V - to persuade by flattery - page 138 - chapter 6

Canard - (kuh-**nahrd**) - N - false story; unfounded rumor - page 75 - chapter 3

Captious - (**kap**-shuhs) - ADJ - ill-natured; quick to find fault - page 190 - chapter 8

Careen - (kuh-**reen**) - V - to swerve; to switch from side to side - page 74 - chapter 3

Caustic - (**kaw**-stik) - ADJ - marked by incisive sarcasm - page 130 - chapter 5

Cavalier - (kav-uh-**leer**) - ADJ - marked by disdainful dismissal of serious things - page 74 - chapter 3

Cephalic - (suh-**fal**-ik) - ADJ - of or relating to the head - page 42 - chapter 2

Champion - (**cham**-pee-uhn) - V - to fight for; support - page 146 - chapter 6

Chicanery - (shi-**key**-nuh-ree) - N - trickery; deceitfulness - page 52 - chapter 2

Churl - (churl) - N - a rude person - page 130 - chapter 5

Clout - (klout) - N - influence - page 103 - chapter 4

Coax - (kohks) - V - to manipulate to obtain a desired outcome - page 116 - chapter 5

Compatriot - (kuhm-**pey**-tree-uht) - N - fellow contryman; a colleague - page 205 - chapter 8

Compendium - (kuhm-**pen**-dee-uhm) - N - a summary; an inventory - page 55 - chapter 2

Compunction - (kuhm-**puhngk**-shuhn) - N - uneasiness caused by guilt; remorse - page 152 - chapter 6

Confraternity - (kon-fruh-**tur**-ni-tee) - N - fraternal union; a society devoted to a similar purpose - page 148 - chapter 6

Consternation - (kon-ster-**ney-shuh n**) - N - dread that results in utter confusion; dismay - page 225 - chapter 9

Contraband - (**kon**-truh-band) - ADJ - forbidden; prohibited from import - page 142 - chapter 6

Contretemps - (**kon**-truh-than) - N - an embarrassing event - page 172 - chapter 7

Convoluted - (**kon**-vuh-loo-tid) - ADJ - twisted; confusing - page 73 - chapter 3

Cosmopolitan - (koz-muh-**pol**-i-tn) - ADJ - at home in many places; internationally sophisticated - page 61 - chapter 3

Coterie - (**koh**-tuh-ree) - N - a group of close associates; a circle of friends - page 22 - chapter 1

Counterpart - (**koun**-ter-pahrt) - N - one of two things that fit together - page 137 - chapter 6

Covert - (koh-**vert**) - ADJ - secret; hidden - page 11 - chapter 1

Crag - (krag) - N - a steep rugged rock or peak - page 215 - chapter 9

Crescendo - (kri-**shen**-doh) - N - the climactic point; peak - page 197 - chapter 8

Crux - (kruhks) - N - the central point; the essence - page 80 - chapter 3

Cryptic - (**krip**-tik) - ADJ - mystifying or mysterious - page 14 - chapter 1

Culinary - (**kyoo**-luh-ner-ee) - ADJ - relating to cooking or the kitchen - page 104 - chapter 4

Culpable - (**kuhl**-puh-buhl) - ADJ - guilty; responsible - page 70 - chapter 3

Cunning - (**kuhn**-ing) - ADJ - clever in deceiving - page 68 - chapter 3

Curt - (kurt) - ADJ - brief; short - page 188 - chapter 8

Customary - (**kuhs**-tuh-mer-ee) - ADJ - habitual - page 26 - chapter 1

Demur - (dih-**mur**) - V - to make an objection, esp. on the grounds of morals - page 119 - chapter 5

Derelict - (**der**-uh-likt) - ADJ - abandoned; forsaken - page 27 - chapter 1

Destitute - (**des**-ti-toot) - ADJ - without means of subsistence; lacking food, clothing, and shelter - page 126 - chapter 5

Dexterity - (dek-**ster**-i-tee) - N - skill; agility - page 114 - chapter 5

Dilettante - (**dil**-i-tahnt) - N - a person who dabbles in the arts - page 88 - chapter 4

Discombobulate - (dis-kuhm-**bob**-yuh-leyt) - V - to upset the composure of; frustrate - page 151 - chapter 6

Disparity - (dih-**spar**-i-tee) - N - lack of similarity; difference - page 213 - chapter 9

Disseminate - (dih-**sem**-uh-neyt) - V - to scatter or spread widely; to broadcast - page 171 - chapter 7

Doff - (dof) - V - to take off - page 37 - chapter 2

Doleful - (**dohl**-fuhl) - ADJ - sorrowful; filled with grief - page 109 - chapter 4

Dolt - (dohlt) - N - stupid person - page 28 - chapter 1

Dossier - (**dos**-ee-ey) - N - a file containing detailed records - page 212 - chapter 9

Effigy - (**ef**-i-jee) - N - a likeness of someone, especially in expressing ridicule - page 245 - chapter 10

Emanate - (**em**-uh-neyt) - V - flow out; originate - page 219 - chapter 9

Ennui - (ahn-**wee**) - N - boredom - page 131 - chapter 5

Espouse - (ih-**spous**) - V - adopt or embrace - page 176 - chapter 7

Espy - (ih-**spahy**) - V - to catch sight of something - page 46 - chapter 2

Estrange - (ih-**streynj**) - V - to make unfriendly or hostile - page 77 - chapter 3

Ethereal - (ih-**theer**-ee-uhl) - ADJ - heavenly - page 98 -
     chapter 4
Evanesce - (ev-uh-**nes**) - V - disappear; fade away; vanish -
     page 128 - chapter 5
Execrable - (**ek**-si-kruh-buhl) - ADJ - utterly detestable -
     page 80 - chapter 3
Exhume - (ig-**zoom**) - V - to unbury; unearth - page 219 -
     chapter 9
Extort - (ik-**stawrt**) - V - to compel (something) of a person -
     page 232 - chapter 10
Farrago - (fuh-**rah**-goh) - N - confused mixture; hodgepodge -
     page 222 - chapter 9
Faze - (feyz) - V - to bother; to upset - page 43 - chapter 2
Felicity - (fi-**lis**-i-tee) - N - the state of being happy - page 95 -
     chapter 4
Fetter - (**fet**-er) - V - to restrain - page 179 - chapter 7
Finesse - (fi-**ness**) - N - delicacy of movement; skill in
     handling a situation - page 50 - chapter 2
Flaxen - (**flak**-suhn) - ADJ - yellowish in color - page 166 -
     chapter 7
Flouter - (flout-er) - N - mocker; scoffer - page 159 - chapter 6
Frowzy - (**frou**-zee) - ADJ - having a slovenly or unkempt
     appearance - page 109 - chapter 4
Fulsome - (**fool**-suhm) - ADJ - repulsive; disgusting; of poor
     taste - page 237 - chapter 10
Furtive - (**fur**-tiv) - ADJ - secret; underhanded - page 20 -
     chapter 1
Gambit - (**gam**-bit) - N - a scheme to gain an advantage;
     clever manuever - page 208 - chapter 8
Glower - (**glou**-er) - V - to stare angrily - page 48 - chapter 2
Grandiloquent - (gran-**dil**-uh-kwuhnt) - ADJ - pompous;
     colorful speech; bombastic in style - page 132 -
     chapter 5
Grapple - (**grap**-uhl) - V - to seize - page 201 - chapter 8

Grievous - (**gree**-vuhs) - ADJ - flagrant; deplorable - page 145 - chapter 6

Halcyon - (**hal**-see-uhn) - ADJ - peaceful; calm - page 13 - chapter 1

Hapless - (**hap**-lis) - ADJ - unlucky - page 36 - chapter 2

Harbinger - (**hahr**-bin-jer) - N - herald; something that foreshadows - page 58 - chapter 2

Heinous - (**hey**-nuhs) - ADJ - shockingly evil - page 15 - chapter 1

Hermetic - (hur-met-ik) - ADJ - closed off; protected from outside influences - page 68 - chapter 3

Homage - (**hom**-ij) - N - respect given to acknowledge worth - page 92 - chapter 4

Homogeneous - (hoh-muh-**jee**-nee-uhs) - ADJ - of the same kind - page 177 - chapter 7

Imprecation - (im-pri-**key**-shuhn) - N - a curse; malediction - page 232 - chapter 10

Incontrovertible - (in-kon-truh-**vur**-tuh-buhl) - ADJ - indisputable - page 107 - chapter 4

Indomitable - (in-**dom**-i-tuh-buhl) - ADJ - invincible - page 164 - chapter 7

Ineluctable - (in-i-**luhk**-tuh-buhl) - ADJ - unavoidable; inescapable - page 212 - chapter 9

Ineludible - (in-i-**loo**-duh-buhl) - ADJ - inescapable - page 86 - chapter 4

Infatuated - (in-**fach**-oo-eyt-ed) - ADJ - possessed by a passion, often foolishly - page 245 - chapter 10

Inimical - (ih-**nim**-i-kuhl) - ADJ - hostile; harmful - page 180 - chapter 7

Inquisition - (in-kwuh-**zish**-uh n) - N - the act of inquiring - page 73 - chapter 3

Insouciant - (in-**soo**-see-uhnt) - ADJ - unconcerned - page 167 - chapter 7

Intrigue - (in-**treeg**) - N - evil plot; use of underhanded schemes - page 228 - chapter 9

Intrinsic - (in-**trin**-sik) - ADJ - essential - page 185 - chapter 8

Jaded - (**jey**-did) - ADJ - dulled or worn out - page 141 - chapter 6

Jaunty - (**jawn**-tee) - ADJ - lively - page 92 - chapter 4

Jejune - (ji-**joon**) - ADJ - juvenile; childish - page 174 - chapter 7

Juxtapose - (**juhk**-stuh-pohz) - V - to place side by side in order to compare - page 64 - chapter 3

Lambaste - (lam-**bast**) - V - to attach violently - page 158 - chapter 6

Laurel - (**lawr**-uhl) - N - a small evergreen bush - page 201 - chapter 8

Legerdemain - (lej-er-duh-**meyn**) - N - sleight of hand; trickery - page 99 - chapter 4

Lissome - (**lis**-uhm) - ADJ - nimble; limber - page 178 - chapter 7

Lugubrious - (loo-**goo**-bree-uhs) - ADJ - dismal; mournful; melancholy - page 149 - chapter 6

Lummox - (**luhm**-uhks) - N - a large, ungainly, dull-witted person - page 23 - chapter 1

Lurid - (**loor**-id) - ADJ - harshly shocking - page 69 - chapter 3

Machination - (mak-uh-**ney**-shuhn) - N - harmful or crafty scheme - page 168 - chapter 7

Maharajah - (mah-huh-**rah**-juh) - N - ruling Indian prince - page 62 - chapter 3

Mania - (**mey**-nee-uh) - ADJ - crazed, excessive excitement - page 71 - chapter 3

Materialistic - (muh-teer-ee-uh-**lis**-tik) - ADJ - excessively concerned with wealth and possessions - page 100 - chapter 4

Maudlin - (**mawd**-lin) - ADJ - silly and overly sentimental - page 194 - chapter 8

Mellifluous - (muh-**lif**-loo-uhs) - ADJ - sweetly flowing - page 96 - chapter 4

Meretricious - (mer-i-**trish**-uhs) - ADJ - gaudy or falsely attractive - page 129 - chapter 5

Milieu - (mil-**yoo**) - N - environment; setting - page 21 - chapter 1

Mollify - (**mol**-uh-fahy) - V - to soften; to pacify - page 152 - chapter 6

Moribund - (**mawr**-uh-buhnd) - ADJ - on the verge of death; in a state of dying - page 118 - chapter 5

Nebulous - (**neb**-yuh-luhs) - ADJ - hazy; vague - page 82 - chapter 3

Necessitate - (nuh-**ses**-i-teyt) - V - to make unavoidable - page 223 - chapter 9

Nepotism - (**nep**-uh-tiz-uhm) - N - favoritsim to family - page 175 - chapter 7

Nimbus - (**nim**-buhs) - N - halo; aura around a person; rain cloud - page 127 - chapter 5

Noisome - (**noi**-suhm) - ADJ - offensive or disgusting - page 165 - chapter 7

Nugatory - (**noo**-guh-tawr-ee) - ADJ - worthless; insignificant - page 193 - chapter 8

Oblivion - (uh-**bliv**-ee-uhn) - N - total forgetfulness - page 24 - chapter 1

Obtrude - (uhb-**trood**) - V - to force itself upon; to intrude - page 199 - chapter 8

Ocher - (**oh**-ker) - N - a range of colors (relating to the metal) from pale yellow to reddish yellow - page 91 - chapter 4

Offal - (**aw**-fuhl) - N - rubbish; garbage - page 139 - chapter 6

Officious - (uh-**fish**-uhs) - ADJ - annoyingly eager to help or advise; meddling - page 126 - chapter 5

Omnidirectional - (om-nee-di-**rek**-shuh-nl) - ADJ - coming from all directions - page 224 - chapter 9

Opaque - (oh-**peyk**) - ADJ - not translucent; not allowing light to pass through - page 202 - chapter 8

Opine - (oh-**pahyn**) - V - to state an opinion - page 77 - chapter 3

Opprobrious - (uh-**proh**-bree-uhs) - ADJ - disgraceful or shameful - page 234 - chapter 10

Orotund - (**awr**-uh-tuhnd) - ADJ - marked by strength and fullness - page 91 - chapter 4

Orthography - (awr-**thog**-ruh-fee) - N - a part of language study that deals with letters and spelling - page 224 - chapter 9

Ostracize - (**os**-truh-sahyz) - V - to exclude from society, by general consent - page 169 - chapter 7

Paltry - (**pawl**-tree) - ADJ - trivial - page 172 - chapter 7

Parse - (pahrs) - V - to analyze with detail, esp. grammar - page 15 - chapter 1

Pedagogue - (**ped**-uh-gog) - N - teacher - page 144 - chapter 6

Peerless - (**peer**-lis) - ADJ - better than all others - page 69 - chapter 3

Penitent - (**pen**-i-tuhnt) - ADJ - repentant; apologetic - page 86 - chapter 4

Perdition - (per-**dish**-uhn) - N - eternal punishment; utter destruction - page 235 - chapter 10

Peregrination - (per-i-gruh-**ney**-shuhn) - N - expedition; especially on foot - page 44 - chapter 2

Perfidy - (**pur**-fi-dee) - N - treason; treachery - page 223 - chapter 9

Phlegmatic - (fleg-**mat**-ik) - ADJ - impassive; apathetic; sluggish - page 95 - chapter 4

Pied - (pahyd) - ADJ - multi-colored - page 214 - chapter 9

Pithy - (**pith**-ee) - ADJ - brief; terse - page 186 - chapter 8

Plummet - (**pluhm**-it) - V - to fall hard - page 110 - chapter 4

Pratfall - (**prat**-fawl) - N - humiliating mishap or failure - page 175 - chapter 7

Proclivity - (proh-**kliv**-i-tee) - N - natural leaning; predisposition - page 236 - chapter 10

Prowess - (**prou**-is) - N - exceptional ability, skill, or strength - page 177 - chapter 7

Pusillanimous - (pyoo-suh-**lan**-uh-muhs) - ADJ - lacking firmness of mind; cowardly - page 34 - chapter 2

Qualify - (**kwol**-uh-fahy) - V - mitigate; make less harsh - page 88 - chapter 4

Quarry - (**kwawr**-ee) - N - a victim; object of a hunt - page 33 - chapter 2

Quaver - (**kwey**-ver) - V - to shake or tremble, as in voice or music - page 26 - chapter 1

Quell - (kwel) - V - to put an end to - page 138 - chapter 6

Quisling - (**kwiz**-ling) - N - traitor - page 190 - chapter 8

Rampant - (**ram**-puhnt) - ADJ - widespread; unchecked - page 172 - chapter 7

Rapport - (ra-**pawr**) - N - relationship of mutual understanding and trust - page 108 - chapter 4

Raucous - (**raw**-kuhs) - ADJ - harshly loud - page 114 - chapter 5

Raze - (reyz) - V - to erase; to destroy - page 207 - chapter 8

Rebuff - (ri-**buhf**) - V - to snub; beat back - page 199 - chapter 8

Recalcitrant - (ri-**kal**-si-truhnt) - ADJ - stubbornly defiant - page 171 - chapter 7

Rectify - (**rek**-tuh-fahy) - V - to correct; to set right - page 170 - chapter 7

Refection - (ri-**fek**-shuhn) - N - refreshment by food and drink - page 97 - chapter 4

Reflective - (ri-**flek**-tiv) - ADJ - marked by meditation or cogitation - page 232 - chapter 10

Reiterate - (ree-**it**-uh-reyt) - V - to repeat - page 81 - chapter 3

Relegate - (**rel**-i-geyt) - V - to exile; to give a lower position - page 65 - chapter 3

Remedial - (ri-**mee**-dee-uhl) - ADJ - tending to remedy -
     page 196 - chapter 8
Remonstration - (ree-mon-**strey**-shuhn) - N - disapproval;
     objection - page 63 - chapter 3
Renegade - (**ren**-i-geyd) - N - traitor - page 204 - chapter 8
Repercussion - (ree-per-**kuhsh**-uhn) - N - consequence -
     page 25 - chapter 1
Reprehensible - (rep-ri-**hen**-suh-buhl) - ADJ - deserving rebuke -
     page 235 - chapter 10
Reprisal - (ri-**prahy-zuh** l) - N - the act of taking revenge -
     page 159 - chapter 6
Repudiate - (ri-**pyoo**-dee-eyt) - V - disown; reject - page 106 -
     chapter 4
Rescind - (ri-**sind**) - V - to cancel; to annul - page 244 -
     chapter 10
Reticent - (reht-**uh-suhnt**) - ADJ - quiet; reserved - page 12 -
     chapter 1
Revered - (ri-**veerd**) - ADJ - loved and respected - page 126 -
     chapter 5
Revilement - (ri-**vahyl**-muhnt) - N - scolding; harsh language -
     page 203 - chapter 8
Rhapsodize - (**rap**-suh-dahyz) - V - to speak or write enthusias-
     tically - page 132 - chapter 5
Riposte - (ri-**pohst**) - N - a retaliatory movement - page 177 -
     chapter 7
Rivet - (**riv**-it) - V - to engross - page 18 - chapter 1
Rogue - (rohg) - N - a dishonest person; scoundrel - page 209 -
     chapter 8
Rout - (rout) - N - a rabble or mob; a defeat - page 157 -
     chapter 6
Rue - (roo) - N - sorrow; repentance; regret - page 148 -
     chapter 6
Sally - (**sal**-ee) - N - any sudden start into activity; outburst or
     flight of passion - page 114 - chapter 5

Satirize - (**sat**-uh-rahyz) - V - criticize with mockery - page 120 - chapter 5

Savoir Faire - (**sav**-wahr-**fair**) - N - polished sureness in social behavior - page 156 - chapter 6

Scenario - (si-**nair**-ee-oh) - N - a sequence of events - page 35 - chapter 2

Schism - (**siz**-uhm) - N - a division - page 163 - chapter 7

Scintilla - (sin-**til**-uh) - N - trace; hint - page 143 - chapter 6

Scrupulous - (**skroo**-pyuh-luhs) - ADJ - very thorough - page 216 - chapter 9

Sedentary - (**sed**-n-ter-ee) - ADJ - settled; characterized by little exercise - page 197 - chapter 8

Sedition - (si-**dish**-uhn) - N - treason; insurrection against lawful order - page 208 - chapter 8

Sententious - (sen-**ten**-shuhs) - ADJ - terse; pithy - page 140 - chapter 6

Sequester - (si-**kwes**-ter) - V - to keep apart; separate - page 181 - chapter 7

Serenity - (suh-**ren**-i-tee) - N - state of peacefulness - page 242 - chapter 10

Shibboleth - (**shib**-uh-lith) - N - catchphrase; slogan; something that distinguishes - page 189 - chapter 8

Shrewd - (shrood) - N - sly; crafty - page 21 - chapter 1

Skittish - (**skit**-ish) - ADJ - nervous; cautious - page 64 - chapter 3

Slake - (sleyk) - V - to quench; satisfy a craving - page 48 - chapter 2

Sneer - (sneer) - V - smile scornfully - page 122 - chapter 5

Solemnity - (suh-**lem**-ni-tee) - N - seriousness; gravity - page 34 - chapter 2

Soliloquy - (suh-**lil**-uh-kwee) - N - the act of talking to one's self - page 135 - chapter 6

Spawn - (spawn) - V - to bring forth - page 231 - chapter 10

Squelch - (skwelch) - V - to put down, suppress, or silence with crushing effort - page 86 - chapter 4

Staid - (steyd) - ADJ - fixed; sober; steady - page 121 -
chapter 5

Stealth - (stelth) - N - the act of proceding with secrecy -
page 58 - chapter 2

Strategem - (**strat**-uh-juhm) - N - a plan to trick an enemy;
ruse - page 173 - chapter 7

Subpar - (suhb-**pahr**) - ADJ - below average; not qualified -
page 223 - chapter 9

Subterfuge - (**suhb**-ter-fyooj) - N - a ruse - page 105 - chapter 4

Subversion - (suhb-**vur**-zhuhn) - N - an attempt to undermine
the government - page 205 - chapter 8

Succumb - (suh-**kuhm**) - V - to submit; to die - page 16 -
chapter 1

Superficial - (soo-per-**fish**-uhl) - ADJ - on the surface; shallow -
page 206 - chapter 8

Superfluous - (soo-**pur**-floo-uhs) - ADJ - excessive; more than
enough; extravagant - page 94 - chapter 4

Suppliant - (**suhp**-lee-uhnt) - ADJ - humble and earnest -
page 246 - chapter 10

Surplus - (**sur**-pluhs) - N - amount greater than needed -
page 220 - chapter 9

Surreptitious - (sur-uhp-**tish**-uhs) - ADJ - sneaky; secret -
page 166 - chapter 7

Svelte - (svelt) - ADJ - slim; slender; having clean lines -
page 23 - chapter 1

Sybarite - (**sib**-uh-rahyt) - N - person devoted to luxury and
pleasure - page 63 - chapter 3

Sycophant - (**sik**-uh-fuhnt) - N - one who sucks up to other;
self seeking flatterer - page 122 - chapter 5

Tacit - (**tas**-it) - ADJ - implied; subtle - page 187 - chapter 8

Taint - (teynt) - V - to contaminate - page 137 - chapter 6

Talisman - (**tal**-is-muhn) - N - a charm - page 238 - chapter 10

Taunt - (tawnt) - V - mock; insult - page 192 - chapter 8

Temerarious - (tem-uh-**rair**-ee-uhs) - ADJ - reckless; rash - page 157 - chapter 6

Tenuous - (**ten**-yoo-uhs) - ADJ - shaky; extremely thin - page 78 - chapter 3

Thwart - (thwawrt) - V - to hinder - page 155 - chapter 6

Timorous - (**tim**-er-uhs) - ADJ - full of fear - page 118 - chapter 5

Titillate - (**tit**-l-yet) - V - to excite - page 99 - chapter 4

Toady - (**toh**-dee) - N - fawning flatterer; a sycophant - page 137 - chapter 6

Toil - (toil) - V - work hard; to struggle - page 42 - chapter 2

Torpor - (**tawr**-per) - N - dullness; apathy - page 132 - chapter 5

Tremulous - (**trem**-yuh-luhs) - ADJ - fearful; trembling - page 217 - chapter 9

Trenchant - (**tren**-chuhnt) - ADJ - keen; sharp - page 202 - chapter 8

Trompe l'oeil - (**trawmp ley, loi**) - N - a detailed style of painting that gives an illusion of being a photograph - page 99 - chapter 4

Truncate - (**truhng**-keyt) - V - to shorten by cutting off - page 212 - chapter 9

Tumult - (**too**-muhlt) - N - an uproar or outburst - page 101 - chapter 4

Uncanny - (uhn-**kan**-ee) - ADJ - mysterious; extraordinary - page 174 - chapter 7

Undermine - (uhn-der-**mahyn**) - V - to impair; to work against - page 233 - chapter 10

Underwrite - (uhn-der-**rahyt**) - V - to sponsor; to subsidize - page 125 - chapter 5

Unflappability - (uhn-**flap**-uh-bil-uh-tee) - N - self assurance; calm - page 89 - chapter 4

Ungainly - (uhn-**geyn**-lee) - ADJ - clumsy - page 136 - chapter 6

Unimpeachable - (uhn-im-**pee**-chuh-buhl) - ADJ - reliable beyond a doubt - page 171 - chapter 7

Unkempt - (**uhn**-kempt) - ADJ - disheveled; messy - page 12 - chapter 1

Unlettered - (uhn-**let**-erd) - ADJ - unsophisticated; ignorant - page 163 - chapter 7

Unobtrusive - (uhn-uhb-**troo**-siv) - ADJ - inconspicuous; unassuming - page 149 - chapter 6

Vacillate - (**vas**-uh-leyt) - V - to waver - page 28 - chapter 1

Vanquish - (**vang**-kwish) - V - conquer; overpower - page 179 - chapter 7

Vehemently - (**vee**-uh-muhnt-ly) - ADV - with passion - page 117 - chapter 5

Vendetta - (ven-**det**-uh) - N - enmity marked by bitter hostility - page 227 - chapter 9

Vex - (veks) - V - annoy; pester; confuse - page 17 - chapter 1

Vim - (vim) - N - energetic spirit; vitality - page 24 - chapter 1

Vitriolic - (vi-tree-**ol**-ik) - ADJ - caustic; harsh - page 151 - chapter 6

Voluble - (**vol**-yuh-buhl) - ADJ - talkative; glib - page 143 - chapter 6

Voracious - (vaw-**rey**-shuhs) - ADJ - very hungry - page 102 - chapter 4

Wan - (**won**) - ADJ - faded; pallid - page 45 - chapter 2

Wily - (**wahy**-lee) - ADJ - shrewd; cunning - page 40 - chapter 2

Wont - (wawnt) - N - habit - page 155 - chapter 6

Wry - (rahy) - ADJ - disdainfully ironic - page 194 - chapter 8

15 Secrets to Free College

Learn <u>1800</u> SAT-Level Words!

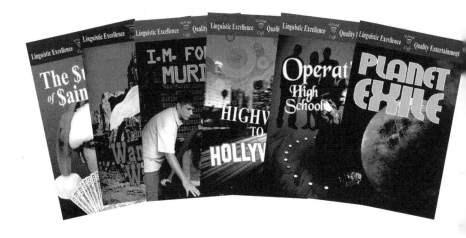

The VocabCafé Book Series:

Retail: $12.95 per book

Sick of boring old flash cards? Learning vocabulary words just got infinitely easier with the help of the VocabCafé Book Series! Each original story contains more than 300 of the most popular vocabulary words found on standardized exams.

Learn new word definitions through the context of an engaging story! From Sci-fi to Mystery, each book features new characters, unique advanced vocabulary, and exhilarating adventure!

Find out more at <u>www.VocabCafe.com</u>!